Savage Love

Cassie Edwards

WHEELER
PUBLISHING

Published in 2002 by arrangement with Leisure Books,
a division of Dorchester Publishing Co., Inc.

Wheeler Large Print Romance Series.

The text of this Large Print edition is unabridged.
Other aspects of the book may vary from the original edition.

Set in 16 pt. Plantin by Elena Picard.

Printed in the United States on permanent paper.

Library of Congress Cataloging-in-Publication Data

Edwards, Cassie.
   Savage love / Cassie Edwards.
     p. cm.
   ISBN 1-58724-356-3 (lg. print : hc : alk. paper)
   1. Cree Indians — Fiction.   2. Women archaeologists
 — Fiction.   3. Large type books.   I. Title.
   PS3555.D875 S26 2002
   813'.54—dc21   2002032764

*To my wonderful grandson David Edwards,
with much love and pride.*

POEM

Smoke fills the night,
Silhouettes dance on the light.
Bellows of songs,
Spirits that long.
Folk dances and chants of power
That linger in the dark hour.
Exotic faces painted to perfection,
The howls of wolves that bind
   the connection.
Figures that glow by the embers of fire,
That fill the heart of your soul's desire.

         — Debbyette Ruiz
         friend and poet

Chapter One

For those may fail or turn to ill,
So thou and I shall sever;
Keep therefore a true woman's eye,
And love me still, but know not why.
So hast thou the same reason still
To dote upon me ever.

— Anonymous

*Fort Meyers, on the Green River near
the Utah/Wyoming border, 1843*

The room was filled with sunlight as Dayanara Tolliver sat at her father's bedside. Her mother was on the opposite side of the bed, her hand twined with her husband's as he lay asleep, his black hair contrasting with the white pillow upon which his head rested.

Dayanara leaned over and smoothed wrinkles out of the patchwork quilt that lay over her father.

"He's sleeping too much," Dayanara's mother said. Dorothea's pale blue eyes revealed her concern for her husband. "Dayanara, we never should have left Saint Louis. We were all happy there in our beautiful home. Why did we have to take this journey north, chasing after a bunch of dried-out bones? Why did those people at the Smithsonian Institute have to involve your father in this project?"

"Mother, they involved Father because they knew of his love of such things," Dayanara murmured. "Also, they knew that I share the same sense of adventure as Father. That is the main reason why we are here, because we were intrigued by the 'monster bones,' as they are called."

"Monster bones, hogwash," Dorothea said, her eyes flashing angrily. "I am so tired of having to leave my home and . . . and . . . follow you and your father's pipe dreams. And now . . . look at your father."

"Father is going to be all right," Dayanara said, hoping it was true. She gazed at his pale face, yet the gauntness of the past several days did seem to have lessened.

And the fort doctor had said that Daniel was past the crisis. His temperature was lower now and he slept much more comfortably, no longer groaning in his sleep.

"I pray for your father's return to good health with every waking breath," Dorothea said, a sob lodging in her throat. "Should he die —"

"Mother, *please*," Dayanara said.

She gazed at her mother, wondering if she resembled her as much as people said.

Dorothea had a curvaceous figure, though like Dayanara she was tiny.

Dayanara smiled to herself as she recalled her father teasing her mother and herself, saying that if they weren't careful, a breeze might lift them from their feet and sweep them away as though they were no more than two pretty feathers.

The only true differences between Dayanara's appearance and her mother's were the slight wrinkles on her mother's face, and their hair. Dayanara's hair hung down past her waist in beautiful waves, as golden as winter wheat, whereas her mother's golden hair was now threaded with gray and was always worn in a matronly swirl atop her head.

"Where's John this morning?" Dorothea asked, gazing out the window.

She hated this fort that housed only men. There were no women with whom she could sit and have morning tea. Oh, she so missed her home in Saint Louis.

She didn't understand how her husband could have been struck down. He had never been ill in his entire life. Not until they boarded that dreadful paddle wheeler headed north for what she called "the wild country."

Dorothea shivered at the thought of coming face to face with one of the redskins who inhabited this wilderness. She planned to stay safe inside the fort where she belonged. She only wished that she could talk

Dayanara into doing the same.

But she knew better. Her daughter had been born with a sense of adventure.

As soon as she was old enough to understand that her father was a naturalist, she had decided she wanted the same sort of life.

And she had succeeded, but not by going to college, which was mostly a young man's privilege. She had learned by doing, and by watching her father.

"Uncle John? I imagine he's already out there looking for hops plants," Dayanara said. She, too, longed to be outside the fort, beginning her own search.

Dayanara was excited about being at Fort Meyers. She had hardly been able to wait to begin the journey north after receiving the package from Washington — a trunk which held something exciting.

Dayanara and her father had both worked as naturalists at the Smithsonian Institute while they lived in Washington, D.C. But recently they had returned home to the family mansion in Saint Louis, Missouri. The move had been made for the sake of Dorothea's health. Dayanara had not wanted to leave Washington, yet neither had she wanted to abandon her mother during her time of sickness . . . a sickness that was later discovered to be all pretense.

Her mother had found there was only one way she could get her husband to leave the life that usually excluded her —to pretend to be ill.

Upon discovering that his wife had lied, had even paid a doctor to lie in order to get her husband to pay more attention to her, Daniel had grown distant from his wife. He was not a man who took to being deceived, even if it was by a woman whose loneliness drove her to it. Nor was he a man who believed in divorce.

It was a strained household that received the wire from one of Daniel's former colleagues, telling them about the monster bones. Dayanara's father had leapt at the chance to join in the search.

Dayanara would never forget her mother's angry shouts and threats. But she finally settled down when she realized that she was near to losing her husband over her lies, as well as her ranting and raving. In the end, she had chosen to make the journey north with him and settle for whatever attention she could get.

Dayanara was so excited about this journey of discovery, she found it hard to sit there and not go right out to search for the ancient bones of prehistoric animals that lay near Fort Meyers.

But her father's illness was not the only impediment facing her. The bones were on Indian land and had never been seen by any whites.

Her father's dear friend Dr. Frank Jones had uncovered a map to the land of the monster bones, forgotten in ancient trunks that he had been going through in the cavernous pit of the Smithsonian Institute's basement.

This map was in one of the many trunks of things that had been confiscated through the years from Indian tribes.

This particular map had been rolled up, scroll-like, among other Indian drawings made on buckskin. It had been well hidden amid various Indian relics and paintings and apparently had never been unrolled or seen by white people until Frank Jones opened it.

After Jones consulted an expert to read the inscriptions written around the edges of the map, he learned what a valuable find he had made. The map was drawn by someone of the Cree tribe, and showed the location of bones from creatures called *Wan-wan-kah* . . . creatures that had lived during what the Indians called "the monster era."

According to the writing on the map, these creatures had special powers, and their bones must not be disturbed. But Frank sensed that the bones were something unique, something that must be found and studied.

Prevented by ill health from pursuing the discovery himself, Frank had passed the map on to the only naturalists he could trust — Dayanara and her father.

Frank waited even now for word of whether or not the map was real, and whether or not there were such things as prehistoric bones in the area.

"Dayanara, you have that look in your eyes," Dorothea said, drawing Dayanara from her deep thoughts. "Daughter, you are *not* going out there to Indian territory alone. Promise me, daughter, that you aren't considering that."

"Mother, please don't worry so much," Dayanara said, sighing.

"Your father told you not to go alone," Dorothea said, her voice tight. "Perhaps John can accompany you — but no, that would make your father even more uneasy. Your Uncle John is here for his own purposes. I'm afraid your father's brother is worthless. Absolutely worthless."

"Mother, I don't want to talk about Uncle John," Dayanara said, her eyes flashing angrily at the very thought of her father's younger brother.

John had been living in the Saint Louis area for several years. With the inheritance he'd received when Dayanara's grandfather died, he had established a small brewery on the banks of the Mississippi. He had become a successful, shrewd businessman, but he was also an alcoholic. In fact, he had brought his own supply of liquor with him.

He was never without a flask of whiskey on

his person, yet he specialized in making beer. He knew everything about the creation of the brew.

John had accompanied Dayanara's family to this wild land for only one reason — hops plants. He had heard that there was acre after acre of wild hops growing on Indian land just waiting to be harvested and re-seeded. This could give John an unending supply of hops for his brewery.

On their way to Wyoming, John had explained to Dayanara that the hops plant was essential to the brewing process. Once the dried flower clusters were boiled in malt, they gave the beer a delicate aroma and also aided in its preservation.

Dayanara tried not to concern herself over John's welfare. She had her problems to worry about, for she had decided to try to find the location of the prehistoric bones without her father.

She prayed that the Indians wouldn't keep her from searching for the bones, and then studying them if she was successful.

She knew that her father even had hoped to take some of the bones back to Saint Louis so he could ship them to Washington.

She gazed at her father, who lay so still, his eyes closed. On the boat a strange illness had killed some of the passengers, and weakened others. Dayanara's father had taken sick almost as soon as they reached Fort Meyers, which they had planned to make their home base until their return to Saint Louis.

Since Dayanara was a naturalist in her own right, who had accompanied him on many such expeditions as this, she knew she was capable of searching for the monster bones without him.

The sooner she could find the bones, the better. Once her father was well enough to travel, she wanted to take him home where he would be more comfortable as he continued recuperating.

She was also uneasy about her uncle's presence among the Indians. She could not help worrying how they might react to such a man as he. Spoiled and headstrong, John was even despised by his own brother. Until John had established his brewery, he had done nothing positive with his life.

Dayanara had always been uncomfortable with the way her father taunted her Uncle John about being a lazy, spoiled playboy. But the taunts were true. John had spent his time gambling and drinking, and Dayanara's grandfather always paid to get John out of trouble. After his father's death, Daniel had continued the practice, paying to keep the news from spreading to their friends and colleagues in both Washington, D.C. and Saint Louis.

Tired of having to bail out his younger brother from one scrape or another, Daniel taunted him over and over again, reminding him that he was not worthy of the name Tolliver.

When Dayanara's father chose to move back to Saint Louis, to live in the family mansion, John had resented his brother's proximity, especially when Daniel constantly claimed John would gamble away whatever money he made in the brewery business while in his drunken stupors.

Thus far, John had proved his brother wrong. He had proved himself capable of owning and running his business. He had even succeeded in hiring some of the soldiers at the fort to accompany him looking for wild hops. The men were willing to desert their posts if it meant gold coins in their pockets and good whiskey, which John had promised them.

Neither Dayanara nor John was truly afraid of the Indians in this area; for the most part they were Cree, who were known to be friendly with whites. The map had surely been stolen from the Cree by another tribe, since the Cree had never been known to war with whites.

Dayanara and John also knew that the Cree were weakened now in number by a terrible outbreak of smallpox some months back. The disease was no longer a threat, yet many of the Cree people were still weak as they recovered from the disease.

Dayanara still couldn't believe that John had managed to get soldiers who were willing to desert their posts to accompany him on his venture, whereas none had agreed to go with her. It seemed the men were fearful of the supernatural aspects of the bones.

Before her father had drifted off into these lengthy sleeps, he had begged Dayanara not to go off on her own to search for the bones.

Yet even as he pleaded with her, he must have known that his words were falling on deaf ears. Being an only child, she had learned the art of independence long ago from a father who never discouraged it, or held her back. He had always admired her spunk.

Knowing what this venture meant to her father, and knowing that he would never be well enough to go on the search with her, Dayanara had decided to find the bones herself. She knew how to ride and shoot as well as any man, so why shouldn't she go out on her own?

The map would lead her to the bones.

As far as she was concerned, the soldiers who refused to help her were yellow-bellied cowards!

She gazed at her father. A part of her told her not to leave him, yet the doctor had reassured her, time and again, that he was past the crisis . . . that he was going to be all right.

The fact that he was resting so peacefully made her believe that he would be all right.

"Mother, I'm leaving now," Dayanara blurted out. "And say no more about it. I must go. Please, Mother, when Father awakens and asks about me, find a way to make him understand so that he won't get upset. We can't chance getting him upset, now can we?"

"Dayanara, this is so wrong," Dorothea said, stifling a sob of fear behind a hand. "You're risking your life for . . . for bones? How can you? Don't you see the foolishness of it? It was bad enough worrying about you and your father exploring Indian country. But the idea of you going alone makes me sick to my stomach!"

"I'm truly sorry, Mother, but I must go and find the bones as quickly as I can. Then I can return to Father with the good news that our venture here was a success," Dayanara said, standing.

She smoothed her hands down the front of her beautiful yellow silk dress. The white lace collar contrasted with the tan of her face . . . a tan she had gotten from her outings with her father in early summer.

Dorothea turned her eyes away from Dayanara. "Go, then," she said, sobbing. "Hurry along, Dayanara. I can't watch you leave."

Dayanara wanted to give her a fierce hug,

but knew that the better thing to do was to leave. She was afraid that if she talked much longer with her mother, their voices might awaken her father.

And she didn't want her father to be awake when she left. She wouldn't be able to bear the worry in his eyes.

She *had* to go. It was a fever in her that nothing but success could extinguish!

Dayanara bent low, gave her father a soft kiss on his brow, then left his bedroom and walked down the dark, narrow hall of the drab cabin that they had been given for the duration of their stay at the fort.

She hurried into her assigned room, where she had left the map in the top drawer of her dresser. Her pulse raced with excitement as she went to the dresser and opened the drawer. Her excitement turned to dismay, and then anger, when she saw that the map was no longer there.

"Someone has stolen it," she whispered harshly to herself. "But . . . who?

"Uncle John!" she gasped, knowing that he would take pleasure in thwarting her.

He didn't want her or her father to succeed. He didn't want them to receive the acclaim he knew they would earn in all the newspapers. His jealousy had surely driven him to steal the map.

Her eyes filled with rage, Dayanara looked toward the window as she heard a horse's

19

hooves outside their cabin.

She ran to the front door and stood on the tiny porch just as John tied his horse's reins to a hitching rail.

"Uncle John, you are a low-down thief," she said. "Give me back the map. I know you have it."

When he didn't reply but instead gave her a cold, lengthy stare, one that made chills race up and down her spine, she inhaled a nervous breath, then swung around and went back to her room.

There had been something in that stare that frightened her. It proved just how much he detested her.

She knew she couldn't prove that he had stolen the map. And who but she would even care?

The colonel at the fort had scoffed at her when she said she would go alone to find the bones since his men were too cowardly to accompany her.

And even though she knew that the colonel and his men were against her disturbing the burial spot of the bones, she was sure that no one had entered this cabin except her family. John could be the only one who had access to the map.

After closing the door to her bedroom, she began pacing. She must accept the fact that she would not have the map to lead her to the monster bones.

She tried hard to recall some of what she had seen on the map while going over it earlier. She smiled as she began remembering the details of the map, for she had studied it extensively with her father as they made their plans.

"Yes, I do believe I can find my way," she whispered to herself.

She hurried to her trunks to get a change of clothes. She had brought several riding skirts and blouses.

She had even made certain to bring sturdy leather boots. She had heard about the snakes that inhabited this country and hoped the knee-high leather boots would protect her from such bites.

"Dayanara! Dayanara!"

The panic, the hysteria in her mother's voice caused Dayanara's heart to go cold. Surely her mother's frantic call had been prompted by her husband's condition. Dorothea seemed to have accepted Dayanara's determination to leave, so her sudden, distraught behavior had to be because of something even more upsetting.

As Dayanara opened her bedroom door, her mother rushed in, tears pouring from her eyes.

"Mother?" Dayanara said, her throat suddenly dry.

"He's dead, Dayanara," her mother wailed. "I . . . I . . . saw him gasp and then take a long, lingering breath . . . and then he stopped breathing altogether. He is gone, Dayanara! Your father is dead!"

Dayanara was struck dumb by the news. She had thought that her father's deep, peaceful sleep was a sign of his recovery. The doctor had assured her that it was.

He couldn't be gone!

She had to grab the edge of the door to keep her knees from buckling.

Chapter Two

After weeping tears of dew;
Above the wind and fire, love,
They love the ages through!
— R. W. Raymond

The morning sun painted the waters down below a soft pink as Quick Fox, a young Cree chief of twenty-five winters, knelt on a bluff high above the winding Missouri River.

He wore only a breechclout and moccasins this day. His hair was as lustrous as the raven's wing and fell across his broad, muscled shoulders, rippling down his back to his waist. One thick lock covered the left side of his bronzed face.

Due to a recent bout with smallpox, which had left him scarred, Quick Fox's face, with its lean features, was no longer as smooth as it had been. He hid those scars beneath his hair like he would hide a dark sin that shamed him.

Eagles soared majestically overhead, their shadows joining the pink waters beneath them. Tall marsh grass had turned mustard-yellow at the water's edge, and ferns had mellowed into the rich cocoa color of late summer against a backdrop of hemlocks and pines.

Farther still, in a broad, gently sloping pass backed by mountain peaks and distant bluffs, stood many conical tepees.

Quick Fox felt a sense of melancholy as he gazed with keen and restless midnight dark eyes at his people's village. He was saddened by the abrupt changes that had affected them so tragically. Too many had been killed by the smallpox epidemic.

Quick Fox had been spared the worst of the disease. He had not been as ill as many of his people.

When the disease first struck the village, those who were not yet sick separated themselves from those who were.

Chief Quick Fox, being young and strong, and thinking he was healthy enough to fight off the terrible sickness, had stayed behind with those who were ill. He had temporarily named his best friend, Brown Shield, chief of those who departed. Brown Shield would lead their people to a new camp, where they could wait for the disease to pass.

When the epidemic was over, the village would be reunited under one chief's rule.

Quick Fox thought back to the beginning of the epidemic five winters ago, during the year of 1838. Smallpox had broken out first among the Blackfoot and Dakota, but because the Cree did not war with either the Blackfoot or the Dakota, his people had been spared the horrors of the disease for a time.

But they could not protect themselves forever from the ravages of the ugly disease. They had been exposed eventually by wandering groups of refugees infected by smallpox.

Quick Fox's counting sticks showed that six months had passed since the parting of his people.

Now, with supplies running low, and unable to replenish them at Fort Meyers or the nearby trading post because of the white man's fear of the epidemic, Chief Quick Fox was worrying about those of his people who had stayed behind in his village.

His people were known for being great bison hunters. But those warriors of his village who had been downed by smallpox still were not strong enough to go on a big hunt. Only a few rabbits and other small game had been caught to sustain their people.

Quick Fox knew that he must send for the other part of his band soon, or those with him would perish.

Huh, yes, the stronger warriors, those who had not been touched by the terrible disease, would be able to participate in a big hunt; his people's lives depended on their success in hunting and trapping.

His spine stiffened when he reached a hand up to the left side of his face and slid his fingers beneath the lock of hair. He grimaced when he felt the smallpox scars. There were not many, but even a few were too much for him. He was a proud man, a man who did not like to think there was anything about him that might make a woman turn away in disgust.

He shuddered and slowly lowered his hand from his face. *Huh,* he was afraid that the scars *would* make women turn away from him, and that made him angry and sad at the same time. Just before the smallpox came upon his people he had planned to seek a wife, perhaps from the friendly tribe of Assiniboines whose village was a half day's canoe ride away on the Missouri River.

Now he did not think that any woman would want to join him in bonds of marriage.

One woman in particular came to mind. As he had stood outside the trading post three sunrises ago, trying to get the courage to enter for the first time since his recovery, he had seen a *yo-oh-habt-popi,* a yellow-haired white woman.

Since he had seen her, he had had the same dream for three nights running, a dream about the awesome beauty of the white woman.

He had been taught long ago by an ancient uncle that dreams and visions gave a man the power to foretell future events. When a dream came to a man three times, it was a sign that it had been sent from above.

It was not to be ignored.

And how *could* a man ignore such a dream of such a woman? Yet how could he forget his scars and his fear that the yellow-haired woman might shudder with disgust at such a sight if she saw them?

It was the dream about the yellow-haired woman that had brought him to the bluff this morning, a bluff where he had gone to pray one day long ago and had been guided to an object which was now his "medicine." It was a small rock carved by wind and time into the shape of a buffalo. Bleached by the sun, it had the appearance of the sacred white buffalo.

He had placed his newfound medicine in a small buckskin bag for safekeeping, for if it was lost, it would cause him great difficulty in life. The medicine bag hung suspended from a pole outside his lodge at all times, except when it rained, when it was taken inside and hung on a pole just inside the entrance flap.

Religion and ceremony were highly valued by his Cree people. They were a means of fostering success in war, fortune in the bison hunt, and good health.

Through prayer Quick Fox hoped to obtain

greater wisdom about this white woman; he needed to learn how he might gain the power to make her look past the scars and see the kind and noble man he was. Once he knew that, he would try to become acquainted with her.

He felt a sensual warmth at the thought of having her to take to his bed each night, and to wake up with each morning.

The Cree were an intelligent people, who adapted to the habits of other peoples readily. After allying themselves with the Assiniboines, they adopted many of that tribe's customs. Quick Fox and his people spoke a mixture of languages . . . among them English.

Huh, if he ever did get to meet the white woman face to face, he could talk with her in her language. He smiled at how impressed she would be by his intelligence.

If she was as generous-hearted and kind as she was beautiful, surely she would look past his scars and see the good man that he was, as he had already looked past the fact that her skin was white.

He knew that her people would label any relationship between them as *tehinda,* forbidden. But he hoped to convince her that their future could be bright.

He reached his hands heavenward and prayed first for his people, and then for the woman.

Chapter Three

For to be wise, and love,
Exceed man's might;
That dwells with Gods above.
— Shakespeare
Troilus & Cressida

A full week had passed since Dayanara's father's funeral. He had been laid to rest outside the fort's walls, beneath the gentle shade of a cottonwood tree.

As Dayanara had stood there while a preacher said the final words over her father's grave, the wind whispered through the soft rustling of the leaves . . . as though her father were speaking to her . . . calming her . . . telling her that things would be all right.

Then that night, as she slept, he had come to her in a dream and told her again that things were all right . . . that he was in peace, that he was happy.

In that dream he had urged her to continue with the mission, to find the bones and study them and make history by doing it.

She had awakened feeling calm and, oh, so loved by her father.

She had also awakened with a determination she had never known before. Her father had died, but not his dream.

Although her mother knew that Dayanara would not leave this land until she succeeded at what she had come to do, Dorothea was waiting for the next riverboat to take her home. Her mother wanted to mourn her loss alone in her own way, in her own home.

As for Dayanara, doing her father's bidding was the only way she could deal with her own grieving.

Dayanara was at the trading post that was located just outside the walls of the fort, down by the river. She was excited about what lay ahead, yet somewhat afraid too. She had never set out on such a venture alone. Her father had always accompanied her.

And she could tell by the way the men in the trading post were looking at her that she was an oddity to them. Surely women never came to the trading post alone.

She tried to ignore the way their eyes followed her and how some whispered and laughed mockingly.

She just lifted her chin and continued what she was doing. She was there for a purpose, and no one was going to make her so uncomfortable that she would leave. She needed a few more supplies, and several shovels, which she had not wanted to bring on the boat with her.

Outside the trading post her horse and a pack mule, loaded with the supplies she had brought from Saint Louis, awaited her.

Trusting no one, not even her own uncle who she believed had stolen the map, she had hidden a rifle and shotgun among her supplies on the pack mule. On her person she carried a tiny, pearl-handled pistol, and a knife sheathed to her upper left thigh beneath her leather riding skirt.

Feeling protected, she continued making her way down the narrow aisles of the small, dirty, smelly trading post. The place was crowded with a mixture of grungy mountain men, hunters, and trappers.

Surprisingly, there were no Indians visible, even though she knew that a Cree village was located somewhere nearby.

She stopped and stood behind a tall stack of pelts while she listened to what a man was saying about the Indians to the proprietor of the trading post. He was laughing and poking fun at the neighboring Cree tribe, saying that with the Cree, no coins, shells, wampum, or any other thing except pelts was used for trade. They weren't acquainted with the white man's money.

A man with a loud voice spoke up, saying that if a coin and a button were presented for trade to a "dumb Injun," there'd be no question but that the Indian would take the damn button!

When the men broke into loud, boisterous laughter, Dayanara was filled with loathing for these men who had so little respect for Indians.

She wished she could become acquainted with the Cree and teach them about such things as money, especially after seeing one Indian in particular the other day.

Yes, she'd been impressed by the Indian as he stood outside the trading post in the shadows of the trees, watching the activity as men came and went from the establishment.

He had been so noble in bearing, so muscular and dignified, and oh, so wonderfully handsome, he had stolen her breath away.

Then suddenly he was gone, as though as he had been nothing more than an apparition. She wondered if she would ever see him again.

Would she come across Indians while she was looking for the burial grounds of the "monster bones"? She hoped that if she did meet them, it would be on friendly terms. She couldn't forget that the Cree might see the bones as holy.

She hoped that if she did have to explain her presence in the area, the Indians would understand that she meant neither them nor the bones any harm.

Yet she *did* hope to take some samples to

send to Washington. But if that wasn't possible, she would make do with recording all that she discovered about the bones. Her report would be well received by those at the Smithsonian Institute in Washington who anxiously awaited news about the prehistoric find.

She thought about the handsome Indian and wondered again, as she had the day she had admired him from afar, why he wore one thick lock of hair down the left side of his face.

Her thoughts were brought abruptly to a halt when she felt eyes on her.

She looked quickly to her right and saw a movement. Then she spotted a child, a boy, who had been peeking at her, and who now slid quickly out of view behind a stack of folded pelts a few feet from Dayanara.

Intrigued by the Indian attire the boy wore, she started to go to him.

She stopped suddenly when Pete Orndorff, the proprietor of the trading post, suddenly appeared, roughly grabbing the boy by an arm.

Dayanara's lips parted in a horrified gasp as the child was yanked hard from behind the pelts. Now that she could see him better, she realized that although the child wore an Indian breechclout and moccasins, he was white. His skin was tanned by the sun, but he was definitely white.

Dayanara remained hidden as she listened to Pete Orndorff scold the child.

"You know better than to come inside this trading post around whites. The Cree you live with have been sick with smallpox," the man shouted as he shook the child hard by the arm. "I've told you time and again to stay out of my trading post. How do I know that you aren't contaminated with the smallpox? Even this minute you may be spreading it not only to me, but everyone here."

Dayanara studied the young boy's gauntness and listened as Pete continued shouting at him, calling him a beggar and hurling other insults as he dragged the child from the trading post.

Dayanara was stunned by the cruelty of this man toward the boy, for surely he could see the child's gauntness, too. It was obvious that the boy hadn't been eating well.

She had been told that Cree warriors were excellent hunters who kept their people fed well, so why hadn't this child been eating enough?

Then she remembered what Pete had said about smallpox, and she guessed that the child had been ill with the disease and had lost weight because of it. But she hadn't seen any scars on his body or face.

Feeling more sorry for the child by the minute, and angry at the sight of a grown man mistreating such a small, innocent child, Dayanara rushed from hiding and stamped up behind Pete.

"Unhand that child this minute!" she ordered, one hand on a hip as she held the handle of the basket filled with her supplies in the other.

When the man stopped abruptly and, still clutching the child's arm, turned around and glared at Dayanara, she didn't recoil in fear.

"Sir, you are treating this child worse than you would treat a stray dog," she said, her voice softer now, her eyes darting back and forth between the boy and Pete. "Can't you see that he isn't ill with smallpox? If that is your only reason for manhandling him, you have no cause to treat him so unjustly."

"Ma'am, whoever the hell you are, you'd best mind your own business," Pete grumbled as he towered over Dayanara from his lanky, six-foot-four height. "I don't know where you came from, or why. All I know is that no woman comes into my establishment and tries to push her ideals on me. This brat is no better than a snake I would kill in an instant if one crossed my path. Even if he was born into the white world, he lives with heathen Injuns now, so that makes him no better than one of them."

He held his face inches from Dayanara's. "And if you side with the likes of Injuns, you're no better than a redskin yourself," he said, sneering. "Now I'd suggest you be on your way, or else —"

"Or else what?" Dayanara said, holding her ground. "If you think you can scare me, you've got another think coming. I'm not just any woman. I don't bow down to any man. My father taught me independence, and, sir, that means I am independent of men like you."

She stood on tiptoe so that her eyes were level with his and her nose almost touched his. "Now, *sir*, I suggest you let go of the boy this minute or I will go to the fort and tell the commander that you don't have the decency it takes to run a trading post near his fort," she said, her voice tight with anger. "And, *sir*, I have come for supplies. I intend to leave with them."

"One day you'll speak out of turn to the wrong man," Pete said, yanking his hand free of the child. "But if you want those supplies, get 'em paid for and get outta here. Pronto. Do you hear?"

Pete stepped away from Dayanara and glared down at the boy. "Get outta here and stay away," he growled. He gestured with a wide swing of his hand toward the door. "Git, you little whippersnapper. Now! And don't come back!"

Dayanara saw the boy's eyes go to her as he wiped tears from them; then he leapt around and ran as fast as he could from the building.

Hoping to be able to talk with the child, to help ease his hurt feelings and embarrassment, Dayanara hurriedly paid for her supplies and went outside.

She looked slowly around and spotted the boy standing beneath a tree, his head in his hands, his body trembling with hard sobs.

Dayanara stared at the child for a moment longer. His long legs were slender and he did not yet have the breadth of shoulder and depth of chest that would come as he grew into manhood. He was still such a young thing, probably ten, and she couldn't help feeling a deep sympathy for him.

She wondered how he had come to live with the Indians. Where were his parents? How long had he been among the Cree? And why?

She moved cautiously toward him, and as she approached him, his eyes rose to meet her gaze.

"Thank you, lady, for helping me," the boy said weakly, a sob catching in his throat.

Dayanara was glad that he still spoke English even though he made his home with Indians now. She smiled down at him. "It was my pleasure," she murmured. "My name is Dayanara. What is yours?"

"My name is Little Fox," he said, the tears having finally dried in his eyes. "I am the adopted son of Chief Quick Fox of the Cree Fox Clan. In the white world, though, I was called Jeremy, short for Jeremiah, but please call me by my Indian name."

Dayanara laid her armload of supplies on the ground beside her and knelt before Little Fox, bringing her eyes level with his.

She placed a gentle hand on his gaunt, tanned cheek, glad that he did not recoil in fear from her gesture of friendship.

"Why did that terrible man call you a beggar?" she asked guardedly.

She was hesitant about asking him why he lived among Indians. She was afraid she might discover that he had been captured and forced to live with them as a white captive, a boy slave, even though she had been told that the Cree were friendly to whites.

Little Fox ducked his head, then looked quickly up at Dayanara again. "There has been much sickness in my village," he said, his voice cracking with emotion. "You heard the mean man talk of smallpox? That disease has killed many of my people and caused many more to leave. There are only a few warriors left to hunt, to keep those remaining at our village in food."

"I'm so sorry," Dayanara murmured. She searched his face and saw no signs of smallpox scars. "You have not been ill with the disease, yourself?"

"Only for a day or so, and then, after many prayers were said to the heavens, I grew well again," Little Fox said. "Unlike so many of my Cree brothers and sisters, I survived and I was not left with much scarring."

She saw the child swallow hard, as though what he wanted to say now hurt him.

She drew her hand away from him and waited until he was ready to speak again.

"Even my adopted chieftain father was downed for a while with the sickness," Little Fox gulped out. "But the prayers were answered as well for him, and he is now well and able to hunt. Still, he is only one man. He cannot go on a large enough hunt to fill all of his people's stomachs. And the other warriors are still too weak to hunt for the larger game with my father."

Suddenly his gaunt face broke into a wide smile. "But soon this will change," he said. "All of my people will be reunited and there will be a big hunt. There will be much food on the Cree's plates, for soon those who left to avoid the disease will return. You see, the disease has left my village now. Hope is in my people's eyes once again."

His eyebrows lifted as he looked even more closely at Dayanara, his eyes closely scrutinizing her. "Why are you, a woman, at the trading post, when usually there are only men there?" he blurted out. "Are you married? If so, why is your husband not at the trading post with you?"

Dayanara laughed softly. "I'm not married," she murmured.

Then her laughter waned.

"My mother is at the fort," she murmured. "My father . . . he . . . he . . . became ill on the voyage to this land. He . . . he . . . went to heaven a week ago."

She chose not to mention her uncle, for even saying his name left a bitter taste in her mouth. She detested him.

"Was your father's sickness smallpox?" Little Fox asked.

Dayanara sighed. "No one knows what the sickness was, but no, it wasn't smallpox," she said. "It was a strange sort of malady that came on many of the people on the paddle wheeler. Some died almost instantly. I . . . I . . . feel so fortunate that I had a few more days with my father before he died."

Dayanara did not want to talk about her father. It hurt too much. And she wanted to know the reason Little Fox was living with Indians, even dressing like them.

She had to ask and hope that he would not think her too nosy.

"Were you taken captive and forced to live with the Cree?" she asked cautiously.

When he smiled softly at her, she knew without his telling her that he was not with the Indians by force. He was there, somehow, because he *wished* to be.

And she could understand that if he had to choose between such men as those she had seen at the fort, and Indians who surely treated him as though he were a person, not a dog, he *would* choose to live with the Cree instead of the whites.

"No, I'm not a captive of the Cree. I never was," Little Fox said softly.

"I ran away from a tyrant of a drunken father and a mother who sold her body on the streets of Saint Louis," Little Fox explained. "After hearing adventure stories about Indians, I decided to find a tribe who might take me in and let me live with them. I hid away on a riverboat and when it arrived at these shores, I fled the boat and Chief Quick Fox found me. I begged him to take me to his home and let me stay with him. When I explained about my parents, he agreed. I was seven then. I am ten now. I have lived among the Cree these three years and am the adopted son of Chief Quick Fox."

"Didn't anyone come looking for you?" Dayanara asked softly. "Didn't your parents suspect that you might have stowed away on one of the boats docked on the riverfront at Saint Louis? Didn't they send out a search party for you?"

"No, no one came looking for me," Little Fox said, his voice drawn. "My family was glad to be rid of me, for I was nothing to them but another body to feed and clothe. I have been very happy with the Cree and hope never to have to live among whites again."

He reached a hand out and gently touched her golden hair. "Your hair is so pretty," he said softly. "It looks like sunshine."

"Thank you," Dayanara said, laughing softly. "And I like yours. It's long and shiny. Is that the way all boys at the Cree village wear their hair?"

"Yes, we take pride in our long hair," he said. He reached up and ran his fingers through his thick tresses. "My father Quick Fox taught me how to use bear grease to make it more shiny."

Then he quickly changed the subject. "Why are *you* here?" he asked, cocking an eyebrow. "Without the protection of a man, aren't you afraid? If not, where do you find your courage? I heard how you spoke to the owner of the trading post. You are a very brave woman."

"Brave, huh?" Dayanara said, smiling. "Well, maybe it did take some courage to speak in such a way to such a large man when most men are in the habit of only looking at women, not listening to them."

"I am proud of your courage," Little Fox said, his eyes beaming.

"Thank you," Dayanara murmured.

She knew that he would be asking her again why she was there, since she hadn't answered that part of his question. But she wasn't sure if she should tell him what her plans were. It was obvious that he was devoted to the Cree, and she didn't know how his adopted people would feel about her mission to study the prehistoric bones.

While she debated the wisdom of confiding in Little Fox, she heard his belly grumble hungrily. Knowing how hungry he must be, she rose quickly and took him by the hand.

"Come with me," she said, walking toward her mule with the child at her side. "I have something for you, Little Fox."

His eyes were wide with wonder when they reached the mule and she released his hand.

He watched almost breathlessly as she reached inside one of the travel bags tied to the mule's back and took out a bright, shiny, red apple.

"Here," Dayanara said, smiling down at him. "This is for you."

Little Fox's eyes were fixed on the apple. Dayanara could see his eagerness to take it, yet he didn't.

She forced it into one of his hands. "Eat," she said, glad when he finally sank his teeth into the juicy apple and gobbled it down in no time flat.

Seeing how truly hungry the child was, Dayanara took cheese and bread out and gave them to Little Fox as well.

He ate these even more ravenously. When he was done, he softly, almost bashfully, thanked her.

It was then that he noticed she had just

purchased shovels, and he gazed in wonder at the pack mule loaded down with so many other things.

"Why *are* you here?" he blurted out. "Why do you have digging tools?"

Dayanara hesitated, but as he continued to look at her with wide, dark, trusting eyes, she knew she must tell him the truth. He trusted her, so she would trust him.

After she explained her reason for coming to Fort Meyers, Little Fox did something that made her eyes widen in wonder.

"I will take you there," Little Fox said in a rush of words. He smiled broadly up at her. "I will take you to the monster bones. You fed me? I, in turn, will help you."

Dayanara was taken aback by his reason for suddenly offering her his help. "I did not give you the food as a bribe," she explained hurriedly. "I gave it to you because I am your friend."

"As are you *my* friend," Little Fox said, his white teeth sparkling as he grinned even more widely up at her. "And, yes, I know that you did not use food to bribe me. I can tell that you are a woman of honest heart and surely would not bribe anyone in order to gain something for yourself."

"Thank you," Dayanara said, touched by his innocent sweetness . . . by his total trust.

"Come with me?" Little Fox said. "I will lead you where you want to go."

"Are you certain that you should?" Dayanara asked, hesitating because she didn't want the child to get in trouble.

"Yes," Little Fox said, shrugging. He took it upon himself to go and retrieve the articles she had purchased at the trading post.

He brought them back and handed them to her, one by one, until she had them loaded on her pack mule.

"There is one thing, though," Little Fox said as she tied the last utensil on the mule.

Hearing the caution in his voice, Dayanara turned and gazed down at him in question. Was he about to give her some sort of ultimatum?

"What?" she asked guardedly.

"We must go with much caution to the graves of the monster bones," Little Fox said.

"Why?" Dayanara asked.

"There are many snakes we must watch out for," Little Fox said. "Sometimes the snakes guard the monster bones. Sometimes they don't. Just in case, we must carry a stout willow branch. It is the Cree's weapon against the snakes."

"Truly?" Dayanara asked, in awe of the child's knowledge of such things. He was so young, yet he knew so much about the ways of the Cree.

He nodded, then went to a nearby willow and broke off a branch. He came back to Dayanara with a smile. "We can go now," he said.

45

"There's room on my saddle for both of us," Dayanara suggested, motioning toward the saddle with a hand. "But first, let's secure that willow branch with the other things on the mule."

After she had tied the branch to the mule, and had situated Little Fox on the saddle behind her, his tiny arms twined around her waist, they rode away from the trading post in the direction that he had pointed out to her.

"Even though I had no part in the cruel way you were treated at the trading post, I apologize for it anyhow," Dayanara said. "Pete Orndorff is a mean, heartless man."

"I know very well about heartless, mean men," Little Fox said, his voice suddenly bitter. "My father was the meanest of them all. He had no idea how to raise a son. I have learned much from my adopted father that my true father could never know."

"I have met men like your white father who mistreat their children," Dayanara murmured. "I'm so lucky that my father was always loving and kind."

"My adopted father is also loving and kind," Little Fox said, beaming. "I have learned much from him that my true father could never teach me. I have also taught my Cree father some of my own ways. It has been good between us, very good."

Dayanara recalled the men at the trading

post mocking the Cree and calling them ignorant.

"Have you taught the Cree the knowledge of coins?" Dayanara asked. "Do the Cree know they could get paid well in coins for the pelts they take to the trading post?"

"There is no need," Little Fox said, shrugging. "The Cree barter their furs for the goods they need. What use are coins to the Cree?"

He laughed into the wind. "The white men at the trading post call my chieftain father and my Cree people ignorant," he said. "It is the white men at the trading post who are the ignorant ones, not the Cree. The Cree's wealth is constituted of far more than mere coins. Their wealth is in their knowledge of the land . . . of the animals . . . and the One Above who blesses them."

Dayanara was in awe of this young man's way of speaking and of his philosophy of life. In everything, he seemed twice his age.

Dayanara was excited about having found someone not only to help her, but to be her friend. She also hoped that through Little Fox, she might eventually meet the handsome Indian she could not forget.

She would find the right time, though, to ask the boy about that warrior. Now she had to concentrate on finding the way to the monster bones.

Her heart was beating with excitement at

having found a way to learn the location of the bones without the map. She would show her uncle that his theft of the map had not stopped her from finding the prehistoric bones.

Chapter Four

The birthday of my life
Is come, my love is come to me.
— Rossetti

His heart aching, Quick Fox stood with his warriors, preparing to begin their hunt. Most were not strong enough to ride their steeds, so Quick Fox and his warriors were on foot. They were not far from their village when they saw a vast herd of buffalo in the distance, their shaggy coats and loud bellows like a mockery to the warriors who could not pursue them.

"These will be someone else's food . . . someone else's warm robes," Quick Fox said, his voice drawn.

He clutched hard at his bow and for a moment was lost in memory of his last hunt. He had been so proud and strong on his powerful black steed as he rode into the throng of buffalo. He could not even count how many of those buffalo he had proudly brought down.

All that he knew was that the food from that hunt was now gone and the clothes made from the skins were worn thin and needed to be replaced. Even their lodge coverings must be renewed.

"We will hunt buffalo soon," Two Feathers said as he drew closer to Quick Fox. "When our stronger warriors return, we will go on that hunt. Even these same buffalo we are now looking at will surely feel the pierce of our arrows."

"The Blackfoot will see them and kill them first," another warrior said, his voice filled with sadness and gloom.

"The Blackfoot no longer come so close to the land of the Cree," Quick Fox said, thrusting his muscled chest out proudly. "They know the wrath of us Cree if they do."

"But surely they have heard about our weakened warriors," Two Feathers said. "Will not they take advantage of that?"

"Remember that they, too, were weakened not long ago by the same vicious disease," Quick Fox said. His eyes narrowed angrily. "It is partially because of them that the disease finally spread to the land of the Cree. Had those few Blackfoot who mingle with others not come to our land months ago, none of our people would have died so needlessly."

"It was cowardly how they professed to be from another tribe in order to be admitted to our village as they fled their own in hopes of leaving the illness behind, while all along, they were already infected with the disease and did not know it yet," Two Feathers snapped angrily. "We only realized what had happened when the dreaded sores erupted on the flesh of so many of our people."

He looked uncertainly at Quick Fox. "Even you, my chief, were damaged by the scarring," he said, glancing at the long, thick lock of hair that lay across the left side of his young chief's face.

"*Huh,* I will carry these scars to my deathbed," Quick Fox said, raising a hand to his face. He slid his fingers beneath his hair and sighed heavily as once again he felt his damaged flesh.

"But your *life* was spared," another warrior said. His eyes suddenly filled with sadness. "I lost my entire family — my wife, my child, and my parents. Oh, but if I could join them at the burial ground, I would."

"Only cowards wish to join the dead," Quick Fox scolded. "And, Brown Eagle, you are anything but a coward, so do not speak as though you were."

Brown Eagle nodded slowly. "You are right," he said, his voice cracking with emotion he could not completely hide. "I shall say it no more."

"Do not even think it, Brown Eagle," Quick Fox flatly instructed.

Quick Fox turned slow eyes to the other men. "*Keemah,* come, warriors, we must hunt now, not talk," he said. He slid his bow onto his shoulder. "And you know the target of our hunt today and our plan."

His twelve warriors nodded in agreement; none of them was happy about the tactics they must use since their bodies were still not strong enough to hunt for large game.

They would take whatever food they could today and be happy for it. They would thank their Father Above for any food on their families' plates, no matter how small or insignificant.

Meat was meat.

First they drove as many groundhogs as they could find from their holes with sharp, barbed sticks and killed them.

They each had brought large bags to fill with their kill. They placed the groundhogs in a few of the bags, then, still on foot, proceeded with their hunt.

They scampered after squirrels and chased them into hollow logs, then plugged the holes with sagebrush. As the animals squealed and tried to dig their way out, the warriors set fire to the sagebrush and fanned smoke into the openings.

When the animals were all dead from the smoke, the warriors unplugged the holes and took them out.

After this kill joined the groundhogs in the

bags, Quick Fox and his warriors moved to a spot where many rabbits were nesting. Once there, they hung several nooses of tough bark from trees and hid and waited.

As the rabbits came sniffing the strange apparatus hanging from the trees, the warriors yanked hard on the nooses and captured rabbit after rabbit, until they had enough food for several more days.

By the time this food ran out, his people would be reunited. Quick Fox was eager to see their faces and to feel their warm embraces. His people were his world, and when they were separated into two entities, it was as if his heart was torn in two.

"*Keemah-namiso,* come, hurry, let us return home with our catch," Quick Fox said, lifting a heavy bag and slinging it over his shoulder. "The women will have these cleaned soon and we will smell the aroma of grease dripping from the meat into our lodge fires. Tonight our bellies will be filled with the blessedness of food."

Quick Fox smiled as he envisioned his son, Little Fox, eagerly eating his fill of today's kill.

His smile waned then, as he recalled the gauntness of his adopted son. Quick Fox often felt less than a man these days because of his inability to make things as they should be in his village, or even in his own lodge.

Many moons ago, when Quick Fox's

mother and father were alive, his parents never failed to put an abundance of food on Quick Fox's plate each night.

And it had been the same for Quick Fox as an adult with responsibilities of his own in his lodge. He had always made certain his son never went to bed hungry, until the ravages of the scarring disease changed everything in his village.

There was not one lodge that had been left untouched by the disease. Even those who had been sent away had not really escaped because they had left behind loved ones who were ill.

Quick Fox was anxious for the first buffalo hunt, not only for the food it would give his people, but for the skins that could replace those that now covered the lodge poles of each family's tepee.

He wanted fresh, new skins wrapped around the lodge poles. He didn't ever again want to see those skins that had housed the ill. He felt it was important to burn them, and at the same time burn the last scent and reminder of smallpox. There were enough reminders as it was . . . the scars that had pitted too many of the faces of his people.

Oh, how he despised the scars that he had been left with, yet he thanked *Tomah-upah, tomah-vond,* Our Father Above, for sparing his life so that he could continue to lead his beloved people.

Quick Fox had prayed over and over again during the worst of the disease, saying, *"Tomah-upah, tomah-vond undiddahaidt soonda-hie"* — "Our father who is above, have mercy upon your children."

He always looked heavenward into the blue sky when he prayed. Neither he nor his Cree people ever prayed directly to the sun, although he knew that because the Cree looked heavenward when they prayed, white people thought his people were looking at the sun and praying to it.

Quick Fox smiled as he envisioned the eagerness in his son's eyes when Little Fox saw the bags of food being brought into the village. Quick Fox had heard his son's belly rumbling with hunger too often of late. But tonight there would be no cause for such noises.

As he and his warriors approached their village, Quick Fox saw the Cree women and children waiting anxiously at the outer edges. He knew that the elderly would be sitting in the cool shade of the trees, their eyes anxious.

It made his heart ache to think that things had come to this . . . that his people had been put in the position of waiting for a fresh kill so anxiously.

He hated thinking about the emptiness of most of their bellies at this very moment. It made him feel less a man, and less a chief.

But soon it would all change.

As he came closer to those who waited, Quick Fox began looking for his son among the crowd. He even expected him to break free and meet Quick Fox's approach with eagerness in his steps and in his heart.

But to Quick Fox's surprise, he did not see Little Fox anywhere.

He looked more closely at the various clusters of children who were standing in groups away from their parents. Still he did not see his son.

Was Little Fox at the white man's trading post? He had been forbidden to go there long ago, even before the sickness came to his people.

Quick Fox didn't trust the white men at the trading post, especially the one who owned it. He would never forget how the men there made Quick Fox feel less than human.

He wished he did not have to do business there, but the trading post was the only place nearby where the Cree could trade with whites.

He knew that the women of his village, especially, enjoyed the goods that could be acquired at the trading post. For them, Quick Fox had put his anger toward the white men aside, as well as the shame he felt when he allowed them to look at him as though he were no more than a worthless snake. He had done trade with the whites.

It had stopped, though, of late, for the whites knew of the smallpox outbreak among the Cree and had made certain the Cree did not enter the trading post to spread the disease to them.

Soon, though, when his people could prove they were well again, trade must be reactivated with the whites. Winter would soon be upon his Cree people, and they needed a good supply of almost everything before the snows isolated them from the rest of the world.

When several children came squealing toward the approaching warriors and Quick Fox still didn't see his son among them, his brow furrowed. Where was Little Fox? As soon as Quick Fox saw that the kill was divided equally among his people, he would go and find his son, bring him home, and scold him.

But the scolding would be brief this time, for his son would be anxious to eat, and one did not digest food well if one's belly was tight with shame.

Quick Fox would not allow the scolding to go so far that he would ruin his son's feast, or his own. But if Little Fox disobeyed him again, ah, then Quick Fox would not spare the rod!

Chapter Five

Where love is great, the
Littlest doubts are fear;
When little fears grow great,
Great love grows there.
 — Shakespeare
Hamlet

"Little Fox, will you get in trouble for taking me to the prehistoric bones?" Dayanara asked as she continued to ride in the direction that Little Fox indicated.

She didn't want to plant the seed of doubt in his mind, yet she hated to think that he might get punished for taking a white person to a place that was surely forbidden to outsiders.

The child was so dear. And now that she knew he had been raised by an abusive father, she didn't want anyone else to be given a reason to mistreat him.

In fact, the more she thought about it, the more she was inclined to tell Little Fox to go on home.

Surely she could find the burial grounds now without his help. Probably all she had to do was continue riding in the direction she was already headed.

"Lady, I —"

"Dayanara," Dayanara said, interrupting him. "Please call me Dayanara, or Day. Some of my closest friends call me Day."

"I will call you Day because it is much easier for me to say than Dayanara," Little Fox said, laughing softly as he found himself stumbling over her full name.

Then he grew serious as he pondered her original question, as to whether or not he should be taking her to the monster bones. He knew he would be scolded by his adopted father, for no one but the Cree knew of the burial ground.

But he trusted this woman. Surely she would only tell friends about the bones. And just maybe the pretty lady had more delicious food in her bag that she would share with him.

He glanced heavenward and saw that the sun was high in the sky, which meant that it was almost dinner time for white people. Day would be stopping soon to eat, wouldn't she?

His Cree people did not stop automatically at any given time to eat. But from having lived in the white world for seven years, he knew their habits.

He could not forget the delicious apple that Day had given him. He had savored each and every bite, especially the sweet juice as it had rolled down his throat. He had enjoyed every bite of the bread and cheese.

If she had something else as wonderfully delicious, oh, surely she would share that with him, as well!

But she kept her horse going at a steady trot, without any sign of stopping. Even if she didn't stop to eat, he still knew that he would tell her whatever she asked of him. She was perhaps the kindest white person he had ever known.

Back in Saint Louis, where people had seen him as a derelict nuisance, some had even kicked him to get him out of their way.

He had worn the clothes of a beggar, which were all that his mother could provide for him to wear. Most of the money she earned as a prostitute was put into clothes and face paint to attract the gentlemen who paid for her services.

What she hadn't spent on clothes and makeup had gone into whiskey. She had reeked of whiskey even more than his abusive father.

Little Fox had been overjoyed to get away from the filthy smell, as well as the disgrace of being their son.

Just at that moment Dayanara drew a tight rein and stopped.

"Why are you stopping?" Little Fox asked warily, unsure whether she was stopping because he had not answered her question, or because it was the noon hour and she was going to share food with him.

He hoped it was the latter.

"I'm hungry, are you?" Dayanara asked, now guiding her horse over to the shade of a huge tree.

"I . . . am . . . always hungry," Little Fox gulped out, then lowered his eyes in embarrassment when he realized how horrible that must have sounded.

"I'm so sorry that conditions at your village are so difficult," Dayanara murmured.

She drew a tight rein again and slid out of the saddle. She reached for Little Fox and lifted him to the ground. While doing so she saw how he eagerly gazed at one bag, the one from which she had taken the food.

She wondered just how hungry the rest of his people were. Should she go to the village and see? Should she take food to them?

But, no, she quickly thought. She couldn't stretch her luck too far about being friends with the Indians. Surely this boy was an exception because he was, in truth, white.

She had been told that the Cree were on friendly terms with whites. But surely they blamed their smallpox epidemic on whites. It was said that Indians had never known the disease until whites brought it to their land.

She reached inside one of her bags and got a blanket. She turned to Little Fox. "If you spread this beneath the tree for me, we'll have a picnic," she said, smiling. "Is that a bargain?"

Little Fox's eyes widened and his pulse raced. "A picnic?" he gulped out. "I've never been on . . . an . . . actual picnic."

"Well, you are going to now," Dayanara said, already lifting the bag of food from the mule's back.

"Do we sit on the blanket?" Little Fox asked as he glanced from the blanket to Dayanara. "Or do you just put food on it?"

"It's for us *and* the food," Dayanara said. She placed the bag in the middle of the blanket, then settled on it herself.

She arranged the tail end of her skirt around her legs, and even slipped off her tight boots to give her toes a breath of air before traveling onward.

She smiled as Little Fox sat down close beside her, his eyes never leaving the bag as she opened it and reached inside.

"More cheese?" Little Fox asked hopefully.

His eyes widened even more as he watched the food being placed on the blanket. Here were comestibles he had only seen while standing outside restaurants in Saint Louis, peering through the window as people in fancy clothes and hats ate at the fancy tables.

Honey!

Bread!

Preserves!

And there was even a banana. He hadn't seen bananas since his flight from Saint Louis.

"It all looks so good," he said, his voice filled with wonder.

"Eat whatever you wish of it," Dayanara said. She took a knife from the bag and placed it beside the bread.

She then brought out two napkins and spread one out on the blanket before them both.

"I can have something of all of it?" Little Fox asked.

After Dayanara nodded to him, he licked his lips hungrily. She took the lid from the jar of preserves, then with the knife spread a thick layer on a piece of bread and handed it to him.

"Try this first," she said, her eyes dancing. "Our family cook in Saint Louis makes excellent jams and preserves. This is strawberry preserves made from huge, ripe strawberries."

Although she was hungry herself, she couldn't keep from just watching Little Fox for a moment longer. He gobbled down a piece of bread heavy with preserves, then grabbed a piece of cheese and ate it. He went on until he had sampled more than one piece of each . . . except the banana.

There was only one. He didn't want to be rude by taking it.

"Aren't you going to eat?" Little Fox asked, a blush rushing to his cheeks when he realized that he had been doing all the eating.

He felt ashamed for showing the pretty woman his bad manners. But the food was so tempting, how could he not have eaten it?

"Yes, I think I will eat some cheese and bread," Dayanara said, placing a slab of cheese on the bread, which was still fresh from the morning baking at the fort.

"Thank you so much for everything," Little Fox said, nodding a thank you when Dayanara handed him another piece of cheese. "You are the most generous person I have ever known, except, no, I can't say that. My adopted father has been so kind to me, as have the Cree people as a whole. But for someone like you, a beautiful white woman, to suddenly appear in my life and treat me as though I am worth something, after I was always treated so badly by the white people in Saint Louis, I . . . I . . . am just stunned. And I'm so grateful. There has been too little food in our village for so long now."

"Will that be changing soon?" Dayanara asked softly. "Are your warriors well enough now to hunt?"

"They are still weak, but each day they grow stronger, and soon all of the people who fled the ravages of the smallpox will be returning, and then our hunts will resume and everyone's belly will again be as full of food as mine is today," Little Fox said, smiling broadly.

"I wish I could take enough food to your

people to feed them as I have fed you," Dayanara said. "But I doubt that they would receive me as easily as you have."

"I *do* want you to go to my village sometime soon and meet everyone, but my people's pride is too great to accept food from you," Little Fox said. He lowered his eyes. "Perhaps *I* shouldn't have been as eager."

"Yes, you should have," Dayanara said. She reached a soft hand to his cheek. "And I have loved seeing you eat and enjoy it so much."

"You asked something before that I did not reply to," Little Fox said, reveling in that momentary touch of her hand. She had lifted it away now, but he would never forget the softness of her flesh, as well as the kindness that had prompted her to touch him in such a way.

"You don't have to tell me, you know," Dayanara said, slowly putting things back inside her bag. She stopped before placing the jar of honey and the banana there. "I shouldn't have even asked."

"You can ask Little Fox anything and Little Fox will tell you," he said in a rush.

"Please don't feel that you must," Dayanara said, relaxing comfortably for a moment before mounting up again. She had to keep an eye on the movement of the sun. She wanted to return to the fort before it got dark. She did not like to think of being out there all alone on strange land in the dark.

"Here is something delicious that you have not yet eaten," she said, smiling at him. She opened the jar of honey, peeled the banana, then dipped the banana into the honey. "There isn't anything more delicious than this."

She gave him the banana with the honey dripping from it and watched as he ate it.

In his eyes she saw heaven and knew that he loved this special treat as much as she always had from the time her mother first gave it to her when she was a child of five.

When Little Fox was through, he slowly licked his lips clean of the remaining honey, then handed her the empty banana peel.

"I'm sorry," he said, blushing. "I ate it all up."

"I intended for you to," Dayanara said. She pitched the peel over her shoulder into a thick stand of brush, then slid her feet into her boots.

"And as for the monster bones . . . I do not see the same sanctity in those ugly monster bones as the Cree do," Little Fox said. "I wish you could carry them all away. All they have been to me is a source of nightmares. For too long now monster animals have visited my dreams, dreams caused by the constant talk of monster bones among the children my age. The Cree children see those bones in a much different way than I.

If the bones are gone, surely my dreams will be friendlier!"

"I imagine it *could* be scary thinking about buried bones and monsters," Dayanara said, nodding. "But I'm sure your father makes you feel safe enough, doesn't he?"

"I want you to meet my father soon!" he blurted out. "Will you come to my village? Will you meet him?"

"One day soon you can take me, if you wish to," Dayanara said, standing and taking the bag back to the mule and securing it in place as Little Fox brought the blanket to her. She had decided she would like to meet his people. After all, she might find the handsome Indian among them. But would they want *her*?

She had no time to ponder that concern. She needed to reach the burial grounds today. She knew now that she wouldn't have time to study the bones, for the day was passing too quickly. The important thing was to at least find their location. Then she could return the following day and begin her studies.

They got on the horse and rode onward. As the countryside passed by, Dayanara gazed at this new world. The sun bathed the eastern valley in pale yellow, which was spotted with dark clumps of sage. The creek they rode beside now appeared to be a green and silver serpent winding its way to the northeast.

And then Little Fox directed her away from the creek and up a steep slope of land, toward a butte.

"Day, when we reach the summit, we must ascend on the south side where the young men in the old times made a trail when they climbed this butte for their vision quests," Little Fox explained. "There the Thunderers sent rocks to fall on the young men who had little courage. When those with courage reached the top, they were led by the Thunderers to a special place to climb down, a place that was made long ago."

Intrigued by this Indian lore, Dayanara was careful as she guided her horse up the butte, the mule braying when it became frightened by the height.

The ascent suddenly grew steep and difficult. What had looked like a smooth path from the distance was actually rough and rocky terrain.

The trail then spiraled up a sharp incline where Dayanara had to make a detour around fallen rocks. Small pebbles bounced down the slope as they continued onward across the top of the butte.

She winced when she saw a rattlesnake slither out of the way, and sighed with relief as the snake crawled out of sight.

And then finally they began to descend the butte on the other side until they reached a hidden valley.

"We must leave the horse and mule here," Little Fox said, already sliding from the horse as Dayanara drew a tight rein to stop the steed.

Dayanara gave him a quizzical look, but as he stood waiting, she slid from the saddle and secured her reins to the low limb of a tree.

"Come with me, Day," Little Fox said, taking her by the hand. "Be careful."

Dayanara stepped warily over the many cracks and holes that pitted the rocky terrain.

She was curious about the burn scars on the smooth rocky floor they were now walking across. She wondered if they were from ancient man-made campfires.

She started to ask Little Fox, but he seemed strangely quiet now as they continued walking onward.

"This is a sacred place to the old ones," Little Fox suddenly said.

"This is a burial ground of the Cree elders?" Dayanara gasped out.

"No, not the burial grounds, but a place of prayer," Little Fox whispered. "Speak and walk softly."

"Should I even be here?" Dayanara whispered back.

"All places where prayers have been said are sacred to the Cree, so everywhere I take you here is sacred, for this is a place isolated from most things and persons, and is sought out when private prayers are needed," Little Fox whispered, then tugged on her hand. "Come with me over this way. We will leave the prayer places behind and then will enter the land where you will see old bones jutting up from the ground. My Cree people have never come to this particular place to pray. It is a place to see and think about, but not to pray over."

Suddenly they were there.

Dayanara was awed by how many bones she saw protruding here and there from the earth. Her heart pounding, she stopped and stared. This was a discovery of discoveries, and *she* was there to see it.

She eased her hand from Little Fox's and bent on her knees beside some bones that were easily accessible.

She started to reach out and touch one of the bones, but Little Fox was there grabbing her hand, stopping her.

Dayanara gave him a questioning look.

"You must not touch until prayers are said," Little Fox explained. He released her hand and fell to his knees beside Dayanara. "We must pray to get permission from above to be here and to look and touch."

"Tomah-upah, tomah-vond," Little Fox began.

As he prayed, Dayanara saw snakes slithering here and there, in and out of holes in the rocks, and in and out of bushes.

She only now remembered the stick that Little Fox had taken from the willow tree. They had left it with her horse!

Chapter Six

The delight that consumes the desire,
The desire that outruns the delight.
— Swinburne

"*Nei-chat*, I am well!" Quick Fox said proudly to himself.

Huh, he was feeling good. It was wonderful to be strong enough to ride his horse Midnight again, and he urged his steed to a gallop as he raced toward the trading post.

After returning home from the hunt, he had questioned everyone in his village about Little Fox. He had discovered that no one had seen the boy, not since shortly after Quick Fox had left for the hunt with his warriors.

Quick Fox had tried to understand why his son would go against his express wishes and had come to the conclusion that Little Fox missed the white world. Perhaps he could not help wanting to be a part of that world, if only in this small way by going to the white man's trading post.

The first time Quick Fox was aware of his

son's pastime of going to the trading post was when Little Fox brought home what white men called "dice." His son had been given the dice in exchange for guiding white men about the country.

More and more whites came to this lovely land to hunt, fish, and even settle. The Cree, known for their peaceful ways, were no threat to the white men, which meant, unfortunately, that when the white people started to plant their roots in this territory, they were more likely to choose land closer to the Cree than to the Blackfoot, Comanche, or Sioux.

His hair flying in the wind, his bare chest warmed by the sun, his face etched with determination, Quick Fox rode onward. His gaze was set on the trading post that was a short distance from the white man's fort. He saw no canoes in the nearby river, which meant that Indians had not yet returned to the post to trade. Since the outbreak of smallpox, all Indians had been banned from the trading post.

Even his son, whose skin was white, knew better than to go there, for all who knew him knew that he belonged to the Cree world now.

Yet his son *had* gone there more than once. Quick Fox knew that Little Fox had even sneaked inside to watch the trading as long as he could before getting caught and thrown out.

Quick Fox was going to make sure this time that if his son was there, it would be the last. Quick Fox hated having to resort to a punishment, but he must make certain his son understood that when Quick Fox forbade him something, it was forbidden!

Another, even more disturbing, thought came to Quick Fox. If his son was *not* at the trading post, then where was he? Little Fox had been gone for many hours, and Quick Fox could not imagine his son being able to elude the white men at the trading post for that length of time. He was no longer a small child with short legs and a small body who could hide easily. He was growing into a young man who would be noticed!

If he was not at the trading post, where would he be?

In trouble?

Of late there were more snakes in the area than usual. What if one of the snakes . . .

Ka, no. Little Fox knew how to elude snakes even better than he knew how to elude whiteskins. Never once had his son been bitten.

But there was always that first time. Even the most careful warrior was surprised by a snake now and then, especially when there seemed to be more snakes in the area than humans.

Arriving at the trading post, Quick Fox brought his steed to a halt. He ignored the glares of the white men coming and going from the trading post and tied Midnight's reins among the white men's horses.

Without hesitating, he strode inside the trading post. He had not been there since the outbreak of smallpox at his village. Shortly after some of his people had fallen ill with the disease, he had gone to the trading post for supplies and Pete Orndorff had ordered him out.

Insulted, Quick Fox had left. But a few days later he understood why Pete had not wanted him there, why he had been right not to allow him to stay. Quick Fox had contracted the terrible disease himself. If he had been allowed to continue to come and go at the trading post, he might have exposed all who were there to smallpox.

But that was behind Quick Fox now. Only the scars on his face would remind whites that he had been one of those who had been infected with the deadly disease. He dared anyone to try to send him away today, for his temper was short with worry over his son.

"Just hold on there, Quick Fox," Pete said as he scampered from behind the counter, his eyes narrowed. "Who said you could come in my establishment?"

Quick Fox's own eyes narrowed angrily as he glared at Pete, a bald man dressed in fringed buckskins and reeking of perspiration.

He understood how the man might stink

like a skunk. The trading post was dark and airless, filled with smelly pelts stacked here and there among other supplies that gave off their own strange odors.

Today many whites were crowded together in the post as they bought and traded with Pete. Most were dressed in filthy attire, some blood-spattered from hunting game that had at one time been hunted by solely the Cree.

Quick Fox found it hard to understand the lack of pride in these white hunters. Their hair was allowed to go unwashed and lay in greasy, filthy strands across their shoulders.

That smell alone made Quick Fox's nose twitch with discomfort.

"Let me check you over real good to see if you are free and clear of the smallpox," Pete said, moving closer to Quick Fox, his beady eyes going slowly over his copper skin.

Knowing that he must endure these moments of proof in order to get answers from the white man, Quick Fox stood his ground and with a tight jaw allowed Pete to study him. Just the same, he was insulted by this treatment, and by the other whites in the establishment who were watching with a mocking look in their eyes.

"What's beneath that hair hanging over the left side of your face, huh?" Pete said, lifting it before Quick Fox could stop him.

Quick Fox's first instinct was to knock the man's filthy hand away, but he didn't. He knew it was necessary to prove to the white man that this was all that was left of his illness.

"Ah, *there* lies the proof that you had the pox, all right," Pete said, nodding. He laughed mockingly. "I'd keep it hid, too, Quick Fox, if it were me. Shame how you got all scarred up like that on your face. Shame."

Having had all the insults he could take, Quick Fox wrapped his fingers around Pete's wrist and slowly lifted his hand away from his face.

"Watch it, boy," Pete growled as he yanked his wrist free of Quick Fox's hands. "I'd not get too bold. You're outnumbered here."

Pete placed his fists on his hips, but took a few steps away from Quick Fox. "Now tell me why you're here," he said stiffly. "If it's for supplies, where's your pelts? I don't hand out supplies free to you redskins, you know."

"I have not come to ask for handouts," Quick Fox said, infuriated by the suggestion, yet forcing himself to remain calm so that he could get the answers he sought about his son.

While Pete had been examining his body for smallpox, Quick Fox's eyes had darted around the room. He had not seen any signs of his son there.

"I have come to ask about my son," Quick Fox hurried on to say. "He has been gone from home all day. Has he been here?"

"Yeah, Little Fox was here all right, begging brat that he is," Pete said, flinching when he saw how that insult brought fire into Quick Fox's dark eyes.

When Pete saw that Quick Fox was not going to react to the comment, except to show his anger in the depths of his midnight dark eyes, he chuckled. "Yeah, he was here," he said. "I saw him con a white woman into something, but then the woman seemed to have conned him right back. After she fed him some food from her bag, he left on her horse with her. Lord only knows where they were going." His eyes twinkled. "Perhaps she asked about Injuns and the boy offered to take her to your village so that she could gawk and get an eyeful of the savages."

Quick Fox restrained his impulse to hit the man. His mind was troubled by the news that Little Fox had left with a white woman. Why would he have done such a thing?

"What did the white woman purchase while she was here?" Quick Fox asked guardedly. "Knowing that might help me understand why my son went with her, and perhaps where."

"Let me see now," Pete said. He raised an eyebrow and idly scratched his brow as he cocked his head and looked toward the ceiling. "Yeah, let's see if I can remember."

He laughed throatily and again gazed at

Quick Fox. "She purchased digging supplies, that's what," he said. He took a step closer to Quick Fox and leaned toward him. "She's probably going to go and dig up those monster bones that I've been hearing about."

Quick Fox's spine stiffened.

"Yeah, I'm sure that's where she's going with your adopted son," Pete said, nodding. "I heard tell of a man who came to this area only recently to find the bones. Word is he grew ill and died at the fort. It is this man's daughter who was at the trading post and who is now with Little Fox. Yep, Quick Fox, I think your brat is leading the lady to the graves of the monster bones, 'cause she had a pack mule trailing behind her horse with a good amount of supplies tied on its back."

"A pack mule? Digging supplies?" Quick Fox said, his teeth clenched.

"Yeah, and like I said, I can only assume that your son is leading her right to the bones," Pete said, chuckling.

"The lady came to the trading post alone?" Quick Fox asked.

"Yeah, she seems to be the independent sort of woman," Pete said, shrugging and chuckling. "I like that type. I might look into knowin' more about her. My wife died a few years back. It'd be nice to have a woman to snuggle with at night again."

His mind whirling with thoughts, Quick Fox turned on a quick heel and left the trading post. He stood beneath a tree and considered his best plan of action. There had been only one white woman on his mind of late, and he had seen only one recently at the trading post. Could it be the same woman who'd conned his son into doing something that Little Fox surely knew he should not do?

It made him sad to think that his son was hungry enough to take food for payment to lead the woman to that forbidden place.

"And how does she know so much about the bones?" he whispered to himself. As far as he knew, the monster bones had not been openly discussed in the presence of white people.

Why would his son lead a woman to the bones? Was it because they shared the same skin color? Was his son more hungry for the company of other whites than Quick Fox had realized?

Quick Fox hoped not, for he would not want to lose his son to the white world. Little Fox was his, through and through. Without the child, Quick Fox's heart would no longer be whole.

Huh, Quick Fox understood the weakness caused by hunger of the belly. He hoped that was all this was about, not the sort of hunger of the heart caused by missing one's true people.

If it was only hunger of the belly that led

his son to betray the Cree, that would soon be rectified, for he and the other warriors had brought food to the village.

He must first find Little Fox and the white woman. Her image had been imprinted on his mind from having thought of her so much. He knew he would recognize a description of her at once.

He hurried inside the trading post again and walked up to the counter, where Pete stood sorting through pelts.

"Describe the white woman to me," Quick Fox said, his voice tight.

When Pete described Dayanara, Quick Fox was certain that his son was with the woman he had seen at the trading post and in his dreams. He felt torn. He believed his son was safe with the woman, for she seemed gentle and kind. Yet on the other hand, if this woman was the sort to bribe a child, she was surely not someone he could fantasize over.

"Thank you for the information," he said, then left the trading post.

He mounted his steed and headed for the burial grounds of the monster bones. There was only one good thing that came out of knowing what his son had done. He knew that Little Fox was not in any sort of jeopardy.

Quick Fox was disturbed, though, to think that Little Fox might also be duped into helping the lady dig up the bones. Quick Fox was very aware of how his son felt about the monster bones; he knew Little Fox would like for them to be gone, because he had nightmares caused by them.

Then another disturbing thought made his jaw tighten with disgust: Pete Orndorff had spoken intimately of the woman, had talked of wanting her in his bed.

It was strange how the idea of the golden-haired woman in bed with the vile, stinking Pete Orndorff enraged him. He even felt jealous knowing that some other man was fantasizing about the same woman who had visited Quick Fox's midnight dreams!

"I must stop thinking of her in that way," Quick Fox whispered.

He sank his heels into the flanks of his steed and rode at a harder gallop across the land. He tried to focus on only one thing. His son.

He hoped that his son was not being made a fool of by a woman whose beauty could surely cause any male to lose his head.

"Not me," he vowed. "She will never trick Quick Fox into doing things that are unlike Quick Fox!"

Suddenly he had something else to think about. Up ahead in the distance, he saw several white men in the process of constructing a cabin. The building was on the edge of land where hops grew wild and beautiful.

Although Quick Fox had not personally opposed whites in this area, he did not like the looks of these men or what they were doing.

He wheeled his horse to a halt and walked Midnight into a thick copse of trees. He tied his horse's reins to a low tree limb.

Staying hidden in the shadows, he moved stealthily beneath the trees until he came close to where the men were erecting the cabin from a stack of logs that had been cut from this thick stand of trees.

Quick Fox crouched down onto his haunches as he watched and listened. He hoped to find out by the men's conversation just why they were building a cabin on this particular spot.

Except when they hunted, most whites stayed within the safe perimeters of the fort. There were no dwellings besides the fort and trading post built yet for whites in the area.

Was this the beginning of further expansion by whites into Indian land? Would they begin settling farther and farther from the fort and closer and closer to his Cree village?

That thought caused a bitter taste in his mouth, for with the influx of whites on Indian land came trouble that he did not even want to think about. He had heard about the greediness of whites on other people's lands. Once they began taking, they took and took. Much bloodshed had been caused by the greediness of whites.

He knew the English language well and

had encouraged his people to pay heed to how the English words were spoken, and to learn their meanings. He realized that knowledge of English was necessary in order to deal with the white intruders on his land.

He had heard that when a white man's fort and trading post came to Indian land, white settlers could not be far behind.

Huh, he had prepared his people for this, and had even taught them that hating whites would only bring death to the Cree.

He focused on a man of *yo-oh-habt-popi*, yellow hair. It was exactly the same color as the hair of the woman who was now with his son.

He listened to what the man was saying about the hops plants and how they would bring the whites much money. He heard him say something about a brewery.

Quick Fox also heard him say something about wishing he had a tall mug of beer made from the hops, but that whiskey would do for now.

With that, the men stopped working and the yellow-haired one drew a silver container from his pocket and took a drink from it, then passed it around from man to man until all had had a swallow.

That word "beer" was unfamiliar to Quick Fox, making him even more confused about what these men were up to, and what it had to do with the hops plants.

But Quick Fox knew the meaning of whiskey. It was firewater that burned the gut of a man and stole away his logic. He did not want firewater close to his people. He did not want his warriors to be lured into its clutches.

For that reason alone, he resented the presence of these men. He had heard how whites tricked red men into doing wrong in exchange for firewater.

As the sun began to sink behind the distant mountains, Quick Fox was suddenly reminded of why he had traveled in this direction — to find his son.

He would have time later to find out more about these *che-kas-koi,* these bad-hearted white men. For now he must be on his way to be sure that his son got safely home.

He gave the white men one last look, then ran stealthily back to his horse and rode off in a wide circle around them. He did not want them to know that he had been there spying on them.

"I will spy again and again, until I know exactly what their plan is," he said into the wind.

Chapter Seven

Familiar acts are beautiful through love.
— Shelley
Prometheus Unbound

Just as Little Fox stopped his prayer, Dayanara felt a sudden chill in the air, as though something cold had swept past her face. She shivered and hugged herself as she looked slowly around. Her gaze fell on the bones that protruded partially from the ground here and there.

She wanted to go and study them immediately, but she knew that time had almost run out on her today. The sun had dipped lower in the sky. In the gathering dusk, the nearby butte loomed blue-black as it was outlined by the yellow glow of the fading sun.

Dayanara wanted to be anywhere but here when the world was totally engulfed in black, even if the eerie-looking bones were only of dead animals, not humans.

The sudden coldness on her face made her feel that there *were* graves of Indians somewhere close by, graves that Little Fox hadn't told her about for fear of frightening her.

She had a superstitious fear of Indian burial grounds because she had heard so much about Indian spirits. If they watched over their departed loved ones' graves, they would not want a white woman anywhere near them.

At least the waning light had prompted the snakes to seek shelter for the night. She saw none of them now whereas only a few moments ago she had seen several slithering among the rocks.

"I truly must return to the fort now," she said as Little Fox gave her a questioning gaze. "Thank you so much, Little Fox, for leading me here. Without my map, I never would have found the bones alone. As I recall, even the map didn't show the treacherous rocky terrain that one must cross before getting to the graves of the monster bones."

"Where is this map you speak of?" Little Fox asked as he walked with Dayanara toward her horse.

"I'm not sure, but I believe my uncle has it now," Dayanara said, dreading the walk over slippery rocks and dangerous ledges to get back to her horse.

She dreaded even more the idea of returning to this place alone, yet she knew that she must. She did not want to share her find with anyone, and she knew better than to think that Little Fox would come with her again.

She also knew she wouldn't ask him. When his father discovered what he had already done, he would surely scold the child terribly.

Dayanara felt responsible for whatever might happen to Little Fox, but surely his father would go easy on him, for who could be mean to such a child as Little Fox? He was so precious in his innocence.

"Day, where did you get the map?" Little Fox asked, his hand sliding into Dayanara's and tightening around hers as he felt her slip on the loose rocks.

"A friend from the Smithsonian Institute in Washington discovered the map among old Indian relics and sent it to me and my father," Dayanara said.

She was glad when she finally saw her horse a short distance away.

She now realized that the journey from the burial place was not as bad as it had seemed while going there. Now that she was familiar with the route, it would not ever be as frightening as it was that first time.

"I know of Washington," Little Fox said. He gave Dayanara a wide grin, his white teeth flashing against the dark tan of his face. "That's where the President lives in a huge white house with tall white pillars."

"You remember your studies well," Dayanara said, smiling at him.

She was amazed at many things about

Little Fox. He was so young, yet he knew so much, and she doubted that his parents had sent him to school to learn these things. Surely most of what he knew he'd learned on the streets of Saint Louis. He had sought out knowledge for himself, gaining the insight and courage to flee his brutal life with parents who cared nothing for him, so that he might find something better with people of a different heritage and skin color.

He had learned so much about the Indians and their lore in only three short years. He was obviously an intelligent child. He could have gone far in the white world had he been given the chance to have an education. He might even have gotten a college degree.

"Tell me once again about the Thunderers," Dayanara said as they mounted her horse. "You said something about them earlier. I find Indian lore so intriguing."

"My father . . . my adopted father, I mean, has taught me everything I know about everything," Little Fox said, proudly thrusting out his small chest. "He is a good teacher, so I have tried to be a diligent student. My father has helped me understand so many things that in the white world were mysteries to me."

He nodded toward the butte they had just left behind. "You see the butte?" he said. "Buttes are hills which abruptly rise from the surrounding ground. Certain buttes are sacred places which the Great Spirit recognized."

He stopped and turned to gaze at the shadows being cast by the butte behind him. "Day, the Butte of the Thunderers that I look at now is a holy hill. It is believed that the Thunderers spoke from its flat top and that their message from *Wakantanka*, the Great Spirit, boomed across the plains. It was there that the lightning struck and caused huge rocks that lay around the butte's rim to break away, so that only those who were determined and courageous could make the difficult ascent."

He turned to Dayanara and smiled.

"You proved to be determined and courageous, so you will always be welcome on the butte and the surrounding area," he said. "When you return to study the bones, you do not have anything to fear. The Thunderers will even keep the snakes from getting near you."

"But I would think the Thunderers would not want me to be in this place, which is holy to your people," Dayanara said guardedly.

"If you only touch, not take, there is no harm in your being there," Little Fox said, giving her a solemn stare. "You won't take, will you?"

"I had wanted to, so that I could send some of the bones back to my friends in

Washington, but if you think it's best that I don't, then I won't," Dayanara said. "I will record my findings on paper, though. Is that all right? I will draw pictures of what I see. Is that all right?"

"Recording your findings in words is all right, but I am not sure about drawing pictures," Little Fox said, raising an eyebrow. "Pictures might be the same as taking the bones themselves, for the spirit of the bones will be in the pictures."

Dayanara swallowed hard. "Then I will only write about them," she promised.

She glanced up at the sky and saw that the light was rapidly fading.

"We must hurry onward," she said. "I'm afraid I have already waited too long. I wanted to return to the fort before it got dark."

"Day, do not worry. I will see you safely home," Little Fox said. He thrust out his chest in an effort to prove his strength and courage to Dayanara. "I will make certain no harm comes to you."

"No, I will see *you* safely home, or at least get you close enough on my horse so I will know that you are going to arrive home safe," Dayanara said, urging the horse on.

"I still feel it will be best if I take you to the fort," he said thickly. "This is a strange land to you. And as night falls, many four-legged animals come out from their hiding places and forage for food. I would not want to think of your being attacked by one on your way to the fort."

"What about you?" Dayanara asked. "If you are on foot on your way home and it's dark, what protection do *you* have against such animals?"

"I have my knowledge of the animals and how to elude them," Little Fox said, shrugging.

He held tightly around her waist as they continued at a steady lope, the mule braying as it tried to keep pace with the horse.

Little Fox watched Dayanara's golden hair fly in the wind.

He smiled when the ends of her hair sometimes whipped into his face and he could inhale its perfumed scent.

"Well, Little Fox, I have more than mere knowledge to use against anything that threatens me," Dayanara said as she glanced over her shoulder at him. "I have much gun power."

"You do?" Little Fox said, his eyes wide with wonder. "Where? I do not see any weapons on you."

"My larger weapons are hidden well on my mule, but accessible in case I need them," Dayanara said. She now looked directly ahead, trying not to worry as the shadows deepened on all sides of her. "But it is my constant companion, my pearl-handled pistol, that is my nearest protection."

"I see no pistol on you," Little Fox said. He strained his neck to look more closely at her.

"That is because it is hidden in the depths of my right pocket," Dayanara said. She smiled back at him again. "All I have to do is reach inside the pocket and I will have my pistol. Anyone or anything that becomes a threat had better watch out. I am very skilled with firearms. My father taught me long ago how to shoot and ride as well as any man. He saw that as necessary in a world where men are prone to try to take advantage of women."

Little Fox's look of awe made it clear that he was intrigued by a woman who knew the art of using firearms. From what Dayanara had read in her study of Indians, the Indian women usually did not even know the art of shooting a bow and arrow, much less a gun.

"Will you teach me how to use your tiny firearm someday?" Little Fox blurted out.

Dayanara went suddenly quiet. She didn't know how to answer him, for she didn't believe that this boy's father would want him to handle firearms until he was ready to teach the skill himself.

"I will have to think about that," Dayanara said, looking over her shoulder to judge his reaction.

When he smiled, she returned the smile.

His smile told her he probably believed that she would teach him how to use her pistol, because he knew how grateful she was for his help in finding the monster bones.

"Tell me now how to get to your village so that I can take you there," Dayanara said, keeping her horse at a steady lope.

She could hardly wait until tomorrow when she could finally delve into the true mystery of the prehistoric find.

"Make a wide swing to your right and soon you will be near my village," Little Fox said, telling her a white lie. Instead of leading her to his village, he was guiding her to a shortcut back to the fort.

He would not rest tonight if he wasn't sure she was safely in her own bed when the midnight hour came.

He was drawn to this woman, though he had only recently met her. She was so kindhearted. He wanted his father to become acquainted with her, too.

He hoped that if they did meet, they would both look past the differences in their skin color and customs. He hoped his father would like her as much as he did, for he secretly wished to have this woman as a mother one day.

Chapter Eight

My joy, my grief, my hope, my love,
Did all within this circle move!
    — Edmund Waller
    "On a Girdle" (1664)

Having finally arrived at the hidden valley of the prehistoric bones, Quick Fox saw fresh footprints in the loose dust of the ground. He did not need to kneel to get a closer look. He saw that one set of prints was small, the size that his son's would be. He also saw that the small feet were clad in moccasins.

He looked at the other prints and saw that they were not much larger; they had probably been made by a woman. The shoe prints proved that this person was white, for the prints were not made by moccasins.

He had already studied the hoofprints made by two animals that had been tethered where he had left his own steed beneath the shade of a tree at the foot of the butte. He recognized two sets of prints, one made by a horse, the other by a mule.

He could only conclude that they were

made by the animals Pete Orndorff had told him about, those which had accompanied the white woman to the trading post.

Quick Fox's jaw tightened as he recalled what else Pete had said about the white woman, that she had bought supplies which were usually used for digging.

"Digging the monster bones," Quick Fox muttered beneath his breath.

Again Quick Fox was torn between conflicting feelings. He could not help feeling anger toward his son for being so easily swayed by the pretty woman and the lure of food. At the same time, he could not help being intrigued by the woman.

The fact that he had seen this woman more than once in his dreams made him certain that he was meant to meet her face to face.

But what would he say to her? He knew he should order her away from the sacred burial place of the monster bones, and demand that she never approach his son again.

Yet could he truly do either thing? He feared his attraction to her would make it difficult.

At this moment the welfare of his son was his prime concern. Quick Fox hurriedly left the burial grounds and went back to his horse.

With shadows looming long and dark all around him, he rode off, his eyes scarcely able to follow the hoofprints as the light lessened around him.

Eventually, he lost sight of the hoofprints altogether, but he had seen enough to know the direction the woman was taking. It appeared she was heading back to the fort. Quick Fox sank his heels into the flanks of his steed and sent him into a hard gallop across the land.

Ah, how he reveled in the touch of the wind against his face and the feel of his muscled steed as his legs held tightly to him.

It had been some time now since he had ridden with such abandon, with such wondrous freedom. The disease had kept him in his lodge and at his village for too long. A man needed to ride with the wind often, just as a stallion did, to keep his spirits high.

When the disease had struck him down, he had lain on his furs racked with fever and covered with ugly blisters, and he had thought never to ride his horse again, nor to see many more sunsets and sunrises.

Tonight he was once again fully a man, a man with hopes and dreams, a man who could look toward the future with a smile and lead his people with all of his being.

And tonight he felt blessed that he had the strength to search for his son on his horse. "And I will find him," he whispered beneath his breath.

He glanced heavenward. The sky had

turned a rosy pink as the sun set behind the mountains.

He could not believe there was any land more glorious than that beneath the sky of his people.

But whites had come and would surely spoil everything eventually. The thought of anything disturbing this land of beauty and serenity sent a sadness through Quick Fox.

Yet again his thoughts returned to the white woman.

Was she not as beautiful as a setting sun?

Would she not be something to glory over morning and night if a man had her at his side, sharing his bed, sharing his life?

Not that he did not find his own Cree women beautiful and intriguing. But none had come into his heart in a special way.

He did not enjoy knowing that a white woman had a grip on his heart now, instead of a woman of his own people. But how could one fight destiny when it sent one's heart in search of a woman whose hair was golden instead of raven-colored? How could he deny himself this woman now that he had seen her?

But again he reminded himself he had his son to think about. He had to make certain that his son's welfare was not compromised again by the golden-haired woman.

If Quick Fox was forced to make a choice between his son and the woman, of course his son would come first.

Though Little Fox had been born white, Quick Fox had loved him as though he were of his own flesh and blood. His people had taken Little Fox in as one of them. Would they accept the white woman, too, if their chief requested it of them?

"What am I doing?" he shouted into the wind, looking heavenward. Why couldn't he concentrate on finding his son and sending the woman away with words that would make her fear to return to the monster bones ever again?

When he lowered his eyes to look straight ahead again, his heart skipped a wild beat. He saw movement ahead in the falling dusk.

With a racing pulse, he squinted into the semidarkness and urged his horse more quickly onward. As he closed the gap between them, he discovered that he had finally found the woman riding the horse with the pack mule trailing behind.

A moment later he made out a small figure sitting behind the woman on the saddle, his arms clinging as she rode steadily onward toward the fort. He knew that he had found not only the golden-haired woman, but also his son.

But why was Little Fox still with the lady instead of back at his village? he wondered.

His heart sank when a new thought sprang to mind. Perhaps the woman had convinced

Little Fox to return to the white world and turn his back on the Cree?

Ka, no! Surely not!

Little Fox was as one with the Cree. He awakened each morning with his new people. He went to bed and said prayers to the Great Spirit each night.

Little Fox would not betray his own heart just because a beautiful white-skinned lady told him to!

Determined not to lose this young man who was his son now in every respect, Quick Fox yanked on the reins and urged his stallion to take a wide swing to the right. He would overtake them and stop the white woman's schemes, whatever they might be.

Quick Fox thought back to the day when he had found the young white boy stumbling beside the Missouri River, his gaunt face suggesting that he had not eaten for days. Quick Fox had soon gained Little Fox's trust, and the child had told him about his flight, how he had eaten only bugs and scraps of food that were thrown on the boat. It was then that Quick Fox's heart had opened to the child and welcomed him inside.

Quick Fox very rarely went anywhere without some sort of food in case he was injured and left defenseless until his warriors found him. That day he had carried meat and bread. He would never forget how ravenously the boy had eaten it all up.

Quick Fox had taken Little Fox to his home and had seen that the woman who cared for Quick Fox's lodge bathed and fed the child, then gave him clothes from her own son who was the same size and age.

From that day to this, a bond had grown between Little Fox and the Cree people. He was Cree, not white. Surely the woman could not captivate Little Fox so quickly.

He finally caught up to the white woman and Little Fox. Emerging from the shadows of tall trees, Quick Fox blocked the way of the woman's white stallion.

He was now much closer to the woman than when he had seen her at the trading post. At this distance he could appreciate how exquisitely beautiful she was.

With her wide blue eyes framed by thick golden lashes, and her tanned face contrasting beautifully against her long golden hair, she took his breath away. He fought against his attraction to her, for he would not allow himself to be duped like his son.

"Father!" Little Fox gasped out. "Father, why are you and . . . you are riding Midnight. It has been so long —"

"*Huh,* I am strong enough to ride my steed *and* to search for a son who has been tricked by a white woman," Quick Fox said, his eyes holding the woman's.

"I did not trick him," Dayanara said quickly, glad that she had found her voice.

She had been speechless for a moment or two at coming face to face with the very man she had thought of so often.

"The child came with me very willingly," she explained.

Then her face heated with a blush as she realized how Little Fox had addressed the man who had caught Dayanara's fancy. This handsome warrior was Little Fox's adopted father. She recalled that Little Fox had said his father was a Cree chief.

Her eyes shifted. She noted again that the warrior wore one lock of hair across the left side of his face, and wondered why.

Little Fox was embarrassed by his father's words, yet he could understand why Quick Fox would be so upset.

"Son, why did you take it upon yourself to lead the white lady to the hidden valley of the monster bones?" Quick Fox asked.

He forced himself to look away from the white woman, to try to forget the softness of her voice when she had spoken to him in self-defense. The sound of her voice still sang a soft melody inside his heart . . . one he feared would be impossible to forget.

"You know?" Little Fox gasped, his eyes wide.

When his father said nothing in return, only gave Little Fox a continuing stern look from his midnight dark eyes, Little Fox became concerned that he might have lost some of his father's trust. He felt suddenly guilty for having aided the white woman. He hung his head and slid from Dayanara's stallion, hurrying over to stand beside Quick Fox's.

Quick Fox saw the shame that his words had placed in Little Fox's heart. He loved his son so much, he now felt wrong for having treated him in such a way.

He reached down with a muscled arm and swept Little Fox up from the ground, placing the boy on the saddle before him.

Seeing how hurt, even ashamed, Little Fox was, Dayanara decided to speak her mind.

"You are wrong to blame Little Fox for what happened," she said firmly. "I asked him to take me to the prehistoric bones. And even though it was not my intent to bribe the child by giving him food, it seems that, in a sense, it did appear so. Please believe me when I say that I did not give him food for that purpose. I'm sorry if it was all misconstrued."

"But you did go to the hidden valley of the monster bones," Quick Fox said tightly.

"Yes, I did. What harm have I done by being there?" Dayanara asked. His dark, midnight eyes almost hypnotized her, they were so beautiful, even with the anger present in their depths.

She had never been this close to an Indian warrior, especially a mighty chief.

The Indians she had seen in Saint Louis

had been viewed from a distance as they came and went in their canoes to bargain with the white traders who camped close to the Mississippi at the river landing.

Her father had warned her never to get too close, for she was beautiful. He had feared she might be abducted and taken captive, even though the Indians that came down the Mississippi to trade were known for their peaceful ways.

But this Indian, this handsome warrior, made her feel guilty for what she had done, and fearful of how he might retaliate.

She wished now that she had never included the child in her hunt for the burial site, yet without Little Fox, she would surely be out there in the wilderness even now, lost and afraid; surely she would never have found the bones at all.

She shivered at the thought of the many snakes she had seen. They had posed more of a threat to her than this handsome Cree chief.

After silently listening to Dayanara and actually admiring her spirit, Quick Fox was even more fascinated by her than before.

Yet he could not forget why she was on Cree land, or that she had been with Little Fox.

"Is it your plan to dig up the monster bones, to take them?" Quick Fox asked, his voice harsh.

A strained silence fell between him and the woman as he waited for her reply. He was almost afraid to hear her answer, for he did not want to be given a reason to order her away; everything within him wanted her to stay.

Chapter Nine

So all we know
Of what they do above
Is that they happy are,
And that they love.
— Waller
"Upon the Death
of My Lady Rich,"
1664

The sound of horses approaching, and then Dayanara's name being shouted by her uncle, made her head turn abruptly.

She was alarmed at how quickly her uncle and his soldiers were approaching. If they thought she was being accosted by Quick Fox, would they fire upon him and ask questions later?

No, on second thought, Dayanara didn't think her uncle would attack; he would not risk his own life for hers even if he did think she was in danger.

Quick Fox watched, too, as the white men approached. His attention was focused on one man — the one who was calling a woman's name. Clearly, he knew this woman.

Quick Fox's heart sank at the thought that this man might be the husband of the golden-haired one.

Quick Fox had gotten so carried away with his fantasies about her, he had not stopped to think that she might be married.

He thought about the name the man was calling. Dayanara. He had never heard of such a name.

He moved his gaze slowly back to Dayanara and held his eyes on her as the men came closer.

Dayanara. *Huh,* he liked the name. To him it was almost mystical in its loveliness, like the woman herself.

She seemed unique. Tiny in size, yet strong in many other ways. And she was courageous, for it had taken great courage to venture into land that was strange without the escort of a man.

Dayanara's spine stiffened when her uncle wheeled his horse to a sudden halt behind her. She urged her horse around and gave him a quizzical look.

But before she could ask him anything, he slid a hand down to a holstered pistol at his right side as though he was about to use it on Quick Fox.

"Are you all right?" John asked, glowering as he gazed past Dayanara at the child with the warrior, then looked directly into the midnight dark eyes of Quick Fox. John couldn't help being unnerved by the anger and suspicion in the Indian's eyes.

And he knew that this wasn't just any Indian. When he had first seen Dayanara with the redskin, one of the soldiers had warned him that this warrior was a powerful Cree chief. He was from the village down the river from Fort Meyers.

John called up all his courage to keep his eyes steady as he continued looking into the Indian's gaze. He was frightened of *all* Indians, but positively terrified of this powerful chief. He had had a confrontation one day on the riverfront in Saint Louis, when he had absently spit on the cobblestones close to an Indian. The man had drawn a knife on John so quickly, it was as though his hand was a lightning flash.

The only thing that had saved John that day was a squaw who begged her husband in broken English not to kill the savage white man. She had argued that doing so would bring death not only to himself, but also to her and those who had traveled down the Mississippi River in their canoes to trade.

John had walked away from that frightening moment with weak knees and a dry throat. He had hurried to a tavern and downed many glasses of whiskey, which helped him forget the confrontation . . . until now.

"Uncle John, you can see that I'm all right," Dayanara said, sighing heavily. "What surprises me is why you ask. You know very well that you are only pretending to care."

John shifted his gaze. He looked into Dayanara's flashing blue eyes and could see her anger and distrust.

He couldn't stop the smug half smile that quivered across his lips. Apparently, she had discovered that someone had taken the map from her belongings. She must realize that only he could have taken it.

It gave him a deep feeling of satisfaction to have caused Dayanara such frustration. No matter what she said, she could not prove that he had stolen the map, and without the map, her precious monster bones could not be found.

Dayanara was quite right. He would like nothing better than to allow the Indian, *any* Indian, to take Dayanara. He longed to get her out of his life, permanently, but he didn't dare let harm come to his late brother's only child. Deeply superstitious, he was afraid that if he did, his brother would find a way to come back and haunt him.

"Dayanara, you should come back to the fort with me now," John said stiffly. "It'll be dark soon. Until my cabin is finished, even I will feel safer sleeping at the fort, especially since it's obvious that you've stirred up some sort of trouble with this Injun. I could tell when I rode up that you were arguing."

Dayanara was keenly aware that Quick Fox

had remained silent since her uncle's arrival. She looked at him over her shoulder, flinching when she saw the animosity in Quick Fox's eyes as he glared at John.

Uncle John had not said anything insulting about Quick Fox, yet there was anger in his expression. It was as though Quick Fox had a definite reason to dislike her uncle.

She could not help wondering why, but felt that the question was best left unasked. The anger in the chief's eyes told her that none of them were welcome.

Little Fox saw Dayanara's uneasiness and felt that he should reassure her. She was someone he felt a strange bond with. He wanted to see more of her. He wanted to be with her.

He wanted his father to know and trust her.

This first meeting between Day and Quick Fox had not gone well. There was a strain between them, a strain that Little Fox wished to eliminate.

"Day, you have nothing to fear from my father, or the Cree," Little Fox murmured. "Please come with me and my father now and meet the others at our village instead of going to the fort with your uncle."

John sidled his horse closer to Dayanara's. "Day? This child even knows your nickname?" he gasped. His jaw tightened. "Niece, you should come with *me,* now. Do you hear me, Dayanara? Now. Since your father is dead, I have authority over you."

Dayanara was taken aback by the outright gall of the man. How dare he try to control her doings?

Quick Fox had listened closely to all that was said. One fact gleaned from the dialogue made his heart sing. He had discovered that this man was not Dayanara's husband, and that she had come to this land with a father, not a husband.

That surely meant that she wasn't married . . . that she was free to be pursued and loved.

Little Fox's attachment to her he also now viewed in a positive light. If his son was close to the white woman, would it not be much easier to get to know her, himself, when a more appropriate time was offered them?

For now, he must keep his distance. Silence was better than speaking his mind at this time. If he said what he felt, he would order the white man from the land of the Cree. He would tell him he was not welcome to build here, either.

Soon the lodge would be gone, for Quick Fox would see to that himself.

Despite his resolve, when the white man reached out and grabbed Dayanara by the wrist, his voice a growl as he again insisted that she do as he told her, Quick Fox could no longer keep his silence or his distance. He had to protect Dayanara, even if it meant lying to do so. He did not trust this man alone with Dayanara, even if he was her uncle. There was too much evil in his eyes.

The soldiers who rode with Dayanara's uncle could also prove to be a threat to her. He had seen the men staring with hungry intent at her.

He also knew that there were no wives at the fort. These men had been without a woman for too long now. Rape could be on their minds.

He had heard of atrocities among other tribes when white soldiers came into the villages and killed all but the women, whom they raped viciously and then killed. Of course, that was on land far from Fort Meyers, but who could say when the soldiers here might eventually turn on his tribe?

"Your niece was not on her way to the fort, she was accompanying me and my son to the Cree village for a short visit. Afterward, I was planning to escort her safely to the fort myself," Quick Fox said in a rush of words, making up a quick story which was necessary to protect Dayanara from these men. "When you came upon us, you saw us stopping for a moment to discuss the beautiful sunset, nothing more. You took from what you saw only what you wanted to see, for it is too often a white man's way to suspect a red man of doing wrong against white women."

Dayanara tried not to look too surprised by what Quick Fox had said. Was he trying to protect her? Had he seen the crudeness with which her uncle treated her? Had he seen her reaction to her uncle's ordering her around like she was no more than a puppy with its tail tucked beneath its hind legs?

She smiled slowly from Quick Fox to her uncle, then listened as Quick Fox continued with his tale.

"Your niece will always be safe in the company of Chief Quick Fox," he said. He slid his gaze to Dayanara as she glanced over her shoulder at him. "She should be free to do as she wishes . . . not as an uncle demands."

Dayanara was truly stunned now. She couldn't believe that Quick Fox had actually intervened in such a way. Thrilled at this opportunity to know him better, she wheeled her horse around and guided it next to Quick Fox's.

"Yes, Uncle John, I do believe you were too quick to interpret what you saw. Our conversation was vastly different from what you thought," she said, smiling smugly at him. "I *am* on my way to the Cree village. We would have been there by now had you not interfered."

John gasped. Itching to kill a redskin, especially this one who was fast making a fool of him, he longed to draw his pistol. Instead he forced himself to inch his hand away from the holstered firearm.

"Dayanara, I *demand* that you go with me to the fort," he said. He glared from Dayanara to Quick Fox. "Redskin, you had best encourage her to do as I tell her. You know that I could stir up trouble for you at the fort if I told them you took her by force. The soldiers could sweep down upon your village and take her, you know. And if they were forced to do it in that manner, many of your people would die."

He smiled crookedly at Quick Fox. "Is Dayanara worth that?" he asked mockingly.

"John, you've said way too much," one of the soldiers said as he edged his horse closer to John's. "No one at the fort wants Injun trouble, especially Colonel Potts. He was purposely chosen to establish the fort here because of his gentle manner with Injuns. As long as he's in charge, there'll be no confrontations. And besides, saying the girl was abducted would be a lie. It's obvious your niece wants to be friends with the Cree. Why not let her? Don't you have more on your mind than her? John, let's go and get a good night's rest. We've a lot to do tomorrow."

John's brow furrowed into a frown. He glared at Dayanara. "Dayanara, what am I going to tell your mother if she asks where you are?" he asked stiffly.

Dayanara's eyes wavered, for she knew that this was her uncle's first civil question of the evening. She knew that she should go with him to the fort.

But her mother was lost in her own world now . . . a world of mourning. She would not be aware whether Dayanara returned now or later.

Not wanting to give John the pleasure of thinking he had gotten the better of her, she glared for a moment longer at her uncle, then gave Quick Fox a nod.

"I'm ready to go with you," she said, smiling when he gave her a look of surprise, as though he had not actually believed that she would agree. She exchanged a quick smile with Little Fox, then again gazed at his father. "We've seen the sunset; now I'd like to see your village."

Quick Fox returned her smile, then her nod. He flicked his reins and sank his heels into the flanks of his steed and rode off with Dayanara following him.

"You stupid woman, I hope the redskins scalp you!" John shouted at her.

Dayanara grew cold inside to know her uncle hated her so much. She realized that she must be on her guard now at all times, for her Uncle John was capable of doing anything to her.

She had not known, until now, just how deep his jealousy of her ran.

Chapter Ten

Everything that man esteems
Endures a moment or a day,
Love's pleasure drives his love away,
The painter's brush consumes his dream.
— Yeats

Having never been in an Indian village before, Dayanara couldn't help feeling anxious, especially when so many of Quick Fox's people gave her unfriendly glares when she rode into the village of tepees with him.

Of course she hadn't expected friendly smiles from them. She was white. She was a stranger.

It was almost dark now, and lodge fires burned from within the tepees, emitting a soft orange glow through their buffalo-skin coverings.

There was a large outdoor fire which lit up the area as though it were day. The sparks flying from the flames were like firefly bursts against the darkening heavens.

Only a few Cree were outside their lodges now. Most of those who had been outside quickly fled into the privacy of their lodges when they saw that their chief had brought a white stranger among them.

Dayanara now wished that she had not come. Yet, looking over at Quick Fox, who so intrigued her, and smiling at Little Fox, whom she felt she had known for a lifetime, she realized that nothing would turn her away, unless someone absolutely forbade her to be there.

As long as Quick Fox rode with her, his back straight, his shoulders squared, his demeanor proving that he was not touched in any way by the coldness of his people toward Dayanara, she felt comfortable enough to stay. She had fantasized about this man from the moment she had seen him, dreamed of what it would be like to actually know him. She still couldn't believe that she was being given that opportunity.

Quick Fox drew rein at the far end of the village, before a lodge much larger than the others and somewhat separate from them.

Dayanara saw that the tepee was painted with designs of buffalo grazing amid tall grass, then noticed that some distance from the grazing animals other buffalo were depicted as having arrows shot into their sides.

Her eyebrows lifted when she saw how those slain buffalo were lined up against one another. She concluded that perhaps this was how Quick Fox kept count of the buffalo he had killed.

If so, she was stunned by the number. She had read somewhere that the Indians did not waste much of a buffalo kill. They made use of the meat for food and of all that was not eaten for their homes and clothes.

"We are at my lodge now," Quick Fox said. He lifted Little Fox from his steed and placed him on the ground. "Little Fox, take Dayanara inside while I take Midnight to my horse corral."

He gave Dayanara a look that she found hard to decipher. It was not a smile, yet it was not a frown, and it was definitely not a look of indifference.

She had read that Indians were difficult to read. They were known for their seriousness in all that they did; they were a people who did not take time too often to joke. Their lives were filled with making certain their people were provided for and safe.

"I will take your horse and mule, also, to my corral for safekeeping until you leave," Quick Fox said, dismounting.

Dayanara nodded and handed him her reins, then slid from her saddle.

"Come inside," Little Fox said, his dark eyes dancing as he took Dayanara by the hand. "My father's lodge is large and comfortable."

Dayanara couldn't see how any tepee could be large enough for one person to live in, much less an entire family.

But after Little Fox held back the entrance flap for her and she stepped inside, she was surprised by the spaciousness of this lodge. It was so tall and so wide, she did not have to stoop. Even when she was standing upright, there was plenty of room over her head.

She noticed that there were also drawings on the inside walls of the tepee, designs similar to those on the outside, but in more detail. These drawings depicted many things besides buffalo, and she concluded that this was some sort of calendar of events.

"Did Quick Fox paint his own walls?" Dayanara asked, her eyes studying the different figures, which were similar to the stick figures she had learned how to draw when she was a little girl in school.

"He prides himself on his paintings," Little Fox said, nodding. "No one else is allowed to paint on his walls."

He yanked on her hand. "The lodge fire will warm you," he said, leading her over to a fire built deep into the ground and surrounded by large rocks. "Although this country is hot during the day, it gets quickly cold most evenings."

"Yes, the fire already feels good," Dayanara said. She sat down on a pelt beside the fire, yet her eyes continued to scan her surroundings.

Along the walls were rolled-up blankets and pelts. There were also buckskin bags which bulged with whatever was stored within them. She saw several bows and many arrows lying in a pile.

Then she remembered something she had briefly seen outside the lodge. She looked at Little Fox. "Why was there a bag hanging on that pole outside the lodge opening?" she blurted out.

"That is my father's medicine," Little Fox began. He stopped and smiled up at Quick Fox as he appeared in the lodge entrance and lowered the flap behind him.

"Is your skin warm yet?" Quick Fox asked as he gazed down at Dayanara. "If not, Little Fox can get you a blanket or a robe."

"I'm fine," Dayanara said. Her eyes held his. She was keenly aware of a sensual warmth in the pit of her belly as Quick Fox looked at her. It was no longer so impersonal a gaze, but something more gentle and caring.

The way his lips tugged into a slow smile made Dayanara's heart skip a beat. It was as though he was allowing himself to relax in her presence.

Her attention turned sharply toward the entrance flap when it was shoved aside and a woman came into the lodge carrying a tray of cooked meats.

Dayanara gave Quick Fox a quick, questioning look as the woman handed the tray to him, glared down at Dayanara, then left the lodge almost as quickly as she had come.

Dayanara shivered uncontrollably, for the woman's look had been so cold and unfriendly, Dayanara felt as though she should leave immediately. It was obvious that her presence was resented in the village, perhaps especially because she was a guest of their chief.

"I really can't stay," she said.

She started to stand up, but Little Fox grabbed her hand and yanked on it until she sat back down beside him.

"Why would you come and then leave so quickly?" Quick Fox asked, an eyebrow lifting. He nodded toward the pelts. "You are my guest, and guests share food before they leave."

"But that woman didn't look as though she approved of my being here. I think it's best if I go right away," Dayanara said, her voice drawn.

Little Fox yanked on her hand again. She knew how badly he wanted her to stay, almost as badly as she wished to remain. Yet that look in the woman's eyes still worried her.

"Not many whites have entered my people's village," Quick Fox said, kneeling to place the platter of food on the bulrush-mat-covered floor. "But she was wrong to make you so uncomfortable you do not feel welcome, for you are her chief's guest, someone who should be respected."

"It's mainly because of the food she brought for you," Little Fox blurted out in his honest way. "Food has been so scarce of late, she resented sharing it with you, especially since you are white."

"Oh, no," Dayanara said. She felt awful now that she understood. "She shouldn't have brought it." She sat down between Quick Fox and Little Fox. "Why did she bring the food? I did not tell anyone that I'm hungry." She laughed softly and blushed. "Even though I must confess that I am."

"It is my policy that when someone comes inside my lodge, food is offered as a kindness to the guest," Quick Fox said.

He reached up to make certain that his hair still covered his scars. He would conceal them for as long as he could, for he feared seeing a look of disgust on her lovely face. That look would cause him to die a slow death inside.

"I am saddened to see that so many of your people were harmed by the smallpox epidemic," Dayanara murmured. "I am sorry that your people are hungry. Little Fox told me how your hunting has been affected by the sickness and how much less food your people now have for their families."

Her eyes brightened as a thought came to her. "I could bring food from the fort for your people," she said. "Tomorrow. I shall bring food and fresh supplies of all sorts to-morrow for you and your people."

"It is best that you do not do that," Quick Fox said stiffly. "Neither I nor my people wish for white people's charity."

"But I don't see it as charity," Dayanara dared to argue. "I see it as an act of friendship."

"No, my people would resent your help," Quick Fox said.

He then looked toward the closed entrance flap when he heard the usual evening sounds around the outdoor fire.

He was glad that Dayanara's presence in the village did not dissuade his people from doing what made their hearts lighter for at least a little while.

He smiled as the drums began to beat and the songs of his people began.

"Is some sort of ceremony being performed outside around the fire?" Dayanara asked.

"No, no ceremony, only songs that give my people moments of happiness," Quick Fox said, smiling and nodding. "Do you hear the singing? At least for a while, it brings light-ness and sweetness into the hearts of my people. Tonight there is even more joy in the songs, for they know that soon all of those who left to avoid getting the scarring disease will soon return. We will be as one again, and the hunt will be good and strong. I hear hope in the voices of my people again. I feel it strong inside my own heart."

"I can't forget the resentment in that woman's eyes as she brought food," Dayanara said. She again shivered involuntarily as though the woman were still there, glaring icily at her.

When she saw a dark look in the depths of Quick Fox's eyes, she wished she could call the words back. She was so angry at herself for reminding him of how the woman had reacted to her, she doubled a hand into a fist beside her.

The tepee was filled with silence; even Little Fox no longer smiled or talked. He seemed to be avoiding her eyes, gazing instead into the flames.

She was keenly aware that Quick Fox had gotten up and moved across the fire from her. When he bent to his knees and lifted logs into the fire-pit, she hoped that tending the fire was his only reason for moving away from her.

She was getting more uneasy by the minute. Even Little Fox seemed to be purposely avoiding conversation. Inhaling a nervous breath, Dayanara gazed again at Quick Fox.

Looking across the fire at him, she saw how the flickering light sharply etched his high cheekbones and noble nose. His eyes were fathomlessly black and reflected the dancing flames as he gazed quietly into them.

She noted how often his hand strayed to the lock of hair lying across his left cheek.

Again she was aware of the merriment outside. She could hear the stamping of feet in time with the drum's beating and the songs. She knew that the Cree people were dancing now, as well as singing.

She was amazed that these people, though downtrodden, poor, and weak, could still sing and dance as though there was nothing wrong.

Quick Fox was battling conflicting emotions. The more he thought about how Yellow Flower had behaved toward Dayanara, the more he realized it would have been better if Dayanara had not come to the village.

Yet here she was.

He had brought her. He had wanted to ask her the details of her life. He had wanted to know everything about her.

Yet how could he pursue her when he knew that she was not wanted among his people, and even she knew that she was not wanted?

He now knew that he must fight his feelings for her.

He vowed that once he returned her to her people, he would forget her.

He had seen how often her eyes had strayed to the strand of hair which he used to hide the scars on his face. If he brushed the hair aside, would she be aghast at the sight? Would she pity him?

Or could she look past the scars and see the true man . . . a man who already adored her with every fiber of his being?

But he should not care how she felt about him or his scars. He had to be strong enough not to want her in his life.

He must get her back to her people, for the longer she sat in his lodge, filling it with her sweet scent, and brightening it with her goodness, the more she was a threat to him.

Quick Fox suddenly leapt to his feet. "I will escort you home now," he said tightly.

Dayanara was so stunned by the suddenness with which he wished to remove her from his lodge, she was rendered speechless. She was also keenly aware of Little Fox's continued silence and the way he kept avoiding her gaze.

Somehow she had lost them and their respect almost as quickly as she had won them. A slow ache of regret filled her heart.

"Truly?" she dared to say, hoping that he might change his mind. "Must I go? I haven't eaten yet. The . . . the . . . meat does look and smell delicious."

When she saw how Little Fox winced, she realized that she had overstepped her bounds. She should have made a graceful exit while she could.

Yet how could she not question Quick Fox

when she saw so much emotion in his eyes? She could see that he cared, yet he seemed to be fighting his feelings for her.

For her part, she was falling more in love with him by the minute, but she knew that this relationship could never work.

It was not only that his people resented her; her own people would find the relationship scandalous and distasteful.

If she fell in love with an Indian, she would be shunned forever by all who knew and loved her.

She wasn't sure if she could give up everything for any man.

Knowing that she must leave, she rushed to her feet and hurried out of the lodge.

The moon was bright and high in the sky, the stars twinkling beautifully against the dark heavens.

The people had returned to their lodges, leaving her alone with Quick Fox as he came from behind his lodge with her steed and pack mule, as well as his own midnight-black horse.

She gazed over her shoulder at the tepee. Little Fox had remained inside.

She supposed that he felt he must shun her, as his father would surely do from now on, and that saddened her. She had grown so fond of the child in the short time she had known him.

Feeling low, she mounted her horse.

She glanced over at Quick Fox. "You don't need to escort me home," she said, scared to death that he might not. She truly didn't want to set out on her own.

She knew now, though, that all she had to do to find her way back to the fort was follow the river. But it was those things in the dark between here and the fort that terrified her.

"I will see you safely home," Quick Fox said, moving his horse up beside hers.

"Thank you," Dayanara said hesitantly. "I . . . I . . . don't like the dark too much, especially on land unfamiliar to me."

Their eyes met and held for a moment, the fire's glow on his face again revealing his handsomeness to Dayanara, and something more. In his eyes there was still such warmth of feeling toward her, yet she knew that he was fighting his feelings.

He had to put his people before her. No doubt that was the reason he was suddenly more enemy than friend to her.

As they rode out of the village, the moon still high and bright overhead, Dayanara glanced frequently at Quick Fox. She noted that he still fought to keep that one strand of hair over the left side of his face while the wind threatened to blow it aside.

Was he hiding something horrible beneath that hair, perhaps a deep scar from a battle with an enemy? She wanted to tell him that no matter what was there, or how ugly it might be to him, nothing could take away from his handsomeness.

When they finally reached the fort, Dayanara started to thank him, but without even a goodbye he wheeled his horse around and rode away.

She noticed that he no longer kept his hand on the lock of hair and she knew why. His back was to her now and she couldn't see his face. She wondered now if she would ever know what he was hiding.

Feeling strangely alone and dejected because of his attitude toward her, Dayanara rode into the fort.

Her thoughts went to her mother. She wondered if Dorothea was more aware of things now. Had she been concerned about Dayanara? Would she even care to hear about Dayanara's discovery of the monster bones?

A sudden worrisome thought struck her. If Quick Fox had decided not to treat her cordially, would he deny her the chance to go and study the prehistoric bones?

Tomorrow when she went there, would he have warriors posted at the entrance to the hidden valley?

She was angry with herself for spoiling things between them. She was too prone to speak her mind without thinking first.

"What if he orders me away himself?" she whispered.

Her shoulders slumped, she dismounted her steed, removed everything from the mule, and led both animals into the corral where feed and water awaited them.

She made several trips into the cabin until everything had been carried in, then went to her mother's bedroom and slowly opened the door.

Dorothea was asleep. Or she was pretending to be.

Sighing heavily, Dayanara went down the narrow hallway. She stopped just outside her Uncle John's room. She was tempted to open the door to see whether he was there or not.

But she was still so angry with him over the map, and his arrogant demand that she return to the fort with him, she knew it was best not to risk another confrontation.

She wanted to be alone, anyway, so she could think things through and plot a strategy that would still get her the opportunity to study the bones.

If Quick Fox wanted to play games with her, so be it!

Chapter Eleven

Love kindled by virtue always kindles
   another,
Provided that its flame appear outwardly.
                                    — Dante

The moon was still high in the sky as John
and his friends lay on their bellies on a bluff
overlooking the Cree village.

John would never forgive the Cree chief for
usurping his authority with his niece. He
would not rest until he got the best of that
Injun chief.

He smiled ruefully as he thought of
Dayanara and her insulting behavior toward
him. After thinking about it, he had decided
it was ridiculous to worry about his dead
brother seeking vengeance. There was no way
that his brother could reach down from
heaven and punish him for whatever he chose
to do to Dayanara. Therefore he had determined to kill her at his first opportunity.

For the first time since he had been born,
John felt truly free. He no longer had an
older brother preaching at him about this or
that. There was no one taunting him or

making him feel useless.

And as soon as he did away with Dayanara, he would not only be free, but also much richer. He was certain that his brother's widow wasn't going to make it through her grieving. She would pine away until her heart gave out on her. That would leave the entire family fortune to him.

He wouldn't even have to continue with his brewery if he chose not to. And with his tormenting brother dead, he no longer had anything to prove to anyone.

But the brewery meant a lot to him now. He had enjoyed being recognized by the community as one of its leading citizens because of the wealth his brewery brought into the city of Saint Louis.

"John, let's get outta here," whispered Luke, the soldier who was his nearest confidant. "Don't you know what being caught here spying on the Indian village could mean? The redskins would scalp us." He reached up and ran his fingers through his shoulder-length red hair. "I'm not hankering to have my hair attached to any redskin's scalp pole."

"Don't you see down there how everyone is in their lodges and how their lodge fires have burned low?" John whispered back. "When we first got here you could see the glow of fires through all of the buckskin coverings. Now you see only a faint flickering.

That has to mean that the fires have been let go and the Cree are asleep."

"Not Chief Quick Fox," Luke argued. "You saw how he rode off with your niece at his side. If he left his village to escort her back to the fort, he should be back any minute now. What if he comes to this bluff to say a prayer to his God? I hear the Injuns like to climb to high places to pray because that gets them closer to their God so the prayers are answered more quickly."

"You worry too much," John snorted. "From this vantage point, we can see in all directions. We'd see him long before he could get up here to catch us spyin' on his people."

"Not if those clouds that are creeping in from the west cover the moon," Luke said, glancing at the clouds that had built up during the past half hour. "It'd even make it hard for us to see our way back to the fort."

"You've lived here longer than me, yet you forget that the river winding alongside the Injun village is the same one that goes by the fort," John said scornfully. "All we have to do is follow the river and we'll get back to the fort."

"If nothing jumps out at us in the dark to stop us," Luke grumbled. "Come on, John. Let's go while the gettin' is good. I *have* been here longer than you. I know the sort of animals that lurk in the dark, and I don't mean only four-legged. The Injuns are a clever sort. They have scouts keepin' watch. I don't even know how we made it up here without being caught." He gulped hard. "If we get back to the fort without being scalped, honest to God, I'll say a quick prayer of thanks to heaven."

"I see now why you gave up your post at the fort to come harvest hops," John said, giving Luke a dark scowl. "You're too much a coward to fight Injuns with the rest of the cavalry."

"I'd watch who you're callin' a coward," Luke said, leaping to his feet. With his hands on his holstered pistols at each hip, he glared down at John. "If you want to argue that point any longer, we can do it with guns. John, your mouth gets mighty tiresome. Right now I'd like nothing better than to shut you up, permanently."

John pushed himself to his feet. He drew a pistol more quickly than Luke could blink his eyes.

"Now who's threatening who?" John said, inching closer to Luke, his pistol aimed at his gut. "Luke, I thought you had become my best friend. Seems I was wrong, now doesn't it?"

"You two better shut up and get back down here so's no one can see you," said a soldier named Lorrie. "I see someone coming in the distance. I imagine it's Quick Fox. I don't think you'd want him to glance up here and see you two facin' off on one another, do you? He wouldn't care if you shot each other. But what he would care about is why you are so close to his village."

His heart leaping almost into his throat, John slung his pistol back into its holster, then grabbed Luke and shoved him down to the ground, falling down beside him.

"You two best get your heads on straight about things," Lorrie grumbled. "You can't forget for one minute that you're in Indian country and that they'd as soon kill and scalp you as look at you. You know that whites are being blamed because the Injuns have smallpox, don't you?"

"I don't care who they're blaming, but I do know that it wiped a good portion of this band of Cree out," John said, watching the Indian coming closer and soon realizing it wasn't Quick Fox, after all. It was some other warrior who had probably been out scouting and was now returning home for the night.

"Yeah, they're a puny lot, that's for sure," Lorrie said.

John smiled ruefully. "Yeah, too puny to protect themselves against an attack, wouldn't you say?" he asked with a snarl.

"What's on your mind, John, besides hops?" Luke asked, gazing at him. "Why did you really want to come up here tonight to spy on the Cree?"

"I wanted to see if what I suspected was

true. And I wanted you to see how few Indians are left here at the village," he said dryly. "From what I've heard, many of their own people, including the healthier warriors, fled their village when others came down with smallpox. Cowards? Yes, *they* are the true cowards. They left their people defenseless. Many died. It wouldn't take much to bring these weakened Indians to their knees, now would it, especially the young chief who made a fool of me today?"

"John, what you're thinking is dangerous as hell," Luke said, his voice tight. "I don't think I'd want a part in it."

"You going to prove what a coward you are by backing down?" John taunted. He had learned the art of taunting well from his brother and was enjoying having someone to use it on.

"John, we've already been through this 'coward' thing, but if you want to pursue it to the end, just keep it up," Luke grumbled. "I'm game, John. I'm game."

"Oh, all right, I'm wrong to do that, but I'm right to want to go against these redskins," John argued. "They will surely try to stop us from harvesting the hops, and if we wait to see if they will, by then they could have their full strength back and be a threat, whereas now they're just pitiful souls all scarred up and ugly."

"Where'd you learn your hate for the red

man?" Lorrie asked, raising an eyebrow. "You have to hate them to want to annihilate them."

"It's a long story and one that I don't like tellin'," John grumbled. "It's in my past. But this is my present, and by God, I want those hops without interference from redskins."

"I truly don't believe you've anything to worry about, John, for the hops mean nothing to the Cree," Lorrie said flatly. "So let's not plot against the Cree, all right? They've already had too long a run of bad luck, as I see it."

"I'm paying your paycheck now, ain't I?" John said, glaring at Lorrie.

"Well, yes —"

"Then shut up and do as I say."

"Okay, John, tell us your plan," Luke said, sighing heavily. "We're with you all the way."

Chapter Twelve

All thoughts, all passions, all delight,
Whatever stirs this mortal frame,
All are but Ministers of Love,
And feed his sacred flames.
                            — Coleridge

The sky that had been lit only by the brightness of the moon now had another color added to it, the color of shimmering, orange flames.

Quick Fox stood back and watched the flames grow higher and higher in the sky.

On his way home he had purposely taken a side trip to this place where the white man had a partial cabin built.

Not wanting the white men to establish homes anywhere near Quick Fox's village, especially now that he had seen the ugly side of this man who was Dayanara's uncle, he had set fire to the cabin and was enjoying the sight as it burned.

With a tight jaw and his arms folded angrily against his bare chest, he continued to watch the fire eating away at the logs.

He smiled as the burning wood tumbled to

the ground, bit by bit, sparks scattering into the air like beautiful orange sequins.

He knew he was taking a chance of being caught by the white men if they were nearby, yet still he did not leave. He remembered now how the white men had said they wanted to get to the fort by nightfall. They were surely there now and in their beds asleep.

The sentry posted at the fort might see the fire, but he would shrug it off. It was far enough away from the fort for the soldiers not to be concerned about it. They would think that it had originated at the Cree village since the village was so close. They might even laugh at what they assumed was the Cree's loss.

Huh, he would stay and proudly watch the fire consuming the half-built dwelling. He wanted every inch of the wood burned so that if the white men still wanted a cabin there, they would have to start all over again by chopping down trees.

He hoped, though, that when they discovered the bed of glowing embers and ash, they would reconsider the wisdom of remaining on land where they were so very obviously not wanted.

On the other hand, they might seek revenge against his people. They would guess that a red man had set the fire tonight.

But he smiled as he thought of the white

soldiers who were no longer soldiers but under the command of a civilian. He thought them cowards for having turned their backs on their duties as soldiers.

No, he did not think men like them would retaliate against any Indian tribe just for the loss of one dwelling made of logs. It was more likely that fear would send them back to where they had come from, far, far from Wyoming.

His eyes slid past the burning debris to where the hops plants blew gently in the moonlight. He was tempted to set fire to the plants, as well, to keep the whites from having them, to take away their reason for being on Cree land. But he decided against it. He was afraid that such a fire would burn out of control and spread to his village; the flames of the burning cabin were contained, for the white men had done a good job of clearing a wide area around their lodge.

As he continued watching the beautiful hops plants waving in the cool night breeze, he was reminded that the leaders of his Cree Fox Clan had set down laws generations ago that even today Quick Fox's people understood and obeyed.

One of these laws was that the most severe penalties were imposed on any person, white or Indian, who set this precious land on fire, whether by accident or on purpose. Even a chief like himself would be punished if he allowed the fire to spread.

Some tribes did not adhere to this rule. They set the land on fire to facilitate hunting, letting the fire flush the frightened animals from their hiding places.

The Cree knew that such an act had a contrary effect. They knew that when animals went on a frenzied run from their homes in the brush or caves, they were driven from the land of those who sought them, into the country of their neighbors, who then had game aplenty for many sunrises and sunsets.

Cree children were taught this law from the moment they were given bows and quivers of arrows of their own. They would not do anything that would chase game from their own precious land to someone else's.

But the fire Quick Fox had set tonight was a different matter, a deed that had to be done. It was for his people's sake.

He wanted to keep white interlopers from planting roots on Cree soil. It would be best if the whites were contained within the fort and trading post.

He was his people's leader. He had to make decisions that would benefit them.

They had chosen him as their leader because they trusted him implicitly. He hoped never to let them down by making a wrong decision.

For now, burning the cabin should be enough to get his point across to these white men. But if Dayanara's evil uncle persisted, Quick Fox would find other deterrents.

These white men were not only a threat to his people, but also to Dayanara. Quick Fox could not help wanting to protect her even though he was struggling not to care for her.

His hand went to his scarred face.

"Surely she is the sort who would look past such imperfection," he whispered to himself.

Especially if she knew that the man with the imperfection was a person whose heart was good and pure, a person who, up until tonight, had sought peaceful ways to solve the problems that arose between his people and whites.

His feelings for this woman were in turmoil. A part of him wanted to go to her this very minute and confess how he felt about her.

Yet another part knew that it was best not to be involved with a woman with white skin. Had not his people looked at her with scorn and mistrust?

He understood all of this, yet the more he thought about her, the more he longed for her.

"Am I so wrong to care for her?" he argued to himself, his eyes on the flames again, seeing in them a face of perfection smiling back at him.

Was it not more wrong to deny his sensual

feelings for the woman with the beautiful name Dayanara? He already knew that she was a woman of compassion from the way she had treated Little Fox.

He would not believe that her kindness to the child had been done as a bribe. She had seen the hunger in his son's eyes and had given him food to alleviate it.

He recalled that Dayanara had also offered to bring food to his village. Had he made the wrong decision by not allowing it? Should he have cast his people's pride aside long enough to take charity from whites?

He firmed his jaw. No, he would not accept charity, for once he did, his people would be indebted forever to whites, and he wanted to owe nothing to his enemy.

Soon . . . soon his people would be reunited. The hunt would be great. There would be no more gauntness or growling stomachs. Everyone would be as they should be again, happy and able to fend for themselves.

His thoughts returned to the white woman. He was still confused about his feelings for her.

"Sleep," he whispered.

Huh, sleep was the answer for now. In his dreams he would escape the realities of life.

He ran to his horse and mounted it in one leap. He rode away from the burning cabin, where all but a few logs had been consumed by flames.

Quick Fox tightened his jaw. If he dreamed of Dayanara again tonight, that would be the answer to his questions. The dream would prove that he should cast aside all his doubts and allow himself to love her freely.

"Dayanara," he whispered, the very breath crossing his lips as he spoke her name warm with need of her.

Chapter Thirteen

That it will never come again
Is what makes life so sweet.
— Dickinson

"Look!"

Luke's exclamation and pointing finger directed John's eyes to the sky, which was lit with an orange glow.

"Fire?" John said in surprise. "I wonder what's . . ."

Then his heart skipped a beat and his throat went dry as he realized where the fire seemed to be originating.

The cabin!

He and his men had been on their way back to the fort when they'd stopped to look at the sky. John knew they weren't far from where they had cleared land for the cabin.

"John, do you think . . . ?" Luke said, his voice fading as John sank his heels into the flanks of his horse and took off.

John's pulse was racing. He could hear the pounding of blood in his ears. He was filled with anger, fear, and frustration.

But most of all, he felt a deep-seated hate.

Once again, he saw Chief Quick Fox's mocking face, the smug smile on his lips.

"You bastard!" John shouted into the wind. He waved a fist above his head. "You set the fire, didn't you? Damn you! Damn you!"

He and his hired men had never seen Quick Fox return to his village. Now he knew why.

Quick Fox had been busy setting fires.

When he got close enough to see the origin of the flames, he saw that it was, indeed, the cabin that had been set alight.

Now there were only glowing embers except when the whipping wind sent sparks from the burned debris into the air like orange stardust.

"God," he groaned.

He slowed his horse to a lope as he continued toward the glowing remains of the cabin.

He was reminded of the hard labor it had taken to chop down the trees for the logs to build the cabin.

In his entire life he had never really had to work for the things he wanted. He had always hired someone else to do the job.

But out here, where workers were scarce, he had been forced to labor alongside the few men he had managed to hire.

And now the cabin was gone.

It would take more hard work just to clean away the charred coals before he could begin building the cabin all over again.

"Damn, damn!" Luke said as he caught up with John and rode beside him. "Who'd do such a thing?"

"Do you mean you really don't know?" John said, laughing throatily at the man's lack of brains. "Indians, Luke! Or should I say *one* Indian. This is the work of Quick Fox. I know it is. Or one of his warriors who he sent to do the dirty work."

Lorrie came up on John's other side on his speckled steed. Lorrie's green eyes were dark with fear as he, too, gazed at the shimmering embers only a short distance away. "I don't like this one bit," he said thickly. "I think this is a message of sorts. They're telling us to leave this land be, or maybe the next thing that'll be set afire is *us*."

"That's just like you. You're provin' to be a coward every time you open your mouth," John said, glaring at Lorrie. "If you don't like what you see, or don't want to keep that trap shut when we run into one trouble or another, you'd best hightail it outta here now. I came to Wyoming for a reason. Do you think I'm going to let one man, a flea-bitten redskin, scare me away? Not on your life."

"What are we going to do about this?" Luke asked as all of them came to a halt alongside the hot coals, keeping enough distance from them so as not to frighten the horses.

"Little did Quick Fox know that we were already plotting against him and his people," John said bitterly. "Now he's given us true cause to kill 'em. I hope I can be the one to sink a bullet in that bastard's heart. I'd like to see that smug look wiped clean off his face by the pain my bullet will be causing him."

"The more I think about what we're planning, the more I think we'd best not do it," Luke said tightly. "You see what that Cree chief did to the cabin? Think of what he and his people will do to us if they beat us when we attack the village."

"You've got to remember that they don't have much manpower or strength now and can't do much to anyone," John argued. "This fire tonight is the work of one man. He overstepped his bounds. His people will pay for it twofold."

Two of the men who usually kept quiet, who just went along with whatever John said in order to get paid, rode up behind John and drew a tight rein.

"I'm out," Abe Janson said, his voice tight. "I've seen enough to know when I'm not wanted in these parts. I don't want to wake up some night with an Injun kneeling beside me ready to take my scalp. I'm headin' back for Missouri on the next riverboat."

"You're not much of a man, now are you?" John said, wheeling his horse around and glaring at the man with the long black hair and tanned face. "If you leave us in the lurch, I hope you don't get far before an Injun *does* overtake you and kill you."

John edged his horse closer to the two men, glaring from one to the other. "I think you forget that the Cree are the ones who are known to be friendly," he said smoothly. "Once you leave Cree territory to try to get back to civilization, you'll be at the mercy of, let's see, the Blackfoot? The Sioux? Or maybe even the Comanche. Now what chances in hell would you have against those savages? And I hear tell they torture white men before they kill them."

Again, John gazed with narrowed eyes from man to man. "I hear some of those Injuns will cut off a fellow's manhood, then stuff it into his mouth so that he can't breathe and is suffocated by the very organ that had up till then pleasured him," he said, chuckling when he saw pearls of sweat pop out on both men's brows. "Now don't that sound like fun?"

"I think I'll stay with you guys," Abe squeaked out.

"Me, too," the other man said, nervously raking his fingers through his stringy brown hair.

"Then let's head on toward the fort and get us a good night's rest. We'll begin building us a new cabin bright and early in the morning. And while we work, we can make solid plans against the Cree," John said.

"I'd like a drink of that whiskey you've got in your saddlebags first, John," Lorrie said. "Whadda you say we go and have a short rest and take a few swigs of rotgut before headin' on back to the fort? What I've seen here tonight has given me a mighty thirst, and I don't mean for water."

"Okay, guys," John said, sighing heavily. "Let's go and sit beside the river. We'll take a rest, drink a few drinks, then go and climb into our beds at the fort. This has been one helluva frustrating day."

He thought of Dayanara and how she had allied herself with the Cree chief, then thought of the white boy with Quick Fox.

His eyebrows lifted as he wondered where the child had come from, and why he was living with Indians.

He shrugged. It didn't matter to him what the child did, or with whom. When he had joined the redskins, he had, in a sense, become one himself. When John and his men attacked the Cree village, the boy's life would not be spared.

No decent person with a right mind would ever want that child to be a part of his life. "Except Dayanara," he thought angrily.

He sank his heels into the flanks of his steed, took one last look at the glowing coals that were all that remained of the cabin, then rode onward.

After John was settled in beside the river with the men, and he had fished more than one bottle of whiskey from his saddlebags, he allowed himself the momentary pleasure of drinking and talking with his friends. But all the while he never really let go of what lay ahead of him.

In the farthest recesses of his mind he was making plans for the day when he would attack the Cree. And Dayanara.

He had to get Dayanara out of his hair once and for all, and by damn, he would!

Chapter Fourteen

It were all one,
That I should love a bright,
  particular star,
And think to wed it,
  he is above me.
      — Shakespeare

The sun was just creeping over the horizon, casting a soft, pinkish glow in Dayanara's bedroom window.

She gave her hair another brushing, then gazed at herself in the mirror on the chifforobe to see how she looked in her new dark green riding skirt and white, long-sleeved blouse.

Something told her that she would be seeing Quick Fox again today and she wanted to look her best.

She was confused by his sudden distant manner last night.

She was afraid something she had said had angered him, yet she couldn't remember saying anything untoward.

She had been friendly to him and had been kind to Little Fox.

"But even Little Fox behaved strangely before I left for the fort," she whispered to herself. She reached back and tied her hair into a ponytail with a ribbon, so that her hair wouldn't get in the way as she traveled on her horse.

She had decided against taking the mule this time. She knew now exactly what she needed to study the bones.

She certainly didn't need the larger shovels, which were the main reason she had taken the mule yesterday. She now knew that she would not be able to dig up the bones and take them away. She would take something smaller that she could use to uncover the bones where they lay, so that she could study them.

She had already gone into the kitchen and packed a bag of food for the day.

She wasn't a heavy eater, so fruit, cheese, and bread would sustain her. All of these foods were given to her by the fort's cook, a man who seemed more knowledgeable than any woman about cooking.

"Mother," Dayanara whispered.

Sadness overwhelmed her at the thought of how her mother had withdrawn from the world. Dorothea now slept her days away for lack of any desire to do anything else.

Dayanara hoped that her mother would eventually come out of her shell. She had heard of women wasting away from grief; she prayed her mother would not be one of them. But no matter how she cajoled her mother to put aside her grief, Dorothea turned a deaf ear to her daughter.

Dayanara stiffened her chin and made herself think of other things. The adventure that lay ahead of her today made her heart thump wildly in her chest.

She believed she could find the hidden valley of the prehistoric bones today without the assistance of Little Fox. She had noted their route carefully yesterday, memorizing landmarks that would lead her back to the bones.

She wished she had the courage to return to the Indian village, so that she could see Little Fox again, and perhaps have a second chance at making friends with his father.

She could only hope he would feel the same yearnings and would seek *her* out. But if he opposed her plans to study and draw the bones, she knew that their friendship could never be. She had come to this land for a purpose. No one, not even a powerful, young, handsome chief, would stop her.

Her hair tied with a pretty bow, her feet in boots that already made her toes ache, Dayanara grabbed up her bag and left her bedroom.

She crept quietly down the hall until she came to her mother's bedroom door. She slowly opened it and gazed at her mother,

her heart leaping with joy when she found Dorothea dressed and making the bed.

"Mother?" Dayanara said, proceeding into the room.

Dorothea turned around and gave Dayanara a soft smile, then held her arms out for her.

"Daughter, come to me," she murmured. "I'm so sorry I've caused you concern."

Dayanara dropped the bag to the floor and rushed into her mother's arms. "Mother, you have worried me so," she said.

A sob caught in her throat as she reveled in the feel of her mother's arms and enjoyed the familiar scent of her freshly washed hair, which had just been brushed dry and hung long down her back.

Her mother wore a beautiful blue silk, flowered dress, and there was a pleasant scent of French perfume on the lace-trimmed collar.

"I'm going to be just fine, Dayanara," Dorothea said, gently moving out of Dayanara's arms. "But I'm ready to go home. I hate this place. I especially hate that we must leave your father buried here."

"Mother, Father is resting in peace, and I know he's all right, for he came to me in a dream and told me that he was," Dayanara said. She placed a gentle hand on her mother's soft cheek. "He lived a life that made him happy. He succeeded in everything he ever did. He achieved much in his life-time, Mother. There was only one thing that he was not able to complete, and that is —"

"The prehistoric bones," Dorothea said, her voice breaking. "He came here to study and dig up some dried-up ugly bones."

"They are much more than that, Mother," Dayanara said, knowing what to expect next. Her mother was going to demand that Dayanara return to Saint Louis on the next riverboat with her, whether or not she was through studying the bones.

She would have to disappoint her mother, for Dayanara would not leave until she had finished what her father and she had come to do.

"Mother," Dayanara said, before Dorothea could begin her argument, "I also came here to study the bones."

Dayanara's eyes lit up at the recollection of what she had seen yesterday. "And, Mother, I found them," she said. "I actually found them. I saw them with my very own eyes."

"You went out there all alone and found the prehistoric bones?" Dorothea gasped out, paling.

"No, not exactly," Dayanara said. She took her mother's hands in hers. "Mother, I became acquainted with the sweetest young man at the fort. He took me to the bones."

"A young man?" Dorothea asked, eyes wide. "You actually trusted a man to take you? You were alone with a man so far from everyone? Dayanara, I've taught you to be cautious about such things. Men . . . most men . . . have only one thing on their minds, and you know what that is. You could've been raped, Dayanara. Raped!"

Dayanara laughed softly. Her eyes danced. "Not likely," she murmured. "Mother, this young man was only ten years old."

She then explained all about Little Fox, his age, where he had lived before stealing away on a riverboat, and who had taken him in.

"Truly?" Dorothea said. "The child lives with Indians? They treat him well?"

"He has been adopted by a young Cree chief named Quick Fox," Dayanara said. Just saying Quick Fox's name aloud caused a sensual thrill to race through her. "Mother, I went to the Cree village."

Then Dayanara's smile faded. "They have suffered so much from the smallpox epidemic," she said.

She saw that the word smallpox caused her mother's face to grow pale. "Smallpox?" she gasped. "And you were there among them?"

"The smallpox epidemic is over," Dayanara said. "It is the weakness the disease left behind that is the true threat. Many died. And those who lived are half starved. The warriors are too ill to really hunt. It is very sad, Mother. I feel so deeply for those people."

"They are not your concern," Dorothea

said flatly. "Your own well-being is. Dayanara, I insist that you return to Saint Louis with me at our first opportunity."

"Mother, you know I can't do that, not until I have finished studying the bones," Dayanara said guardedly. "Please understand. I must finish what Father came here for. It was his dream to succeed at this last venture before retiring."

She could not tell her mother that she had another reason for not wanting to go back to Saint Louis just yet. Quick Fox! Although she had only met him one time, and he was obviously fighting his feelings for her, she felt things for him that she had never felt for any other man.

Just thinking about him made her feel giddy.

She wished she knew how to break through that wall he had suddenly built between them last night. She hoped that somehow Little Fox would intervene and convince his father to seek her out.

"I know that no matter what I say, you will do whatever you want to do," Dorothea said. "So go ahead, Dayanara. Do what you must. Get it over and done with, and then we can concentrate on returning home."

"Thank you, Mother," Dayanara said. She flung herself into her mother's arms. "Oh, thank you, thank you."

"Dayanara, I love you so much," Dorothea

murmured, caressing Dayanara's back. "I loved your father just as much. I only hope he knew that before he died. What I did . . . the lies . . . surely made him lose respect for me. I wish he could have told me that he'd forgiven me before he died."

"I'm sure he did," Dayanara said. She eased herself from her mother's arms. "Mother, he knew how you hated this side of his life. But he just couldn't give it up. Because he understood your feelings, I'm sure he did forgive you. He just didn't get the chance to say it."

"Hearing you say it makes me believe he did," Dorothea said. She grabbed up Dayanara's travel bag and thrust it into Dayanara's arms. "Go on, Dayanara. Do what you must. I'll pray that nothing happens to you."

"Mother, please don't worry about when I'll be back," Dayanara said, thinking back to last night and how her return to the fort had been delayed. "If it gets dark and I'm not here, don't send the cavalry out looking for me."

"Whatever you say," Dorothea said. She nervously clasped her hands together before her. "Have you seen Uncle John this morning?"

The very mention of her uncle made Dayanara's stomach tighten. She hadn't told her mother about his thieving ways. She saw no need to worry her mother about that, since she already had so much on her mind.

"No, I only moments ago left my room," Dayanara murmured. "Why?"

"I was just wondering if he found the hops plants and what he plans to do about them if he did," Dorothea said softly. "It would be nice if he returned home with us. Without your father, I could use John's help back home."

"Don't count on it," Dayanara said dryly. "Mother, Uncle John is a most undependable man. You know that."

"Yes, but under these circumstances —"

"No circumstances will ever change him for the better," Dayanara said, then opened the door. "Mother, I shall try my best to do nothing to worry you, but still, remember that if I'm not home before dark, I will be all right."

Her mother nodded.

Dayanara left the room. As she went out of the cabin, she walked past John's door, which was ajar. When she heard him snoring, she crept to the door and opened it just a little more.

She could tell by the way he was stretched out across the bed in his clothes that he had returned to the fort in a drunken stupor. She could even smell the stench of whiskey heavy in the room.

Disgust heavy on her heart, Dayanara swung away from the room and hurried out to her horse.

She was glad when she was finally riding free of the fort.

Anxious to get to the hidden valley, she sank her heels into the flanks of her steed and thundered onward. She loved the feel of the wind against her face. The sun had not reached high enough into the sky to warm the earth, and the air was still chilly.

Dew clung to the tips of the trees. It even dripped from the leaves of a thick stand of cottonwoods as she rode past.

She traveled onward, watching for the landmarks she had noted.

When she came across a wide expanse of plants that she knew were hops, she slowed her pace and rode beside them. The plants stretched far into the distance, beautiful and blowing lazily in the breeze.

Then she was aware of something else. The wind was bringing to her a smell of smoking ashes.

What could have burned? she wondered.

She drew rein abruptly when she saw a smoldering pile of ashes not far ahead.

"What on earth . . . ?"

She rode onward, then slowed her horse again when she came to the huge pile of ashes from which the smoke was still spiraling. She studied the pile and assumed that it must have been some kind of dwelling.

"How did it catch fire?" she whispered. "And whose was it?"

Then her heart skipped a beat. Had it been John's cabin? Yes, it had to be. It was being built right next to the hops plants.

Yet how had it burned? Did he know?

She dismounted and knelt down beside the hot pile of ashes.

She studied it some more, and then her insides grew tight when she heard the sound of someone approaching on horseback.

"Uncle John . . ."

She leapt to her feet and turned to see who it was, then sighed with relief when she discovered that it was not John, but Quick Fox. If John did not yet know about this fire, she knew he would go into a fit of rage when he made the discovery; she didn't want to be there when he did.

As Quick Fox rode closer to Dayanara, her pulse raced more rapidly. She was thrilled to see him again. To be able to gaze upon his handsomeness, to possibly have a chance to make friends again, was something she had prayed for.

Quick Fox saw Dayanara standing beside the smoking ashes, and his heart skipped several beats.

He knew now that he had been wrong to be so unkind to her last night. She had appeared again in his dreams, and at last he felt free to express his feelings for her.

He brought his horse to a halt beside the pile of burned debris and dismounted.

Dayanara saw how he smiled as he gazed at the ashes and she concluded that surely it was he who had burned the cabin.

"Quick Fox, did you set this fire?" she blurted out before realizing she was going to speak.

"Beneath the moonlight I did start the fire," Quick Fox said, nodding. "I watched until the cabin burned to the ground."

"But why?" she asked, even though she believed she already knew the answer.

"This land, these plants, belong to the Cree," Quick Fox said. "When I saw your uncle building the cabin, I knew that I would destroy it at the first opportunity."

"Then it *was* my uncle's cabin," Dayanara gasped out.

Again Quick Fox nodded. "I destroyed it not only because of the land and the hops, but also because your uncle brought firewater with him onto my land. I do not want my young braves or my warriors to be introduced to firewater," he said tightly. "I will never give up this land to a man such as your uncle. I will fight even to the death, if necessary."

Dayanara went cold inside at his vehemence, and she recalled Quick Fox's sudden coldness to her last night.

"Will you fight me also, to keep me from the prehistoric bones?" she asked guardedly.

She didn't like the way he went suddenly quiet.

Chapter Fifteen

Sweetest love, I do not go,
For weariness of thee,
Nor in hope the world can show
A fitter love for me.
     — Donne
     (Song — "Sweetest Love")

Unnerved by Quick Fox's sudden silence, Dayanara started to mount her steed to leave, but stopped when he reached over and grabbed her by the wrist.

"What are you doing?" she gasped, eyes wide as he turned her toward him.

Everything within her melted when he pulled her to his hard body and kissed her. She found herself twining her arms around his neck and returning his kiss, as though she had done this countless times before.

It seemed perfectly natural, the way their bodies fit into each other, the way their lips pressed so wonderfully together, the way their breath mingled.

She was suddenly filled with conflicting feelings . . . passion for him, yet also fear, for she was vulnerable, completely alone with him. She truly did not know this man enough to know whether he would take advantage of the situation.

Her mother's warning about rape came to her in a flash, but she truly could not imagine this wonderful man being capable of rape.

His embrace was solid, yet gentle. His lips were trembling with true feelings for her. And she could feel his heartbeat thundering against her.

No, she could not imagine this man being capable of anything but honorable deeds. Still, he had set fire to the cabin.

But that was soon forgotten in the delirium caused by his kiss and embrace.

She clung.

She kissed.

She sighed.

Quick Fox slid his lips from hers. "Dayanara . . ." he whispered against her cheek. "I cannot help . . ."

Dayanara was shaken when he did not finish what he seemed so badly to want to say but instead drew quickly away from her and turned his back to her.

Her heart pounding, she gazed in wonder at his bare, muscled back, which heaved with his heavy breathing. She could tell he was battling against the emotions he had just revealed to her in such a sensual way.

She covered her mouth with a hand; her

lips still throbbed from his kiss.

She had felt such joy during their embrace, yet now she felt that joy turning to confusion.

"Quick Fox, what's wrong?" Dayanara murmured as she lowered her hand from her mouth.

Quick Fox could not respond to her question. How could he?

He was breathing hard as he fought the feelings he had just revealed to the woman he desired. *Huh,* he desired her so much that his insides ached.

And, ah, the kiss, the embrace!

She had shared them so willingly and lovingly, yet despite his dream he worried that no good could come of their shared passion.

He was Indian. She was white. There were too many obstacles in the way of their happiness.

Suddenly he was aware of something else. He realized that during the throes of passion he had forgotten to keep his scars covered. His hair had not lain across his cheek to protect it.

Had she seen the scarring?

He quickly covered the scar with his long hair, yet he still could not turn to face her.

What if she *had* seen? Was she standing there even now repulsed by the scars?

Was she wishing that she had not allowed herself to be drawn into his embrace?

167

At this moment, he felt himself less than a man. His spirits were low. His joy was gone.

Still shaken by their kiss, and concerned at the way Quick Fox had turned from her, Dayanara was unsure what to do. Should she question him again about his strange change of mood?

Or should she mount her steed and ride away as though nothing had happened . . . as though he didn't even exist?

But how could she?

That kiss and embrace had brought him into her heart, and she knew that he was there to stay.

Looking at him had made her weak inside. But being held by him had made her mind spin with rapture.

She could not let him leave her again. She knew that there was something special between them and that he was fighting it. He was a proud, powerful chief. She was only a woman, and white at that. Surely a powerful chief should not waste his time with a woman . . . especially one who was white.

But didn't chiefs marry? Did they not want sons to follow in their footsteps? Undoubtedly they did, but only if the sons were borne by women of their own people.

She was suddenly aware that he had lifted his left hand to make sure the lock of hair was again covering the left side of his face. She was almost certain now that he had been scarred by the smallpox.

Dayanara firmed her jaw and took a wide step that took her around to stand directly before Quick Fox.

She gazed into his eyes and felt the passion flowing between them. Before he could stop her, she raised a hand to the left side of his face and slid the hair aside.

Quick Fox's heart ached and his gaze was unsteady as he watched her study the pockmarks on his cheek. He was stunned to see that she was not repulsed by the scars. Instead, there was compassion, understanding, and caring in her eyes.

Had he been wrong to be self-conscious for so long about the scars? Were they not so unsightly after all? Was it only because he was a proud man that he felt ashamed of the scars?

He was so relieved, so happy, he wanted to pick her up and swing her around as he laughed with joy. He forced himself to keep his composure, for he was a chief and must guard his dignity.

"You do not see the scarring as ugly?" he blurted out. "You can have feelings for a man who is disfigured as I am?"

What she did next truly stunned him. His eyes went wide with wonder as she stood on tiptoe and lovingly kissed the scarred cheek, then stepped away and smiled into his eyes.

Never had he felt such awe. Never had he

been so deeply touched.

He reached out for her, placed his arms around her waist, and drew her into his embrace. He was kissing her ever so gently when the sound of horses approaching forced them quickly apart.

They both turned just as John and his cohorts rode up.

John glowered as he stared first at the smoking ashes, then at Dayanara and Quick Fox.

He had seen them kissing. It repulsed him to think that a white woman would belittle herself to kiss a redskin savage!

And not just any woman, but one of his blood kin.

If her father were alive, surely he would kill Quick Fox for having touched Dayanara.

The sight of the two of them standing together beside the smoking debris made him wonder if they both were in on the burning. Perhaps Dayanara had shared in the crime because she knew he had stolen the map.

Quick Fox had probably done the dirty deed because he did not want any white man settling this close to the Cree village. But how would the Injun even know who the cabin belonged to if Dayanara had not told him?

Unless perhaps those at the fort sympathized more with Quick Fox than with John.

John could tell that the colonel had a dislike for him, yet John knew not why. It was that way with many who met him. For some reason there was an instant dislike. It had been very different for his brother, whom everyone had enjoyed and admired.

But his brother was gone now, and John would never again have to walk in his shadow. He was the master of his own destiny and, by God, he would not allow a mere niece and a Cree chief to stand in the way of his success.

"You savage," John hissed as he glared into Quick Fox's eyes. "I will make you pay for burning my cabin and for getting Dayanara involved in the scheme. And you will pay dearly for having kissed a white woman . . . my *niece*. You know it's forbidden, Quick Fox."

Dayanara went cold inside at her uncle's words. As John took off toward the fort, she felt certain that he was going to tell the colonel about Quick Fox's behavior with her.

She had no choice but to go to her uncle and talk some sense into his head, if that was possible. He was a dense, selfish man who thought only of himself. He would report what he had seen because it would be the easiest way to get Quick Fox out of his hair, as well as Dayanara.

She just knew that the colonel would order her and her mother to leave on the next paddle wheeler to Saint Louis.

She couldn't allow that to happen. Like her uncle, she had come here for a purpose, and she would not allow anyone to stand in the way of her success.

She turned to Quick Fox. "I must go to my uncle and make him see reason," she said.

"Let him go," Quick Fox softly argued. "That white man has no power in the land of the Cree. He is foolish to think that he might have. If he or the men at the fort go against my people, they will regret the day they were born."

"But there are only a few of you now," Dayanara said. "And those warriors at your village are still in a weakened condition from the ravages of smallpox."

Quick Fox almost told her that soon the manpower at his village would be more than doubled. As soon as those who had left returned, no man would dare to attack his Fox clan of Cree.

At the last moment he chose not to share this information with Dayanara, for he felt it best that only the Cree knew the movements and actions of the Cree.

When she became his wife, then, and only then, would she know his every movement — his every secret.

He suddenly realized where his thoughts had taken him. He had actually thought of this woman as his wife!

The promise of having her to awaken to each morning and to take to his bed each night filled him with joy.

He knew that she had deep sensual feelings for him. But were her feelings strong enough to convince her to leave her way of life to join his?

"No, Quick Fox, this is something I must do alone," Dayanara murmured. "Please trust me. I know how to deal with the likes of my uncle. I learned it from my father long ago. My uncle has been nothing but an embarrassment to my family for years. It's hard to understand how two men could be so different, but believe me, my father and my uncle were exact opposites."

"If you feel that you must go to him alone, then go," Quick Fox said, placing a gentle hand on her cheek.

He was keenly aware that he need no longer protect his scarred cheek with his hair. It made him proud to know that the scarring made no difference to Dayanara.

He would not feel ashamed of the scars anymore.

Even the evil white man, her uncle, had not seemed to notice his disfigurement. It was as though the scars had disappeared the moment Dayanara had kissed them.

At least it seemed that way inside Quick Fox's heart and mind.

"But, my woman, remember that I am

nearby should your evil uncle try anything that could harm you," Quick Fox added.

Dayanara's eyes shone with happiness when he addressed her as his woman.

"Your woman?" she murmured, swamped by sensual bliss. "You called me your woman."

"You are, are you not?" he said, smiling at her.

"Yes, yes, I am," Dayanara said, squaring her shoulders.

They reached out and held hands for a moment; then she broke away and ran to her horse, swinging herself into the saddle.

Fixing her eyes on her uncle, she rode hard after him.

Quick Fox watched her, his heart filled with so many things.

Huh, his *woman.* Dayanara was his. And she would be his wife.

Nothing would dissuade him from the decision that he had made today about this woman whom most saw as forbidden to him.

The word "forbidden" was no longer a part of his vocabulary.

Chapter Sixteen

Down on your knees,
And thank Heaven,
Fasting for a good man's love.
      — Shakespeare

Dayanara caught up with John and brought her horse alongside his. She thought that surely he would stop when he saw her, but all he did was give her another cold stare and continue riding toward the fort.

"John, stop, we need to talk," Dayanara shouted at him.

"I've nothing to say to you," he shouted back. "You're no kin of mine anymore, Dayanara. Not after letting that savage manhandle you."

"That word 'savage' is an insult to Quick Fox, and your thinking that I'd let any man manhandle me, as you call it, is an insult to me," she shouted back at him. "I was in that man's arms because I wanted to be. And he is a man. Not a savage! If anyone is a savage, it is you, Uncle John. You are so uncouth at times, so terribly insulting. Stop, Uncle John. I insist!"

"To hell with you, Day," John said, still keeping his horse at a steady gallop. "I don't care what you have to say. You've proven your true colors today. If your mother hears about your dalliance with a redskin, she'll be ashamed to call you her daughter."

"I know you had a terrible experience with an Indian in Saint Louis, Uncle John, and that's why you hate them, but you must know that all Indians aren't alike, just as all white men aren't," Dayanara said, keeping up with him on her steed. "You know that you and Father were exact opposites. So don't you see that you might be wrong about Quick Fox?"

"I don't care to discuss it any longer," John shouted back at her. "But let me say this, Day, you've taken sides with the wrong person. I'm going to make that Injun pay for becoming involved in our family's lives."

"And just how do you think you can make him pay?" Dayanara asked, her eyes filled with fire.

John laughed scornfully. "Just you wait and see," he shouted back at her. "Now get away from me, Dayanara. I smell the stink of the savage on you. You probably even have fleas crawling on your flesh, since you allowed him to hold you in his arms."

"Oh!" she screamed. "You are so insulting. How can you live with yourself?"

She looked past him at the other men, who

had kept their silence. "Do you know the sort of man you have allied yourselves with?" she shouted at them. "You'd best reconsider, or he'll take you down with him."

"And who's going to 'take me down'?" John asked mockingly.

"John, with your attitude, you can't last long on land that belongs to the Cree," Dayanara said.

"You're the one who's wrong," he returned hatefully. "I'm going to make Quick Fox pay, not the other way around."

"John, what on earth are you referring to?" Dayanara prodded. "What do you have in mind?"

"You'll see," he said laughingly. "Just you wait and see."

She shivered uncontrollably, for she knew that her uncle meant business. He did plan to harm Quick Fox, perhaps even all of his people, for she knew the sort of man her uncle was. When he got a grudge against someone, he would not let it go until he made that person pay.

She slowed her horse and watched as John rode onward with his men. She didn't have any choice now but to wait and see what he meant.

She only hoped that after thinking through what he was planning, her uncle would reconsider. Surely he would realize he couldn't risk starting a war with the Cree.

She wheeled her horse around and rode back to Quick Fox. When she reached his side and drew her horse to a halt, he took one of her hands.

"He's planning something," she said, swallowing hard. "But I don't know whether or not to take him seriously. I've seen the cowardly side of my uncle too often to think that he'd dare go against you and your people. He had a bad experience with an Indian back in Saint Louis. At that time, it scared him to death. Maybe what he said today is just all talk. I hope that's all it is."

"I will not waste any sleep over what your uncle said, or might do," Quick Fox said, shrugging. "He is a man with a loud voice but small spine."

Dayanara laughed softly at those words. "Yes, that describes him very well," she said. "But still, I just don't know . . ."

"Are you going to go and study the monster bones today?" Quick Fox asked guardedly.

"Would you mind if I do?" Dayanara asked.

"Not if you only look but do not take," Quick Fox said stiffly. "Will that be enough for you?"

"It has to be, for I don't want to do anything that would upset you," Dayanara murmured. "I am so grateful that you will allow me to go back to the secret valley of the prehistoric bones."

"I would go with you, but a meeting is planned in the council house of my warriors this morning and I should return there now as head of the council," Quick Fox said.

He slid his hands from hers and edged his horse closer to hers.

He reached a hand to her neck and gently drew her face close to his.

"My woman, while in council I will find it hard to concentrate on business. My mind and my heart will be filled with you," he said huskily.

"Just as I will find it hard to concentrate on studying the bones," Dayanara said softly, her pulse racing as he brought his lips so close to hers, she could feel their warm breaths exchanging.

"We will be together soon," Quick Fox said, then covered her mouth with his in a hard, demanding kiss. A moment later he swung away from her and rode off.

Her heart throbbing, Dayanara watched him, then sighed heavily as she turned in the direction of the hidden valley. She found she knew the way quite well.

As she moved her horse into a gallop, her thoughts turned back to her uncle.

Although she had chosen to go to the hidden valley alone, she suddenly felt strangely vulnerable, especially with Quick Fox traveling in the opposite direction.

If she screamed for help, only the birds would hear her.

The only one who might be a threat to her was her uncle, but the danger he posed was very real. Today he had looked at her and spoken to her as though he truly hated her.

She realized now that he must harbor a deep-seated resentment toward her since her father, his brother, had always taken her side against John.

But she would not let a man like John spoil things for her now. She had to make this venture a success to honor the memory of her beloved father. She wanted to dedicate the finds to her father.

When she sent her findings to Washington, her father would receive the credit he deserved. He had been a dedicated person, who had worked with the best interests of the Smithsonian Institute in mind for too many years to be forgotten.

"Father, I will succeed," she whispered as she gazed heavenward. "And as for John? He's proving to be the cad you always knew him to be."

She looked over her shoulder. She hoped that Quick Fox had reconsidered and had decided to accompany her instead of going into council with his men.

Or even Little Fox. She missed the child. It would be wonderful to have him with her today to share her discoveries.

She looked straight ahead and shivered at another thought. Snakes. She knew they were a threat. She must keep an eye out for snakes, the two-legged kind like her uncle, and those that slithered on their bellies along the ground.

Sighing heavily, finding courage in thoughts of her father, even feeling that, somehow, he was with her, Dayanara traveled onward. She knew she was not far from the hidden valley now.

The thought made excitement soar within her; all her worry about danger was swept away into the wind.

Chapter Seventeen

I may command where I adore!
— Shakespeare
Twelfth Night

There was an air of excitement in the council house as everyone sat in a wide half circle before Quick Fox.

He sat on a raised platform on comfortable pelts. As usual he wore only a breechclout and moccasins, but his men noticed something different about him. He no longer wore the thick strand of hair across his scarred face.

Quick Fox could still feel the sweet warmth of Dayanara's lips as she kissed the scars. He now thought of the scars as a trophy . . . a trophy of love, for any woman who would accept the scarring of his face as Dayanara did, had proven her love for him.

He would never hide the scars again.

And if anyone looked at them with disgust, he would think again of Dayanara's kiss and just as quickly the scars would be gone, at least from his mind. And that was all that mattered.

He had finally come to terms with the changes in his face. And he had only one person to thank. Dayanara.

His eyes slid down and he smiled as Little Fox turned and smiled up at him, as though he guessed what his father's thoughts were. It was because of Little Fox that Dayanara had come into his father's life.

Although Little Fox had gone against his father's word by going to the trading post again, he had done his father a service with this disobedience.

Quick Fox now knew and loved Dayanara, and she returned his love.

He squared his shoulders and rested his hands on his knees as he looked past Little Fox. "My people, we are gathered here today to discuss our future," he said, determination in both his voice and his eyes. "I feel that it is time for us to send for those who left to escape the wrath of smallpox. But it must be voted on so that we all agree that it should be done. If some of you still fear that it is too soon for your loved ones to return, I will understand. But as you know, I believe there is no more danger from the disease, or I would not have brought the white woman among us."

He saw a sudden resentment in some of his people's eyes at the mention of the woman. This was one of the reasons why he'd called a council today. He was going to share with his people his feelings for the white woman. He had thought long and hard about it and knew that he could not live without Dayanara, just as the heavens could not exist without the moon, sun, and stars.

He did not understand how love could come into a man's life so quickly, but he knew this love was right. He also knew that because he had chosen a white woman for his future wife, he must expect many of his people to doubt his decision.

But he knew with all his being that loving Dayanara was right . . . was good.

The few hours while he had chosen to turn his back on her were sheer torment. Never again would he put himself through such torture.

But he did hope to win his people's approval. He might not convince them today, but in the near future he would.

He wanted Dayanara to move among his people without feeling angry eyes on her. He wanted her to feel at peace even though she loved a man whose culture was so different from her own. He wanted her to become as one with his people.

"This woman," one of the elders said, interrupting Quick Fox's thoughts. "She has come to the land of the Cree not to love you, but to use our people in order to achieve her own goals. She wishes to take from us the monster bones that have lain untouched since the giant animals roamed this land."

"*Huh,* she has brought digging tools, has she not?" another elder said, his old eyes wary.

"She brought digging tools, but she is not going to use them," Quick Fox said, feeling Little Fox's pleading eyes on him. He knew that his son wanted Dayanara to become a permanent part of their lives. He felt sure Little Fox wanted to speak out on her behalf, yet he remained silent because he knew that it was not the place of a ten-year-old brave to talk back to the elders. Little Fox was smart in many ways. His silence now proved just how smart.

"Why did she bring them if she is not going to use them?" another elder asked.

"She did not know it would be wrong to dig up the monster bones until my son and I explained it to her. Now she plans to study them, but not move them."

"This woman, you did bring her among us," one of the women asked. "Why, Chief Quick Fox? Why would you introduce her to our ways when she is from a world so different from ours?"

"Because this woman has become special to both your chief and his son," Quick Fox said, his voice smooth, his gaze direct. "It is not known to me how love can grow so quickly, especially for someone whose skin and ways are different from ours, but it has happened. I feel much for this woman. I want her in my life and my son's for more than just an occasional visit to our village. I plan to pursue her as a man pursues and courts a woman he wishes to make his wife."

He stiffened himself against the groans and moans of displeasure, and held his eyes steady as he looked from person to person.

Then he nodded. "I knew that it would be hard for you to accept, and I understand," he said softly. "But when you allow yourself to know her as I do, and as my son does, you will see that she is worthy of not only your chief's love, but also of yours. She is from a place far away, and her life has been filled with many things mysterious to us, but if she agrees to leave that world behind and come to live among us, then that is how it should be."

He sighed heavily. "I ask you to think on this and remember that your chief has never led you down the wrong path before," he said. "Nor will he now. I know this woman will fill your . . . our . . . lives with goodness. Her smile is like sunshine. Her laughter is like a soft song."

He realized that he might have said too much; there was now a strained silence among his people. Had he gone too far in describing his feelings for Dayanara?

He smiled at his people; then his smile

waned. He became the serious chief his people were more familiar with. He would turn now to the other matter before the council.

"We have met today not to discuss the woman I have chosen, but instead to make a final decision about when we send for our loved ones," Quick Fox said.

He was glad to see a new expression on their faces as they began to think about the importance of getting their lives back to normal.

"It is my opinion that the danger of smallpox has passed," he said. "I vote to bring our people home. A larger number of warriors among us means good hunts, and protection against possible enemies."

He was thinking about Dayanara's uncle and the threat he posed to Quick Fox's people by his mere presence in the area. He had already proven to be a wicked man that no one could trust. Even his own niece did not trust him.

And those men who allied themselves with John were no better than he. For money, they would do anything.

"And, my people, we do not only have enemies on two legs to fear; we must also guard ourselves against the wrath of the wind, snow, and cold, which will be upon us much too quickly," Quick Fox said. "If we do not come together as one unit now, the bison hunt will not be possible. It is important to get the hunt behind us so that we are prepared for the long winter ahead."

"Let us take a vote now," Red Feather said, rising to tower over his people as they sat and looked up at him.

Red Feather went and stood beside Quick Fox. "What is the vote to be?" he asked, feeling his chief's proud eyes on him, for his chief knew that Red Feather would give up his own life if it meant that his chief would live. "Those who wish to send for our people, raise a hand. Those who do not, say *ka,* no."

The vote was unanimous. There were no negative votes among them.

"The vote is good for us all," Red Feather said, still taking charge for a moment longer. "Our lives will be in order again, as they should be. And now I feel that we owe our chief another vote of confidence. He has spoken his mind to us about the woman. Has he ever been wrong in anything he has chosen to do? Does he not have enough insight to know his own mind about a woman? I say we let him know today that we are behind him in this decision, as well. Those of you who oppose having a white woman among us, say *ka.*"

Quick Fox's spine stiffened with anticipation as he awaited their response.

When no one voted against him, he inhaled

a deep breath of relief, for if anyone had voted against his decision to bring Dayanara among them, he would not have felt free to express his love for her.

Although he knew that those who didn't want him sharing his life with a white woman had only stayed quiet because of their love for him, he still felt that when Dayanara came to his village, she would be welcomed.

He felt eyes on him and gazed down at Little Fox. His wide smile revealed his happiness with this latest vote.

Quick Fox would bring his son and Dayanara together again soon, so that their friendship could grow. If everything worked out as Quick Fox hoped, she would one day soon be a mother to his son, and his son would no longer be without a woman's guidance.

He had worried about his son not having a mother's leadership, even though young braves needed a father's guidance more than a mother's. It was the softness of a mother's love that all children needed, and Little Fox had had none of that while living with his true mother.

Dayanara would fill the emptiness in the child's heart. His own mother had known nothing about raising a child, not even how to love one.

He became aware of an excitement in the air. His people were talking among themselves, their eyes filled with anticipation, and he knew that this was because they would finally be reunited with their loved ones.

Husbands and wives had been separated because of the dreaded disease. Children had been separated from their parents. And many elders had been left sadly alone without the help of their children.

The elderly especially, needed the love, the closeness, of their blood kin, to help them survive the later years of their lives.

Quick Fox was anxious for Dayanara to see the full strength of his people. It would be wonderful to witness the reunion of the clan as its members came together again as one large family, whose hearts were bound together, beating like one heartbeat.

He hoped to distract Dayanara from her interest in the monster bones, yet he wanted to go gently in this matter, for he did not want her to think of him as she did her uncle, who tried to dominate her.

And when they were married, he would be sure to allow her to be her true self. He did not want a wife who lived in the shadow of someone else, especially her husband. He knew her to be a woman of spirit, of strength, of substance. He would never do anything to stifle her independence.

"My people, I am glad that we all came together and will now leave the council house with happiness in our hearts," Quick Fox said, bringing silence among his people as they again centered their attention on him.

He looked over at Red Feather and smiled. "My friend, gather together all of our warriors and make plans to travel to those who have waited so patiently for the day they can return to us," he said. "I have something I must do, but I will return soon."

Red Feather gave Quick Fox a warm hug as Quick Fox stepped from the platform. Then Quick Fox left the council house and hurried to his horse corral.

Soon he was riding away from the village, his long, thick hair blowing in the wind. He knew where to find his woman and hoped she had kept her word to him. He prayed that she was only studying the bones today, and nothing more. He was afraid that once she saw the bones again, she might be tempted to dig them up and study them because of her intense curiosity about them.

But he also knew that she was a woman of honesty and good heart. She had said she would not dig them.

Soon he would know if he was right about her; he would know if he was right to have told his people about his feelings for her.

If he'd been wrong, ah, what a fool he would look in the eyes of his people.

Chapter Eighteen

No man has ever lived that had enough
Of children's gratitude, or woman's love.
— Yeats

As Dayanara secured her horse's reins to the low limb of a tree, she stiffened when he whinnied nervously, then shook his head back and forth and pawed at the ground with his right front hoof.

Realizing just how alone she was and how far from the fort, Dayanara swallowed hard and turned slowly to see what might be causing her horse's uneasiness.

Her breath caught in her throat when she saw a coiled-up rattlesnake only a short distance away. It was already starting its staccato whirring clicks, poised to strike at her.

Too afraid to move, to grab her rifle which she carried in a gunboot at the right side of her horse, or to reach in her pocket for her tiny firearm, Dayanara stared with a thudding heart at the snake.

Then she became aware of something else. She heard the sound of an approaching horse. Oh, if only it was Quick Fox.

He had known that she was going to be there. Perhaps he had finished with his council and had decided to join her.

But as she slowly turned her head to see who was arriving, her heart sank and a keen fear swept through her. It was her uncle. He was only a short distance away now, and she knew that he saw the snake and the danger she was in.

"Uncle John, please help me," Dayanara said, even though she was afraid that the sound of her voice would goad the snake into striking her.

John heard the pleading in Dayanara's voice and saw the fear in her eyes. A moment later he understood the reason for her terror.

His gaze fell upon the rattlesnake and saw that it could strike at Dayanara at any moment. If it did, she would die, for he knew nothing about how to save someone from the bite of a rattlesnake.

He gazed at Dayanara again. He was stunned that she had found her way to the prehistoric bones without the map that he had stolen from her belongings.

It was clear she knew the way to the secret valley, for she had been securing her horse's reins so that she could go the rest of the way on foot. He knew that the path there was a treacherous one. He had gone there himself to see the bones.

He had been tempted to destroy the burial site, yet his superstitious fear of Indian spirits avenging such a move had sent him away from the burial site without causing any damage.

He wanted to ask Dayanara how she had discovered the hidden valley without the map, but he knew the answer without even asking.

Surely the Cree chief had taken her there. His actions proved just how much he cared for Dayanara, for surely this site was sacred to the Cree.

"Uncle John, why aren't you doing something?" Dayanara asked, still afraid that her voice would cause the snake to strike at her.

She had on heavy, knee-high leather boots, and her riding skirt hung down over the tops of the boots, which might protect her from the snake's bite. Yet she wasn't sure. She didn't know how deeply a rattlesnake's fangs could sink. If they went through the leather of her boots, then she was a goner!

"John, do . . . something. . . ." Dayanara pleaded, stunned that he was just sitting there. Did he hate her so much that he would let her die? Would he wait and watch after the snake struck her?

"Uncle John, you can't hate me this much," Dayanara said, her voice breaking with emotion.

John heard the plea, and the accusation in her voice.

His brother's face came to him in his mind's eye, a face that John had learned to hate, yet fear. He swallowed hard, reached a hand to his holstered pistol with the intention of saving Dayanara.

Then he slowly eased his hand away from the firearm, a nervous tic twitching his left cheek just beneath his eye as another thought came to him.

His brother was dead. Wouldn't it be a much better world if Dayanara joined her father in death? John had decided to find the means of doing away with her. Wasn't this the perfect way?

No one would ever know that he had been present to save her, so no one could accuse him of not having done it.

Yes, this was the perfect opportunity to be rid of his niece once and for all.

All his life he had walked first in his brother's shadow, and then Dayanara's. He had never been able to best either one of them. That failure had tormented him more than anyone would ever know.

A slow smile slid across his lips as he looked from Dayanara to the snake and back to Dayanara. "It won't be long now, Dayanara. The snake seems to be moving slowly because of the cold last night." He chuckled. "But don't fret too much over it.

Once the snake's body warms enough to strike at you, your death will be quick and merciful. You won't even have time to think about what hit you, or to think about my allowing it. Bye-bye, Dayanara. It's been a misery knowin' you."

"Uncle John, I knew you disliked me, but I never knew how much," Dayanara said, a sob catching in her throat.

Quick Fox had approached the scene silently, suspicion of Dayanara's uncle prompting him to keep himself hidden.

Unsure of what John had on his mind where Dayanara was concerned, Quick Fox leapt from his horse and tethered its reins to a tree. He yanked an arrow from the quiver at his back and fitted it onto the string of his bow, then crept quickly onward until he came up behind John. Not even Dayanara could see Quick Fox hidden in the shadows of the trees.

But from this vantage point, he now saw the snake and the danger that Dayanara was in and realized that her uncle was not going to help her. It was hard to believe that her uncle was actually going to let the rattlesnake bite her.

Making an instant decision, Quick Fox stepped quickly out in the open, at the same time releasing the arrow from his bowstring.

He watched John start as the arrow whizzed just past his face.

He saw Dayanara's eyes widen with surprise when she realized what he had done.

The arrow sank into the snake's skull, stopping its forward momentum. It fell to the side, dead, where ants and flies were already beginning to gather on its mangled head.

Dayanara looked back at her uncle and gave him a questioning stare. Then, sobbing, she ran to Quick Fox and flung herself into his arms, clinging, and thanking him.

John was stunned speechless. He had been caught red-handed allowing his own niece's death.

He now knew that he could never return to the fort, for Dayanara would tell everyone there that he could have saved her but had not.

John felt trapped. He knew that if he tried to flee, Quick Fox could just as quickly sink an arrow into his back.

Obviously, the Indian chief had fallen in love with Dayanara. He'd led her to the monster bones and now had saved her life. Had not the kiss earlier proved the extent of his feelings for her?

Although so many of his plans had been spoiled by his actions today, John could not help laughing to himself as he imagined his niece, a wealthy woman, cooking over the meager cook fire in a mere Indian tepee. He doubted that she would last long among Indians, even one who was a powerful chief.

But John didn't feel altogether defeated. Although the hops were no longer his for the taking, he had other schemes to pursue.

"Quick Fox, you have really done it this time," John said through gritted teeth. "You will pay dearly for interfering in my life again. You don't have enough warriors to stop my next plan . . . annihilating your puny clan. Only a few gunshots will be required and you will all be dead. And then, by damn, I'll return to Saint Louis. I don't need your damn hops to make a success of my business. I don't need them, or you, Dayanara, or our family money. I know you will make certain now that I don't get a cent of my brother's inheritance."

John raised a quizzical eyebrow when he saw that the warning he had just given Quick Fox hadn't bothered him or scared him. Instead, the threat caused a strange, even an amused, glint in the Indian chief's dark eyes.

When Dayanara began talking, John turned to her.

"Uncle John, you are stupid to talk to Quick Fox like that. You are signing your own death warrant. And if he doesn't stop you dead in your tracks, I could go to the fort and tell the colonel what you did, or should I say what you didn't do today. You were actually going to allow that snake to kill me," Dayanara said, feeling safe in Quick Fox's arms.

She glared at her uncle as she continued. "But, Uncle John, I won't do that. I know I don't have to do that for you to finally come to a bad end. You have a way of making bad things happen to yourself. So in time, Uncle John, you will make the wrong move, and it will be your last. As I see it, you've already made a big mistake in telling Quick Fox your plans. Now, do you think he's going to allow what you are planning to do?"

"If he hopes to stop me, he'd better do it now, for by God, Dayanara, I've taken all I can take from Quick Fox," John spat out. He laughed. "Do you see me afraid? Didn't you see that I wasn't afraid to tell Quick Fox what I have planned? He knows that what I said about his people is true. And he isn't the sort to cold-bloodedly murder a man to keep him from carrying out a plot against his people. I see him as the sort to try to fight off my attack, even knowing that it is all but impossible."

"There are only a few of you," Dayanara said, her eyes glittering angrily.

"Are you certain?" John said teasingly. "How do you know that I haven't met with others who are tired of bowing down to the Cree?"

Dayanara gazed with troubled eyes up at Quick Fox.

His smile let her know that John would not get away with any of his threats.

"White man, you'd best be on your way, and if I were you, I would enjoy today's sunshine and tonight's moonglow, because you do not have many more to enjoy," Quick Fox said flatly. "You do not see my people as strong? You do not know the meaning of the word until you see the true strength of my warriors."

John shifted uneasily in the saddle.

Then he smiled boldly. "Of course you would try to scare me," John said. "But nothing much scares me anymore, Quick Fox. Especially not when I know that I have the upper hand."

"You are a fool," Quick Fox said, then shrugged. "Be on your way, fool. Take in each breath and thank the heavens for it, for there will not be many more for you, especially if you attempt to carry out your plan against my people."

"Uncle John, how can you be so stupid that you would threaten Quick Fox and then laugh at his warnings?" Dayanara asked. "Uncle John, go to the fort. Stay there. I won't even come and turn you in. When the next paddle wheeler docks, you must accompany Mother back to Saint Louis. That is the only sane thing for you to do."

John gave her a bitter look and laughed sardonically. But when he looked at Quick Fox, he was intimidated by the chief's attitude of nonchalance.

A shiver raced up and down John's spine as he wheeled his steed around and rode away.

Dayanara took a deep breath, then turned and gazed at the fly-covered snake. "He would have truly let the snake kill me," she said, her voice breaking.

She turned around and gazed up at Quick Fox. "How could he be so hideous?" she said, her voice drawn. "How? He is my father's brother, my *uncle*. We have the same blood in our veins. How can one person be so different from others of his own kin?"

"In life, there are many questions, and this is just one of them," Quick Fox said, twining his arms around her waist. "My woman, I think it is best to abandon your plan of studying the bones today. Come with me to my village. Be a part of my lodge where you will be not only safe, but adored. Let me show you ways to forget everything but the love we share. Forget your curiosity about the monster bones. There are more important things in life. There is *us*."

At the huskiness in Quick Fox's voice, sensual warmth flowed through Dayanara's veins. She knew that he planned to make love with her.

She had never been with a man sexually before. And this was not just any man. He was a powerful Indian chief! It amazed her that such a man as he truly loved her and wanted her.

She had never thought much about marriage or loving a man until she had seen Quick Fox that first time and he had caused her heart to react in a brand-new way.

Until him, she had centered her life . . . her dreams . . . around being a naturalist. She had organized her life around her family.

But now?

Things had changed the moment she had fallen in love with Quick Fox. Not even the thought of leaving behind the family mansion frightened her. Love would help her adjust to anything, even living in a tepee. For now, she was anxious to get away from this place where she had almost died. But she would return. It was important to finish what she had started. She felt she must achieve this last goal of her father's life. She would return. She would study the bones and send her findings back to Washington.

But for herself, she wanted only to stay in Wyoming. She wanted to be Quick Fox's woman, forever.

"I am eager to leave this place today," Dayanara said, visibly shivering. "But, Quick Fox, I *do* want to return. Perhaps you will even come with me. Let me study the bones for a while, send my findings to those who are awaiting them, and then, Quick Fox, I want nothing in life but you."

"As I you," Quick Fox said, pulling her against his hard body.

He gave her a long, deep kiss, one of his hands moving between them, then resting on one of her breasts.

The warmth of his hand through her blouse, the touch of his hand against her breast even through the cotton fabric made Dayanara's knees grow weak with longing.

"Please, let's go now?" she whispered as she drew her lips from his.

She gazed up at him and saw the passion in his eyes. "I have never wanted a man," she murmured. "Not until you. My body is filled with all sorts of strange sensations."

"I shall awaken all your feelings when we make love," Quick Fox said huskily. "My woman, my own body is on fire with need of you. I am not certain I can wait until we return to my village."

"But we must," Dayanara murmured. "We can't make love out here where . . . Uncle John could spy on us."

"You are comfortable about returning to my village?" he asked. "You were treated less than cordially the last time you were there."

"If you feel that I will be welcome, yes, I am comfortable," she murmured.

"Then we shall leave now," he said. "After we get inside my tepee, I will tie the ties at my entrance flap and we will have privacy."

"What will Little Fox think if he tries to enter his lodge and can't?" she asked softly.

"Little Fox has gone with other young

braves today to make their own sort of hunt for our people," he said.

"They hunt for game?" she asked.

"Small game and also fish in the river," Quick Fox said, pride in his voice.

"I fell in love with Little Fox the moment we met and talked," Dayanara said.

"As does everyone fall in love with my son, for he is a young brave with much love to give back," Quick Fox said, smiling broadly.

"He deserves so much more than he ever had in Saint Louis," Dayanara said, suddenly solemn as she thought of the way this child had been treated.

"Yes, that is why he won the hearts of my people," Quick Fox said, helping Dayanara into her saddle.

He took her reins and walked her away from the snake to where he had left his steed tethered.

As he handed Dayanara her reins, he smiled into her eyes. "My son needs a mother as I need a wife," he said thickly. "Would you take both of us into your heart and become a wife and mother as vows are exchanged between you and me?"

Though they had known each other only a day and a night, Dayanara wasn't as stunned by the question as she might have been. She had known the moment they had finally met that her heart was lost to this man.

She had read about love at first sight. Always before, she had scoffed at such a thing really happening. But now she knew that it could, and it had happened for her and Quick Fox.

"I would be honored to be your wife and Little Fox's mother," she said, her voice soft and lilting. "Quick Fox, will your people want me? Or . . . or . . . will my presence among them put you in an awkward position as chief?"

"In council today, I shared with my people some of the feelings of their chief," Quick Fox said.

He loosened his reins from the limb, then swung himself into his saddle. He positioned his bow out of the way on his shoulder, then lifted the reins.

"What sort of feelings?" Dayanara asked as he kicked his horse and they rode off together in the direction of his village.

"The feelings of a Cree chief who is in love with a woman of white skin," Quick Fox said, keeping at a steady lope beside Dayanara's white steed. "I told them I wanted them to accept you into their lives."

"And? What was their reaction?" Dayanara asked guardedly.

"At first there were many who showed their displeasure at their chief's love for a white woman," Quick Fox said. "But in the end, I had their blessing, and therefore, so do you."

"You mean they . . . will . . . truly allow our marriage?" Dayanara said, her heart soaring at the news.

Could this be happening? she wondered to herself.

Was she really riding side by side with a powerful, handsome Indian chief who was telling her that he had coaxed his people into accepting her not only as a white woman amid them, but a white woman who would be their chief's wife?

And then another thought came to her that almost spoiled the moment. Her Uncle John. She just couldn't get his threats off her mind.

It was a terrible thing to realize that her own blood kin could be so vicious and evil.

She knew that if anything or anyone stood in the way of her happiness with Quick Fox, it would be her uncle.

She clenched her jaw and decided there and then that she wouldn't allow her uncle to jeopardize her relationship with Quick Fox. If he tried, she would not hesitate to do whatever it took to stop him.

She realized she must be the one to thwart his plans, not Quick Fox.

She knew the end results of an Indian retaliating against any white man, even if he deserved whatever Quick Fox might choose to do to her uncle. It was no secret that white men awaited any chance to rid the earth of another "savage," as most whites called Indians.

She wouldn't allow anything to happen to Quick Fox. She would protect him at all cost. For she loved him with every beat of her heart.

She thought of the small pistol that lay in the depths of her skirt pocket. Surely John would forget that she was well prepared if he tried to harm her again.

Today, as the snake had lain coiled and ready to strike, she had been too terrified even to consider using her firearm against it. But the next time her uncle threatened her, she would be prepared. She would not stop at drawing her firearm on *him*.

Chapter Nineteen

There is only one happiness in life —
To love and to be loved.
— George Sand

The ties had been secured on Quick Fox's entrance flap, and Dayanara was in a state of wonder. For the first time in her life, she was standing before a man and allowing him to slowly undress her.

She was aware of the scent of the perfume that she had sprayed in her hair. It was a rich fragrance from a bottle that her mother had given to her for Christmas the year before, a bottle that Dorothea had specially ordered from France.

She was also aware of Quick Fox's clean, fresh smell, a scent that she would always identify with him. He smelled as though he had just stepped from a bath in the river.

His hair shone from its morning washing.

Little Fox had mentioned how some braves and warriors wore bear's grease in their hair to give it a more lustrous shine. But she saw nothing like that in Quick Fox's hair. It was thick and shining and long without any assistance from animal grease.

As she held her arms away from herself so that he could slide her shirt off, she felt a strange warmth in the pit of her stomach. For the first time in her life, a man was looking at her breasts.

Quick Fox tossed her blouse aside and then his eyes swept over her breasts, from one to the other, a deep, dark passion in the depths of his gaze.

She felt the heat of his look and was, oh, so glad that her breasts were round and firm, that her nipples formed perfect cones at the tips.

She wanted Quick Fox to approve of everything about her.

She drew in a ragged breath of rapture when he bent his head and flicked his tongue across one of her nipples, then covered it fully with his lips and sucked it into his mouth, his teeth softly nipping her flesh.

Trembling with pleasure, a pleasure that she'd never thought possible, Dayanara closed her eyes and became aware of something else very new to her. There was a strange sort of ache, as well as a throbbing, at the juncture of her thighs, where no man's hands had ever before touched her.

It was as though a man's hand were there even now, caressing her, and the pleasure was wonderful and sweet. But it was his lips and his mouth on her breast that were making her body react.

She had to wonder how much greater the pleasure would be once his hands did touch her secret place. What would it be like when something else was his manhood?

The thought of actually making love for the first time in her life did not frighten her at all, but left her dizzy with a strange need of it.

Quick Fox's heart was pounding like distant drums inside his chest as he tasted the sweetness of Dayanara's nipples. He swept his tongue from one to the other. The nipples had become hard at his touch.

Her breasts were warm, round, firm, and for a woman of her size, large. He filled both hands with them, now, then licked his way up across the column of her neck, and then to her lips.

He swept his arms around Dayanara and crushed her breasts against the bareness of his chest and kissed her with a fierce, possessive heat. He was experiencing a raging hunger never known to him before.

He was aware that she, too, was lost in the moment. She moaned softly and clung to him as she gave herself up to the rapture.

His body was growing feverish with need of her. And he was surprised by his reaction to this woman. He was a man who had women at his beck and call, yet he had not been prepared for the intense passion he felt for

Dayanara. It was as though his body, especially his manhood, had lain dormant until now . . . until he felt this fierce need for Dayanara.

He wanted her fully now, but he did not yet want to end these special moments as his passion mounted and their kisses deepened.

But his body was crying out for hers in other ways and he could no longer deny this want, this need that made his senses spin.

Breathing hard, and keenly aware of how blood had filled his throbbing manhood, its heat now almost maddening, he stepped away from Dayanara. His hands trembled as he gazed at every new inch of her body being revealed to him as he continued undressing her.

And when she stood totally nude before his feasting eyes, his whole body was overcome with a feverish heat he had never known before.

He ran his hands slowly over her body, keenly aware of how his touch was making her tremble and gasp with pleasure, especially when he placed a hand directly over the golden fronds of hair at the juncture of her thighs.

"My woman, you are awesome in your beauty," Quick Fox said huskily.

He watched her expression change from wonder to intense passion when he slid a finger through the fronds of hair and found the swollen mound where a woman's sexual feelings were centered.

He began slowly caressing her there.

Dayanara had never felt anything as wonderfully sensual as now, when Quick Fox's finger caressed her where her entire heart seemed to be centered. The throbbing was so intense. The pleasure spread like warm flames as he touched her and caressed her.

"You feel it, do you not, the pleasure a man gives a woman with a mere touch?" Quick Fox asked, his voice so husky he scarcely recognized it as his own.

He badly wanted to receive the same caresses, but he knew she was an innocent. He would have to be patient until he could show her how it was all done, moment to moment, body to body.

"Yes, I feel it," Dayanara murmured, her face hot with a blush from the building rapture within her. She closed her eyes and felt as though she were melting as the pleasure spread upward and upward. She felt as though she might explode with the wonder of it.

"There is much more than that to feel," Quick Fox said thickly.

When he drew his hand away, Dayanara opened her eyes and gave him a wanton look. "Must you?" she said, hardly believing it was herself being this wanton.

She could hardly believe that she was

standing nude before a man, and not even feeling self-conscious.

It seemed so natural that their love for one another should be revealed like this, a moment at a time, a touch at a time, a heartbeat at a time.

If someone had told her even one month ago that she would be nude with *any* man, she would have called that person daft.

But now? Nothing seemed impossible between her and Quick Fox. Their love was real and deep. Their bodies were crying out for each other.

And she wanted it all today with him, for she had waited twenty years, had kept herself a virgin, so that the right man would introduce her to all ways of making love. Of course she would have preferred to have spoken the vows of marriage first, which was the ordinary thing to do. But their relationship was anything but ordinary.

It was as though if they didn't make love today, they might die from longing. She was going to forget everything that she knew was right and take from the moment all that she could, for who was to say that there would even be a tomorrow for her and Quick Fox?

When word spread of her love for this man, would white people try to stop it? She vowed to herself that she would fight for this man, and the right to love him, even if it meant using a firearm to get her point across.

Her love was so deep, so intense, she knew now that she could never be without it.

Quick Fox stepped away from her.

He held his arms out from his sides. "Undress me," he said huskily, his eyes two pools of passion. "See me. Touch me. And then we will bring our naked bodies together. We will make love as no man and woman have made love before us."

The thought of making love with a man for the very first time in her life made Dayanara's knees grow weak and her pulse race. She knew without a doubt that this man was skilled in all the ways of pleasuring a woman.

She brushed aside an instant of jealousy when she realized that a man as virile as he, as handsome, would have had many women in his life.

She was just glad that none had yet claimed him fully. He had in a sense saved himself for Dayanara, for it was *she* he had asked to marry, none of the other women he had taken to bed.

Her hands trembled as she reached to the waist of his breechclout. Her eyes widened when she saw something large, hard, and long pressing against the inside of his breechclout.

She swallowed hard to know that he was so big, and so ready. But she was ready, too.

She was throbbing unmercifully between

her thighs. She was eager to have him touch her again there.

But she was somewhat afraid to have him enter her for the first time. He was so big. Hers was surely a small passage that had not yet been entered.

Could he push his way inside her? What if she was too small and it hurt too much?

She didn't want to disappoint him. She knew that no matter how much it hurt, she would not allow him to realize it. Surely once she got past the initial pain, the rest would be pure pleasure. That pleasure was what she concentrated on as she slowly began sliding the breechclout down.

She had not gone far before the very tip of his manhood became visible, and the sight overwhelmed her with a feverish heat.

Trying to bring her breathing under control, she pushed the breechclout away from him. His manhood sprang into full view, the sight of it awesome to her.

"Touch me," Quick Fox said, his voice deep and even more husky. "Familiarize yourself with me as I did with you."

Her throat dry, her pulse racing, her knees even weaker now, Dayanara hesitated.

He reached out and brought one of her hands to his manhood. It seemed to grow even larger as he twined her fingers around it. She was acutely aware of the heat of his flesh and of the throbbing of the vein that ran up one side of it.

She was on fire herself, eager to have him inside her, yet she still wanted to touch him like this for a while longer.

"Move your hand on me," Quick Fox said, his voice low and deep.

He closed his eyes and groaned with pleasure as Dayanara began moving her hand up and down on him, watching the loose skin move with her hand, and covering the tip as she became more daring and moved the skin up and over it.

"My woman, you fill me with such pleasure," Quick Fox moaned, his eyes closed, his head held back. "Your fingers are magic . . . magic."

Then, not able to stand much more of this sort of pleasuring, but instead wanting the true wonders of her body, Quick Fox moved her hand away. He swept her into his arms and carried her to his bedding.

Gently he placed her on the thick, soft pelts. He knelt down over her, his knees straddling her.

"I will love you forever and ever," Quick Fox said, then lowered his mouth to hers and gave her a long, deep kiss as he delved low with his manhood.

As one of his knees parted her legs, he sank his manhood into her, slowly, slowly. He could feel her tightness and realized that he was the first to take her sexually. He would also be the last, because she was going to be his wife.

Dayanara twined her arms around his neck as he moved more deeply within her, what seemed an inch at a time, and then a sudden, searing pain roared through her.

Dayanara's fingers bit into his shoulders as she cried out against his lips. A moment later she went limp and relaxed as he continued moving farther into her, the pain soon gone and replaced with a pleasure beyond words.

She clung to him and seemed to know that it would make their pleasure even more intense if she wrapped her legs around his waist, for she did it as though she had done it countless times before.

A tremor went through her body when she felt him now, ah, so deep within her. He moved rhythmically and her own body responded. She clung and rocked with him, his lips now on hers, demanding yet sweet.

Her whole body quivered with the raging passion that was growing, growing, growing.

She experienced a lethargic feeling of floating as the thrusts continued and his kiss deepened.

His hand reached between them to cup one of her breasts, and he kneaded it for a moment. When he slid his hand down across her belly until he reached the place that until tonight had not known the pleasures it could feel, she sighed.

When he began rubbing his fingers around her swollen nub of pleasure, and then stroked it in long, lazy strokes, Dayanara knew she could not take much more without . . .

Suddenly she was filled with a wondrous feeling, as though sunshine were spreading its warmth throughout her.

And then there seemed to be an explosion of sparks within her, as her body trembled against his as his manhood lurched more deeply within her and jerked and throbbed and spasmed over and over again. All the while, his arms held her tightly, his lips crushing hers in a fiery kiss.

And then they both lay quietly, he still above her, her beneath him, still clinging together.

"I never knew it could be like this," Dayanara said, panting softly as the pleasure lingered in liquid heat.

She reached a hand to his sweating brow, then her lips.

She kissed him, even the saltiness of his sweat tasting good to her, for everything about him was wonderful.

"This is only the beginning," Quick Fox breathed against her lips, then gave her a slow, lingering kiss.

Dayanara returned the kiss, her body throbbing again as his fingers swept slowly over her, teasing and caressing what she now knew to be pleasure points.

She grew breathless as he again caressed her between the thighs, stunned when another explosion of ecstasy rocked her body.

She drew her lips from his when she came down from the rapture a second time. "What you just did . . . ?"

"*Huh,* a man's fingers can bring the same sensation to a woman as his manhood," Quick Fox said, smiling devilishly down at her. "And you can bring the same sort of rapture into my heart with *your* fingers."

"Show me," Dayanara said, feeling wicked now, almost as wicked as his smile.

"You already know how," Quick Fox said, yet he reached for her hand and placed it on his manhood. "Just move your hand on me a few times and I shall show you the sort of pleasure you give me."

Wanting to learn all ways of lovemaking with him, Dayanara did as he suggested, and soon she saw how his eyes closed, his teeth clenched, and then she saw the splash of white that came from his manhood and into her hand.

"What on earth . . . ?" Dayanara gasped as she took her hand away and studied what clung to it.

Quick Fox rolled away from her and lay at her side on his back. "What you see is the way babies are introduced into the womb of a woman," he explained. "It is my seed."

Dayanara paled. "Do you mean that is inside me now after our lovemaking?" she asked softly. "Do you think we . . . made . . . a baby?"

He sat up and reached for a cloth in a wooden basin.

"Would it spoil what we just did to think that you might already be with child . . . *our* child?" Quick Fox asked, using the damp cloth to gently wash her hand.

After rinsing the cloth, he lovingly washed the remainders of their lovemaking from between her legs, then dropped the cloth into the water. Next he moved to his knees and knelt over her, and before she could answer his question, he flicked his tongue over her mound of joy.

The sight of him doing that at first startled Dayanara so much that she actually forgot her concern about being with child. She forgot everything in the thrill of passion that his tongue was causing as he continued flicking it over her where she was still tender from lovemaking.

She closed her eyes and enjoyed, and then found herself in the throes of release a third time.

Her heart pounding, her face hot with a blush, she gazed down at Quick Fox and ran her fingers through his long hair as it lay across her legs. He continued to lie there, his lips again almost worshiping her as he kissed her softly on her womanhood.

When he smiled up at her, she was lost to everything but him and what they had shared. If she was with child as a result, so be it. She had waited what seemed a lifetime for the right man. Having found him, she would welcome a child born of their union.

"Please kiss me?" Dayanara murmured, beckoning him with her outstretched arms.

"You did not tell me how you feel about the possibility that you are with child," he said, moving so that he could lie beside her. He twined his arms around her and drew her next to him, belly to belly.

"I would like nothing more than to have your child," Dayanara murmured, then trembled with ecstasy when he fully encompassed her in his arms, his lips warm and soft against hers, yet again demanding.

"Make love with me again," he whispered huskily against her lips. *"Nei-com-man-pe-ein.* In my language I am saying I love you. I cannot get enough of you."

"Nor I you," Dayanara murmured.

He lifted her above him and taught her a new way to make love.

She straddled him.

Her golden hair hung long down her back as she held her head back and sighed with pleasure while he slid himself up into her and again began his rhythmic strokes.

Chapter Twenty

Take heed of loving me.
— Donne

Although Quick Fox knew that his warriors would be ready to leave, to bring back the rest of his people, he just couldn't end these special moments with Dayanara.

He had waited a lifetime for such a love; he wanted these moments to go on forever.

He had heard the commotion outside as his warriors readied their steeds for travel. He knew that Red Feather would have Quick Fox's stallion ready for him; he had instructed his friend to do this for him while he was in the privacy of his lodge with his woman.

All that Quick Fox had to do was to step out of his dwelling; his horse and his warriors would be waiting for him. He and his warriors could leave immediately.

Upon their return, his people would at last be whole again. And while he was gone, there would be enough warriors left behind at the village to stave off any attack that Dayanara's uncle might be planning.

Quick Fox did not expect him to attack soon, though, for he knew the cowardice of the white man and felt that he would need time to build up the courage to seek his vengeance.

It was Quick Fox's plan to keep Dayanara at the village until his return. He did not like to send her into the face of danger, and her uncle's hunger for vengeance against her was also strong.

He had already explained the situation to Dayanara, how he was going today to get his people, and how he truly did not want her to leave his village until he returned.

He would have asked her to go with him to get his people, but he knew that might be putting her in danger, as well.

Now that he knew her uncle might attack his village, he had to separate the women and children from the warriors as they made their way back to their homes. The warriors would ride ahead, returning to the village as swiftly as possible. Only a few would be left behind to guard the women, children, and elderly, who traveled at a slower pace.

"You are in such deep thought," Dayanara murmured as she buttoned the last button of her blouse.

She had hated leaving the pelts, where she had experienced physical love for the first time, but she understood Quick Fox's plan.

The fact that he had asked her to stay in

his village until his return concerned her for only one reason: her mother. She did not want to worry her mother needlessly. Still, her mother knew that Dayanara had a mind of her own. Dorothea would not be surprised at all if Dayanara spent the night away from the fort, even though she had warned her against such foolishness.

Dayanara would do as Quick Fox asked, for he had assured her that it would only take a short while for him to get to the temporary home of his people and return with them. He had said that he planned to be back home before the moon exchanged places in the sky with the sun.

He had also reassured her that he was leaving enough warriors at the village to protect those who were there until he returned with a full force of stronger warriors.

Speed was necessary.

She hoped that the warriors would return before her uncle could take advantage of those left behind.

She had decided that she would be prepared, herself, to fight her uncle, if need be. If he did arrive with vengeance on his mind, she would be the first to stand up against him with her rifle.

"*Huh,* I am thinking of many things," Quick Fox said, sliding his feet into his moccasins. "I have heard my warriors readying their steeds for our journey."

He stood up and went to Dayanara.

He embraced her, then held her away from him at arm's length. "I am thinking about the moments we just shared," he said thickly. "I am thinking about when we can become man and wife so that we can have such moments every night. Will you become my wife soon? Or, *mah-tao-yo*, little one, am I asking you to do something you need more time to think about?"

She reached a gentle hand to his cheek. "I need no time at all to think about marrying you," she said, sighing with sheer joy. "Whenever you say, I will be at your side to speak our vows."

"Even tomorrow?" Quick Fox said, searching her eyes. His belly clenched when he saw her gaze waver. "After our people have been reunited, will you say vows before them with me?"

"Yes, even tomorrow, but, Quick Fox, I still need time to study the prehistoric bones so that I can wire the information to Washington," Dayanara said, her voice drawn. "May I still continue my studies even if we are man and wife? Or would you rather I finish them before we get married?"

"How long will it take for you to study the bones?" Quick Fox asked, dropping his hands from her shoulders.

He knelt before the firepit and slid logs into the ashes, readying them for a fire later this evening when night's dark shadows lengthened around his village.

"Not long," Dayanara said, happy that he was going to allow her to complete her studies.

He rose to his full height and turned to her. "Then, as soon as you are finished, we shall say our vows, but not before," he said. "When we enter into marriage I want you to do so with your mind free of the life you will be leaving behind."

"I understand," Dayanara murmured. "And thank you for understanding about my need to finish this project. I am doing it not for myself, but for my father."

"What of your mother?"

"She is going to return to Saint Louis on the next available paddle wheeler."

"And your uncle?"

"I apologize for my uncle's behavior toward you," Dayanara said. "He has never been very bright. He is so crude, I find it hard to believe that he and my father came from the same womb."

"There must have been many years between the births of those two sons," Quick Fox said. "Your uncle looks closer in age to you than to your father. That is rare, is it not, to wait so many years between children?"

"It isn't the best way to have children, especially if you wish them to be close in heart, which my father and his brother never were," Dayanara said. "Yes, it was seventeen years between sons for Gertrude and Abner Tolliver, who, God rest their souls, died during an outlaw raid in Saint Louis only a few years ago. After having my father, they lost several children due to miscarriage. Then, lo and behold, finally, after many tries, Gertrude carried a child full term. That was John. Most said that by then she was too old to have a child, and that made people believe that perhaps something happened to John while he was in her womb. You see, he was a tyrant almost from the moment he could walk and talk. Everyone hated seeing his parents bring him into their homes. He broke everything. He fought the other children. And then when his parents died and he became the responsibility of my father, my uncle fought everything my father tried to do or say to make his brother's life right. Father finally gave up. He just couldn't do anything about John but detest the very ground he walked on."

"A man of *che-kas-koi*, bad heart," Quick Fox said. "It is sad that John turned out to be so unruly that your father suffered because of it, especially after he tried to do right by his brother."

"Uncle John made not only my father's life miserable, but also mine and my mother's," Dayanara said. "He still does."

"If I am wrong about your uncle, and he does not attempt an attack against my people, then you must be careful, yourself, while you are away from my protection," Quick Fox said thickly. "This man has a grudge against you. That is why you must stay under the protection of my warriors here at the village until I return."

"Thank you, I will," Dayanara said, sighing. "I'm just glad that you won't be gone for long. I would hate for John to arrive and attack while you are away."

"That is why I will return quickly with my strong, healthy warriors. The women, children, and elders will come at a more leisurely pace," Quick Fox said.

He turned away from her and walked toward the side of his tepee. "I have something to show you and then I must leave," he said softly. "It is something I have wanted to show you since I knew of your interest in old things. I have an ancient belonging of my people that you might want to study while I am gone."

A sudden excitement filled her at the idea that Quick Fox was ready to share such a special artifact with her. Dayanara watched him go to a large, long buckskin bag and carefully open it.

He looked over his shoulder at Dayanara. "My son should be home soon. He will keep you company as you wait for my return," he said. "And, Dayanara, what do you wish for me to call you? Dayanara? Or Day?"

"Which do you prefer?"

"Dayanara," he said, smiling at her. "Like you, it has the sound of a soft song."

"Then please do call me Dayanara," she said, going to sit beside him as he nodded for her to come.

"This is something old that my elderly uncle gave me," Quick Fox said, uncovering a willow cane which had been carved and polished with care. "My uncle no longer needs the cane. He is helpless now. He lies in his bed of pelts and blankets and is cared for by the women of our village. His mind dwells on his life long ago and with those who shared it."

"The cane is beautiful," Dayanara murmured, reaching out to run a hand over the carved surface.

"I keep it polished for my uncle in case his mind returns to today's world," Quick Fox said, handing the cane to Dayanara. "While I am gone, you can study the carvings on the cane, if you wish. My uncle's great-grandfather carved some of them into the wood, as did my uncle's grandfather, and then, too, my uncle. It is a valued belonging of my family."

"I would love to study the carvings," Dayanara said, already looking closely at the cane and noticing the shapes of forest animals.

She gazed up at him. "Are there messages in these carvings?" she asked softly. "Are there meanings behind them?"

"I have shown this cane often to my son, Little Fox, and explained each and every carving to him. When he returns from his hunt, tell him that I gave him permission to share these meanings with you while I am gone," Quick Fox said.

He went to his supply of weapons.

He slapped a sheathed knife around his left thigh just beneath the spot where the breechclout's fringed hem lay, and fastened it in place.

He swung his quiver of arrows onto his back, and then grabbed up his carved bow.

Dayanara had noticed those bow carvings earlier. She wanted to ask Quick Fox their meanings, too, but knew that he had already spent too much alone time with her. Now he must give his attention to his warriors.

He bent low and brushed a soft kiss across Dayanara's brow. "I shall return soon," he promised. "But remember, Dayanara, should your uncle stage an ambush on the village, allow my warriors to protect you in my absence."

She wanted to reassure him that she was very capable of caring for herself, that she had a rifle on her horse which would protect her better than bows and arrows, but she kept her silence and only nodded.

"I hope my uncle isn't foolish enough to carry out his threats," Dayanara said, looking up at Quick Fox. "I hope that his cowardice keeps him away."

"A man whose mind is tarnished with evil like your uncle does not know how to weigh wrong and right," Quick Fox said. "I will enjoy showing John the true strength of my combined warriors."

He laughed throatily. "Little does that man know who he has tormented when he mocks this powerful Cree chief," he said.

He smiled as he thought of the shocked look on John's face when he saw the full number of warriors at Quick Fox's command.

Dayanara carefully laid the cane aside, then went to Quick Fox. She twined her arms around his neck. "I shall miss you terribly while you are gone," she said, her voice breaking.

"Soon we will be together all the time," Quick Fox said. He swept his free arm around her waist and drew her against his hard body. "When we are man and wife, we will always be there for each other."

Dayanara melted inside when he kissed her. Although she had loved her life of independence, and always enjoyed helping her father in his work, she had also dreamed of a time when she would put all this behind her and settle down with a wonderful man to have children.

In her wildest dreams she would never have thought the man would be a handsome Indian chief. But even though it had happened so fast, she knew this was right for her.

She couldn't chance that someone might find out about her feelings and try to stop this marriage, which most whites would see as forbidden.

She and Quick Fox had known each other a very short time. A part of her warned that she should wait a while longer.

But another part refused to wait. Nothing in life was certain, especially one's tomorrows. One must accept happiness now, or possibly lose it in the frailties of the future.

And hadn't her own mother fallen in love as quickly? Her mother had only known Daniel Tolliver one week before they married, and they had been married for many years.

"Please hurry home," she softly begged. "Things can happen so quickly."

"That is why I *will* travel in haste to the camp of my people, then return in haste to this village. Thoughts of being with you will hurry my steps," Quick Fox said.

He gave her another long, deep kiss, then wheeled around and left before they could say goodbye.

"Father!"

Dayanara's eyes widened when she heard Little Fox's voice outside the lodge.

"Father, I had a good hunt!" Little Fox shouted as he rode up on his pony with five dead squirrels and five rabbits tied to the side of his saddle. "The new bow you helped me carve worked well for me, Father, as well as the arrows you lent me."

Dayanara went to the entrance flap and raised it. She smiled as Quick Fox mounted his steed, then rode over and stopped beside Little Fox's pony.

A warmth spread through her as Dayanara watched father and son talk a moment longer about the successful hunt.

Then she saw Little Fox look toward her and knew that Quick Fox had explained her presence there. She returned Little Fox's smile, then went and sat down and studied the cane until the boy should enter the tepee.

The weight of the pistol in her pocket gave her an idea. Had not she wanted to teach the child how to shoot it?

This would be the perfect opportunity. While she was with Little Fox just outside the boundaries of the village, she could keep an eye out for her uncle.

Chapter Twenty-one

Did I tell you, I rather guess,
She was a wonder, and nothing less?
— Oliver Wendell Holmes

After Little Fox saw that his father had
shown Dayanara the old cane, he had asked
if she wanted to meet the elderly uncle,
Brave Thunder, who had given it to Quick
Fox for safekeeping.

She sat with Little Fox now beside the old
man's bed of pelts and blankets and listened
as Brave Thunder rambled on about the
things that occupied him.

Her heart went out to the old man, for
surely long ago he had been as handsome
and as muscled as Quick Fox. He still had
the high, pronounced cheekbones that made
Quick Fox so noble in bearing. They were
even more pronounced beneath the leathery
skin that was drawn so taut across his face.

In his eyes, which had paled with age,
there was still much wisdom, and his wide
shoulders had surely been muscled and
proud at one time. He had a thick head of
white hair which lay across his bare shoul-

ders. And the bones of his ribs were so visible, Dayanara knew she could have counted them if she'd wished to.

While he continued telling about things that only a wise old Indian would know, Dayanara held Little Fox's hand as he sat close beside her on a soft white pelt.

The flames in the firepit made the lodge uncomfortably warm, but they were kept burning because the old man complained of being cold, even in the harsh heat of summer.

Dayanara's eyes moved slowly around her, and she found many fascinating things to study.

The yellowed buffalo-skin wall had scarcely a space without pictures on it. Surely as Brave Thunder had aged, he had added more and more drawings to the wall, depicting the events he remembered.

Before entering the ancient lodge, where even the flap had rips and tears in it, Little Fox told Dayanara that Brave Thunder had requested long ago that no one change his lodge covering. He wished to let it age along with him, so that his stories on the skins would be there even after he died.

Dayanara wished she knew the stories behind each drawing. Surely there would be fascinating tales that might even be written into a book for the world to read and thereby understand this old man and his Cree heritage.

The old man lay flat on his back on his bed, day in and day out, and was kept clean by the women of the village. He was spotless in his brief breechclout, his leathery skin shining from a fresh bath today.

She gazed elsewhere and saw the huge supply of weapons in a pile in the shadows at one side of the tepee. She saw bows that looked as if they had been made long ago, their strings now hanging limply from them. But it was the arrows that fascinated her. There was more than one quiver filled to the brim with them, and each had colorful feathers on the end.

Her gaze fell upon a stack of tomahawks and knives. She gasped when she saw something that looked like dried blood on one of the tomahawks.

Then her eye went to a display of scalps hanging on a scalp pole just inside the entrance flap. She was glad when she saw none that looked as if they had belonged to white people. They were all of thick, black hair, surely taken from the old man's Indian enemies.

"There were many enemies in my day," he suddenly said as he caught Dayanara staring at the scalps.

She looked quickly at him, and listened again to what he had to say.

"There were enemies on all sides of my Cree people," he said thickly. "We were not, and are still not, a warring tribe, but when our families are threatened, those who threaten them become the enemy. Scalps were taken as trophies then. But it has been many moons now since Brave Thunder or any of our Fox Clan of Cree used his tomahawk to take hair from anyone. It is good to lie here and know my people are safe under the leadership of my nephew Quick Fox."

He reached a thin, quavering hand out to pat Little Fox's knee. "Did you say that your father Quick Fox will come soon and join us today, as you sit at my side with the pretty white lady?" he asked, his voice a deep, low rumble.

Dayanara glanced quickly at Little Fox just as he glanced at her. They both knew that the village stood vulnerable against a possible ambush by Dayanara's uncle, and both prayed that Quick Fox would return soon so that no one would die needlessly today because an evil white man plotted against the Cree.

Dayanara's and Little Fox's eyes moved back to Brave Thunder.

"You know of the scarring disease, do you not?" Little Fox asked, taking the old hand and holding it affectionately.

"*Huh,* a disease that this old man had many moons ago. Luckily, I was left with my life intact and no scarring," Brave Thunder said, slowly nodding.

"You know then that some of our people left to escape the disease?" Little Fox asked.

"*Huh,* I know, and are they now among us again? If not, when will they be?" Brave Thunder asked, his old eyes looking hard at Little Fox. "It is not good that we are divided. Someone might take advantage . . ."

Dayanara and Little Fox gazed at each other again, then realized the old man had caught their glances and raised an eyebrow over it.

"What are you not telling this old warrior?" Brave Thunder asked.

"Father will return soon, even today, with those of our people who were separated from us," Little Fox said softly, avoiding the complete truth. He did not want to worry the old man needlessly. He changed the subject quickly.

"Tell us more, old uncle, of things you speak about even in your dreams," Little Fox said. "The life you led as a great war chief is so interesting. I could hear the tales over and over again and never tire of them."

"That is good," Brave Thunder said, smiling and revealing a mouth that had only a few chipped, yellowed teeth remaining.

The yellow color came from his love of tobacco. The tepee reeked of it even now, for when he was alone, he still enjoyed puffing on his old pipe and blowing smoke rings into the air of his lodge. The chipped teeth came from battling his enemies long ago.

"My days are filled with so many memories," Brave Thunder said, sighing heavily. "It is with much pride that I lie on my bed and meditate on life and its meaning. . . ."

He continued until his own voice put him to sleep.

Little Fox gave Dayanara's hand an affectionate squeeze. When she looked over at him, he nodded toward the entrance flap. She smiled and returned the nod.

She waited for Little Fox to gently remove his hand from Brave Thunder's. She saw the love of this boy for the old man when he bent over and kissed his brow, then gently covered him with a clean, white pelt.

When she and Little Fox were outside the lodge, Dayanara glanced up at the sun. It had slid halfway down in the sky, which meant that it was mid-afternoon. Quick Fox had been gone for quite a while and was surely even now on his way back to the village.

She slid a hand into her front right skirt pocket and circled her fingers around the small, pearl-handled pistol.

She smiled at Little Fox. "You said you would like to learn how to fire my small pistol," she murmured. "Would you like to learn now? We can leave the village and go stand on the bluff which overlooks it so that we can keep an eye out for your father's return."

She didn't tell him the true reason she wished to climb the bluff. From that vantage point she could see her uncle's approach with his cohorts should he decide to carry out his threat against the Cree.

If she saw him, she would shout down to the warriors in the village and give them fair warning. Her voice would carry that distance, especially since the wind was blowing from the bluff toward the village.

If that didn't work, she would fire her pistol in the air to alert them. Of course, she knew the sharp report of her firearm could carry to her uncle and warn him, as well. Perhaps that would be good, for if he knew that his ambush would not be a surprise, he might retreat and not even carry out his plans.

Either way, she felt that she was doing right by the Cree. While their chief was gone, she would do what she could to help keep them safe.

"Father told us to stay in the village," Little Fox said, frowning uneasily up at Dayanara.

"We will be close enough to feel as though we are still here," Dayanara said, but she felt guilty for urging Little Fox to disobey his father's commands.

She looked up at a bluff that stood opposite the one where she planned to go and was relieved to see a sentry there, armed with a bow and a quiver of many arrows. She was sure he was watching the distance for anything or anyone that might be a threat to his people. Seeing him made Dayanara feel that it would be all right to go to the other bluff with Little Fox.

"I shall go and get my bow and arrows," Little Fox said, then broke into a run.

As she waited for him, she watched the women of the village as they went about their daily chores. When they gazed at her, she smiled and was happy when some smiled back.

She felt a shiver of uneasiness when someone gave her a dark frown. Clearly she was not welcomed by everyone. She could only hope that after they knew her better and realized she meant only good toward them, they would change their minds. If not, her life as the chief's wife would be horribly awkward. . . .

Her thoughts were interrupted by the sound of thundering horses' hooves in the distance. She smiled at the thought of Quick Fox returning to his village.

But that smile quickly waned when the sentry on the bluff shouted down at his people, telling them that white men approached on horses.

"My uncle . . ." Dayanara whispered, her insides turning cold.

Chapter Twenty-two

Love, all alike, no season knows,
   nor climes,
Nor hours, days, months,
Which are the rags of time.
                      — Donne

There was a sudden panic at the village. Although they had been warned of a possible attack, no one, not even Dayanara, had thought it would happen.

Women were screaming and grabbing up their children, others clutching the hands of those who were too big to carry.

The elders' eyes were wild with fear as they tried unsuccessfully to put more haste in their steps than usual.

The warriors who had stayed behind to protect their loved ones were gathering together, shouting at one another as they made decisions as to where they should position themselves.

Dayanara turned to Little Fox. "Go to your lodge and stay there!" she cried.

How could her uncle attack these innocent people? she thought desperately to herself.

The warriors who had stayed behind could not really protect the village from her uncle and his men, even though her uncle did not have that many soldiers following him.

It was their weapons that made the difference. The soldiers had rifles and pistols that fired deadly bullets, whereas the Cree had only their primitive weapons.

"I want to stay with you," Little Fox said, determination etched on his face. "I will go to my lodge and get weapons. I will fight like a man, not go and hide like a child."

"No," Dayanara said as she grabbed him by an arm and tried to forcefully take him to the tepee. "Little Fox, I can't allow anything to happen to you. Please do as I ask."

"I will go to my lodge, but only to get a weapon to fight off the white men," Little Fox said, yanking his arm free.

As he ran toward his tepee, Dayanara went after him. If she had to stay in the tepee herself to keep him safe, she would. The more she thought about it, the more she doubted that her pistol, or even her rifle, would help the Cree. Surely her uncle and his cohorts would never get close enough for her bullets to reach. She knew that her uncle was too cowardly to come into the village. He would be stopping soon, ordering his men to take positions around the village to fire at those they could see.

Dayanara hurried into Quick Fox's lodge

along with the boy, then positioned herself at the entrance flap to block his exit.

"Day, why are you doing that? I must go and help. I *must*," Little Fox cried as he looked over his shoulder at Day, then went on to his father's cache of weapons and began sorting through them.

"Where are they?" he cried. "Oh, where did he put them?"

"What are you looking for?" Dayanara asked, listening for gunfire outside.

"The poisoned arrows," Little Fox said, taking one arrow from a quiver, and then another. "I know that I can strike a blow against our enemy if I can find the poisoned arrows."

"Poisoned arrows?" Dayanara gasped out. "Quick Fox has such things?"

"All Cree have poisoned arrows," Little Fox said, still searching through the arrows. "The white men have the power of guns to wreak their havoc with deadly bullets. The Cree have no firearms, but we do have something just as deadly. Poisoned arrows. Even if an arrow misses the heart, it can still kill. If it enters the flesh of an arm or leg, the poisoned arrow will be as deadly as any white man's bullet."

"It sounds dangerous even to make such a thing as a poisoned arrow," Dayanara said, glad that she hadn't heard any gunfire outside yet. Perhaps her uncle was only trying to scare the Cree. Maybe he was even now riding away, laughing at the confusion and fear he had aroused in the Cree village.

Either way, he had made a deadly mistake. Somehow he would be made to pay. When Quick Fox returned with his warriors, oh, how her uncle would pay for the sin he and his men had committed against Quick Fox's band of Cree.

"It is done with much caution," Little Fox said, stopping to turn and gaze at Dayanara. "I watched Father make his personal poisoned arrows. He dips the point of the arrowhead into a mixture of pulverized ants and the spleen of an animal which has been allowed to decay in the direct rays of the sun. He has used rattlesnake venom, also."

He looked past Dayanara at the closed flap. "I hear nothing," he said. "I wonder what's happening?"

Dayanara's breathing became shallow as she listened, as well. She no longer heard the approach of horses. That had to mean that her uncle and his men had stopped.

Or had they retreated?

Was that why no sounds were being made?

Or were they positioning themselves where they could start firing at any moment?

She gazed past Little Fox at the weapons and made a quick decision.

"I am going out there with my pistol," she explained hurriedly.

"I will go with you," Little Fox said determinedly. "I am very skilled with the bow and arrow. Quick Fox taught me well. But I have a smaller one that I use that my father helped me make."

He positioned his smaller quiver of arrows on his back, and grabbed up his own personal bow. "My father has many sorts of weapons. Some were his father's and his father's father before him. I speak of *pogamoggan*, a war club. He also has a shield made from the tough skin of a buffalo bull, which also belonged to his father and his grandfather before him."

"Grab the shield," Dayanara said quickly. "If you want to go with me to help fight my uncle, I will feel better if you use a shield for protection."

"It will impede my ability to use my bow and arrow," Little Fox argued. He rushed toward the entrance flap. "*Mea-dro,* come on, Day. Let's go and work together to do what we can to help my Cree people."

Knowing that there was no point in arguing with him any longer, Dayanara sighed heavily and left the tepee with Little Fox.

As they got outside, she was very aware of the strained silence in the village now. Everyone but the warriors who were defending their people was inside. The inhabitants of the village were being so quiet, the silence had an unreal quality to it.

And then suddenly she became aware of something else. She heard the thundering of horses' hooves again.

She went cold inside. Was her uncle once more advancing on the village?

Would the soldiers brave the volley of arrows that the Cree would launch against them? Would they come into the village and trample down the tepees with their steeds in order to get to the women and children and the elderly?

"Chief Quick Fox!" a warrior shouted. "It is Chief Quick Fox approaching! He is just in time! The white men are positioned now to fire upon our village!"

"Quick Fox?" Dayanara and Little Fox said in unison, both sighing heavily with relief as the horses kept coming.

Dayanara ran with Little Fox to stand with the warriors at the edge of the village. She could now see her uncle's horses tied in the trees and his men even closer, positioned within firing distance of the village.

She smiled as she saw her uncle and the white men scrambling from hiding. They were running to get to their horses to make a hasty escape.

But they weren't fast enough. Suddenly Quick Fox and his warriors were there, surrounding them, stopping their escape.

"Get them!" Quick Fox shouted. Several warriors leapt from their steeds to follow his command. "Disarm them!"

Dayanara watched as other warriors dismounted and took ropes to where her uncle was standing with his men, their eyes wide with fear.

She was stunned by how many warriors had returned with Quick Fox. Surely there were a hundred!

She now understood why his people had felt so vulnerable without the normal amount of warriors with them at the village. They were used to so many.

She gazed at Quick Fox, who looked both noble and commanding on his horse. The warriors under his command showing great respect for him by responding to his orders as soon as they were given.

Little Fox slid a hand into Dayanara's. She gazed down at him just as he looked up at her and smiled. In his smile, she saw such love and pride for his father.

It made her feel suddenly lonesome. Her beloved father had been dead for such a short time. It always felt to her as though all she had to do to see him again, to hug him again, was to return to the fort, where he would be waiting for her.

Instead, he was in a hole in the ground, dead!

She swallowed the urge to cry, for she knew that she had to accept his loss and go on with her own life. And what a life it was going to be. The man she loved was so special . . . so loving. He had already filled that vacant place in her heart that her father's death had caused.

"Tie the ropes around the white men's necks!" Quick Fox shouted, his eyes only momentarily leaving the captives to find Dayanara standing safely with Little Fox. He gave her a silent nod, then turned back to the business at hand.

"Tie rope around their necks?" Dayanara gasped, only now realizing what Quick Fox had said. "Does he plan to hang them?" Dayanara asked, gazing down at Little Fox just as he looked up at her. "Do your Cree people hang those who . . . who . . . go against them?"

"I don't know," Little Fox gulped out. "I have never seen anyone go against us. I hope . . . they . . . don't hang them. Wouldn't that get the soldiers at the fort angry? Would they not then retaliate against my people?"

"Yes, they might," Dayanara said, her voice drawn. "Although these men were doing wrong, the colonel at the fort might not care."

She waited breathlessly to see what Quick Fox had in mind for her uncle and those he had lured from the fort to be his allies in crime.

Chapter Twenty-three

Love which will never be seen twice.
— Alfred de Vigny

"Warriors, those of you who have been assigned the task, go and ready three canoes," Quick Fox said as he gazed at the warriors awaiting his orders.

The warriors nodded, then rode toward the river.

Quick Fox nodded at the warriors who had placed the ropes around the white men's necks. "You have also been instructed what to do," he said. "Do it."

"What are you going to do with us?" John cried, his eyes wild. "If you aren't going to hang us with these ropes, what else are you planning? Why are you readying canoes?"

"Man with bad heart, soon you will see," Quick Fox said.

Quick Fox looked on impassively as the warriors yanked on the ropes, bringing cries of pain from the white men. He watched his warriors lead the white men toward the river; then he swung around and rode toward the village.

When he reached Dayanara and Little Fox, he gave Dayanara a firm gaze. "You are safe now from your tyrant of an uncle," he said. "You have nothing to fear from him again." He looked over at Little Fox. "You are also safe, my son."

He then looked past them at his people, who had come from their lodges, young and old alike, all giving him a look of utter adoration.

"You are all safe from these white men who came today to kill and maim," he said to them. "They are going far away. Never will they set foot on our soil again."

Dayanara wanted to ask what his plans were for John and his men, but knew that the question might seem as though she were arguing their fate.

John had tried to kill her. He deserved no consideration from her. Whatever his fate was going to be at the hands of the Cree, he had earned it.

She was surprised, though, when Quick Fox reached down and placed his arm around her waist, then lifted her onto his steed with him, placing her before him. Then he pulled Little Fox up behind him.

"It is only right that you, my woman, see the punishment I hand down to your uncle firsthand," Quick Fox said.

He ignored the looks of dismay from his people. Clearly they were surprised that he had singled Dayanara out. But they knew she was his woman. They knew she would soon be his wife.

He gazed over his shoulder at Little Fox. "And, my son, I want you to learn from what happens today to these white men," he said thickly. "I want you to see how peacefully vengeance can be accomplished against one's enemy. Another tribe wronged by whites might instantly kill them, but that is not our way."

"You aren't planning to kill my uncle, then?" Dayanara asked, drawing Quick Fox's eyes back to her.

"*Ka,* not this time, but if he does not do as he was ordered today, and he returns to the land of the Cree, I will not blink an eye before I sink a poisoned arrow into his dark heart," Quick Fox said, then rode off with Dayanara and Little Fox toward the river.

Dayanara was flooded with warmth when he slid an arm around her waist in order to hold her securely on his steed. Her love for this man deepened each time she was with him.

And today he had proven himself to be a man of peace; a man of honor. She admired him for so many things.

The fact that her uncle had been so foolish as to plot against such a man as Quick Fox would always amaze her.

She hated to think that he might have succeeded in killing many Cree today if Quick Fox had not arrived at the very instant when he was needed. But as it was, all was well now among the Cree. The whites who had plotted against them would not get the opportunity to do so again, and their village was now protected by all its warriors.

Her thoughts focused on her uncle again as Quick Fox drew rein beside the river.

Dayanara and Little Fox slid from the horse, and then Quick Fox dismounted. Dayanara held Little Fox's hand as she watched the fate that was planned for her uncle.

"What are you going to do now?" John gulped out. "Why have you brought us to the river? What are the canoes for?"

"Climb aboard of your own free will, or you will be placed in the canoes by force," Quick Fox said tightly. "Divide yourselves up equally so that an equal number of white men are in each canoe."

"But what about our horses?" John asked, his eyes frightened as he gazed at Quick Fox. "Can't we just leave on our horses if we promise never to return again?"

"Your horses, and all of the belongings on the horses, are now the property of the Cree," Quick Fox said with no emotion.

He stepped up to John and lifted the rope from around his neck, as other warriors removed the ropes from the other captives.

"Now get aboard the canoes," Quick Fox said darkly. "Warriors will take you to an island. There you will be left."

"What?" John asked, his eyes suddenly wild. "Do you mean to say that you are going to leave us, stranded, on an island?" Then he smiled smugly. "We can swim. So take us to an island. We won't stay."

"You . . . will . . . stay," Quick Fox said. He stepped closer to John and spoke directly into his face. "You will stay until a riverboat comes past that is headed away from my land, not toward it. You will wave down the riverboat. You will board it. Then you will travel to lands far from here. You will never return. *And* you are not to tell anyone how you got on the island. If you do, and I find out, I myself will hunt you down."

He placed his face even closer to John's, until their noses almost touched. "You would not even want to think about how you would be made to die at the hands of this Cree chief," he warned. "You are getting off easy, you know. I should kill you and be certain I will never have to see your face again."

He stepped away from John and looked in the eyes of each white man, one at a time. He gave them the same warning that he had given John, until all of their faces were drained of color from fear of Quick Fox's wrath.

Then he stepped away from them. He

nodded to his warriors, who climbed aboard the canoes to paddle the white men away.

But even then John couldn't keep quiet.

"Where in the hell did you get so many warriors?" he screamed as the canoe he was in was shoved out into deeper water by Red Feather, the warrior who would be responsible for making certain that John was taken to the island. "What tribe did you get assistance from?"

Quick Fox smiled smugly. "You thought that there would be only a few warriors to fend off your attack," he said. "You were wrong. Those warriors you see today? They are part of my band. And what you see are still not all of my people. The wives and children of these warriors are not far behind. The whole village will soon be reunited. We are strong again in number, and health. No one would dare go up against us now. Especially someone like you, John Tolliver. *Mea.* Go. Go to your own people. But I doubt that they will want the likes of you among them. How could they? You are wicked, through and through."

John waved a fist in the air. "I will return to Saint Louis, all right!" he screamed as Red Feather sat down in the canoe and he and another warrior began drawing their paddles through the water, heading downstream. "I will be glad to get back to civilized country. And to hell with the hops."

He glared at Dayanara. "And, niece, to hell with you," he screeched. "If you marry the savage, you will deserve the life he will give you in a cold, drafty, flea-infested tepee."

Having heard enough, Quick Fox turned to Dayanara and Little Fox. "Son, will you take my horse to the corral?" He spoke to Little Fox, but his eyes were on Dayanara.

"*Huh,* I shall do that for you," Little Fox said, then suddenly hugged Quick Fox. "I'm so glad you came when you did. If not, many would have died."

Quick Fox took the boy's hands, then knelt down before him. "All is well, my son," he said gently. "And you should never doubt your father's ability to care for you and our people. My love is strong for you all. I have been chosen to protect you. So shall I always."

Little Fox flung himself into Quick Fox's arms. "Father, without you, I . . . I . . ." he sobbed, but said no more because he knew that it was wrong to show that he was still fearful.

"There, there, cry no more," Quick Fox said comfortingly. "*Mea,* go. Go now, my son. Be the man that you are. Take my horse. Come soon to our lodge. Dayanara will be there with me."

Little Fox swallowed back a sob, leaned away from Quick Fox, then smiled bashfully up at Dayanara. "Day, you have seen the

256

child in me," he said softly. "I wished always to show the grown-up to you."

Dayanara sank to her knees beside Little Fox. She gently drew him into her arms. "Sweet, sweet Little Fox," she murmured. "There is nothing wrong in showing your emotions like you just did. You might want to be a man, but, honey, you are still only a child . . . a child who needs both a father and a mother. Soon that will be possible. I hope to make your world complete by being your mother."

"And I can hardly wait," Little Fox said. He eased away from her. He was all smiles as he glanced from his father to Dayanara. "I shall take the horse now."

Quick Fox patted him fondly on the head, then gave him a soft shove toward the waiting animal.

And then Quick Fox walked with Dayanara back into the village. The warriors were greeting and hugging loved ones they had not seen for months.

Soon the women and children and the elderly were arriving, too. As Dayanara went into Quick Fox's lodge, she heard singing and shouting and laughing as all of the Cree assembled in the center of the village.

"There will be a great celebration tonight," Quick Fox said, pulling Dayanara into his arms. "Can you stay?"

"I wish I could, but I have been gone from

my mother for too long as it is," Dayanara murmured. "I'll go to the fort and make certain that she is all right."

She ducked her head momentarily, then looked up at him again. "And I have something else to do," she said softly.

"And what is that?" Quick Fox asked, raising an eyebrow.

"I don't want anyone at the fort to know what happened to John," she said, her voice breaking. "If they knew that you had a role in sending *any* white man away, I'm afraid the colonel would come and question you about it. Who is to say what he might assume or do when he knows what you did? I . . . I . . . want to go and do away with John's things so that when everyone realizes he is missing, they will think he decided to leave on his own."

"Will you be putting yourself in jeopardy by doing this?" Quick Fox asked. "It is a brilliant idea, but will it look as though you allied yourself with the Cree by destroying your uncle's possessions?"

"I will be careful not to be seen doing it," Dayanara said, swallowing hard. "I shall wait until everyone is asleep, especially Mother. Then I shall get my uncle's belongings and burn what I can in the fireplace of our cabin. I will hide what is left among my things and bury them later where no one can ever find them."

"We can make firm plans to marry now that your uncle is gone and my people are safely home again," Quick Fox said, framing Dayanara's face between his hands. "We will set a date soon?"

"Yes, soon," Dayanara said, melting inside when he brushed a soft kiss across her brow.

"But . . ." she then said.

"But what?" Quick Fox said. He leaned away from her. Their eyes met and held. "What is it that you wish to do?"

"I need more time in the hidden valley," Dayanara said, searching his eyes. "Is that all right? I haven't recorded much in my journal. I need positive confirmation for Washington that the bones are prehistoric."

"Then go tomorrow while I join my people in celebrating our joy at being reunited," Quick Fox said softly. "Take several days if need be."

Little Fox came into the lodge. He squeezed between Quick Fox and Dayanara. "I'm so happy," he said, his voice breaking. "This doesn't seem real . . . this sort of true happiness just doesn't seem like it could happen to me."

"Well, it is happening," Dayanara said, bending low to hug him.

Then she leaned away from him. "Honey, I'm going to the fort now to be with my mother this evening, and tomorrow I am going to go one more time to the hidden valley. After that, my time will be all yours and Quick Fox's," she said, smiling broadly. "You see, I, too, find it hard to believe that I have found such happiness, but I have. With you and Quick Fox, I will be the happiest woman in the world."

"I will see that you get safely home," Quick Fox said.

"No, you don't have to," Dayanara said, rising to her full height. "With John gone, I feel safe. You should spend this time with your people. You should join the celebration. I wish I could, but I have things that need to be dealt with at the fort."

Quick Fox pulled her into his arms. "Be careful," he said thickly, kissed her, then walked her to the corral and helped her into her saddle.

"I'm so happy for you and your people," she said, tears burning at the corners of her eyes as she looked past him at so many smiling faces.

"They will soon also be *your* people," Quick Fox said.

"Yes, my people," Dayanara murmured. "I love you, Quick Fox. I can hardly wait until I return and can stay forever with you."

"Soon," he said. "Soon."

She nodded, blew him a kiss, then rode off.

She truly did feel safe. Her uncle was finally out of her life!

She did feel some sadness, though, over what had happened to John. But then she recalled the trouble he had always caused her father and she was glad all over again that his meanness had finally came to an end.

"Yes, I feel so safe with you out on some island, John!" she said into the wind, smiling broadly.

Chapter Twenty-four

This bud of love, by summer's ripening
    breath,
May prove a beauteous flower when next
    we meet.

— Shakespeare

Dayanara was startled when she didn't find her mother in their cabin. Since her father's death, her mother hadn't strayed from the cabin. She had remained inside, locked away from the world.

So now where could she be?

When she heard women's laughter coming from the courtyard of the fort, Dayanara rushed to the bedroom window and gazed from it.

What she saw puzzled yet relieved her. Her mother was dressed fit to kill in her prettiest dress, a gathered maroon velvet gown with a lace collar. Her face was radiant with a flush of what seemed unusual excitement as she came from the colonel's cabin with several women and children. They were laughing and chatting, followed closely by several soldiers.

Dayanara recalled having seen a paddle

wheeler docked close to the fort as she rode up. She had thought at the time that when this paddle wheeler went back down the Missouri, it would pass the island where John and his cohorts had been taken. Surely this would be the paddle wheeler that would be flagged down by her Uncle John.

She only hoped that her uncle had done exactly as he had been ordered . . . that he hadn't told anyone how he and the men had gotten stranded on the island.

She would never forget the steely determination in Quick Fox's words as he had warned John about his actions.

Quick Fox *would* kill John if he got the chance, and Dayanara didn't ever want to see that side of her husband's personality.

He was a gentle, caring man, not a cold-blooded murderer.

But she couldn't forget the actions John had taken against the Cree. He had planned to kill them all, if possible, especially Quick Fox. He had even meant to kill her.

"Uncle John, please go on to Saint Louis and stay out of my life, and Quick Fox's," Dayanara whispered. She gazed heavenward. "Please, God, make him do what is right?"

Since her arrival at the fort, she had seen no women there. It was known that the wives and children of the cavalrymen had been made to stay behind.

She then heard the whistle of the paddle

wheeler and realized it was getting ready to depart for its return journey to Saint Louis and all other ports along the Missouri.

She didn't see any of the women scurrying to get aboard the paddle wheeler. That had to mean that they had come to stay, either for a short visit, or for as long as their husbands would be stationed there.

She had noticed that more cabins were being built these past few days, but her mind had been too occupied by other things to wonder why. Could it be that families would now be allowed at this post?

It didn't matter to Dayanara one way or the other. It was just wonderful to see her mother finally coming out of her shell and reentering the world of the living.

Then another thought came to her. The paddle wheeler was leaving without her mother. Had her mother decided to stay at the fort after all? If so, what had caused her change of heart?

Dayanara's eyes widened when she saw the colonel emerging from his private cabin with a lovely woman who appeared to be her mother's age clinging to his arm. They, too, joined the group walking toward the dining hall.

She was not at all surprised when her mother stepped away from the others, indicating that she would not be going into the dining hall with them. Her mother stood there alone, looking suddenly forlorn. She had no husband to join her.

Dayanara hurried from the cabin and went to her mother. She gave her a hug, then ushered her back to their cabin.

"I didn't know a paddle wheeler was due to arrive today," Dayanara said.

She watched as her mother went to a window and gazed at the last of those who were going into the dining hall.

"But I'm glad it did," Dayanara murmured. "The newcomers have finally got you out of this cabin. I'm so glad to see your smile again."

The hoot-hoot of the paddle wheeler's whistle reminded Dayanara that the boat was departing.

"Mother, aren't you returning home on the paddle wheeler?" Dayanara asked.

With a swish of velvet, Dorothea turned to Dayanara, wiping tears from the corners of her eyes. "I have decided not to leave, not until I am able to convince you to go with me," she murmured. "Dayanara, you are all that I have left in this miserable world. I hoped that you would make plans to return with me on the next paddle wheeler. I was told that another one would be here in two weeks. That should give you time to finish your research at the digs. I am counting on your leaving then with me, Dayanara. I won't take no for an answer."

"Mother, I —" Dayanara began, but was stopped when her mother interrupted her.

"Don't say anything right now," Dorothea said. She gave Dayanara a gentle hug. "We have time to discuss it."

She stepped away from Dayanara, laughter in her eyes. "Come with me, Dayanara, and join the others in the dining hall," she said anxiously. "Moments ago, I didn't go with them because I didn't want to sit alone at the dinner table. But you are here now, Dayanara. Please join me."

Dayanara was torn. She knew it was important for her mother to make friends, especially since Dorothea was going to remain at Fort Meyers for another two weeks.

"Mother, are those women and children here to stay, or have they come to visit until the next boat arrives?" Dayanara asked.

"The women and children are here for the duration of their husbands' enlistment," her mother said, turning again to gaze at the dining hall.

Laughter was coming from the open door and windows. The flicker of candles became visible as they were lit to augment the fading light of the waning day.

Again she turned and gazed at Dayanara, a new excitement in her eyes. "Did you know that one of those women is an old friend of mine?" she asked. "Dayanara, we attended school together as children and remained friends into adulthood. Her name is Grace. We haven't seen each other since she and her husband, who is now the colonel, stood up with your father and me at our wedding. It is like a small miracle that she should show up here when I need a friend so much."

Dorothea tilted her head. "Do you know what might be fun?" she said, suddenly giggling like a schoolgirl.

"What, Mother?" Dayanara asked, wondering at this change in her mother.

"If I stay until Grace leaves," Dorothea said, her eyes dancing, "we can rekindle our friendship. I know we could talk for hours and hours and never tire of one another's voices."

"Mother, I think it would be wonderful if you would stay," Dayanara said, sighing at the happiness she saw in her mother's eyes. "Then you wouldn't insist that I leave with you. Mother, I . . ."

Lost in her own private world again, Dorothea didn't even listen to what Dayanara was about to say. She lifted her chin, giggled again, then rushed toward the door. "I am going to join everyone in the dining hall," she said, giving Dayanara a quick glance over her shoulder as she jerked the door open. "Come with me? If you don't want to, I understand. I don't know why I didn't think of it before. I can sit with Grace and her husband."

"No, I don't think I'll join you, not this

time anyhow," Dayanara said. She gave her mother a warm smile. "I think I'd actually be in the way. You and Grace must have so much to talk about. I shall meet her later, Mother. Is that all right?"

"Certainly," her mother said, then hurried from the cabin.

Dayanara went to the window and watched in amazement as her mother actually ran to the dining hall, the hem of her velvet dress held up away from her scurrying feet. She had never seen her mother filled with such excitement, not even when she was doing things with her husband and child.

This Grace, this woman from her mother's past, had worked magic today. Dayanara had feared she would never see her mother give a genuine smile again.

"This is so wonderful," Dayanara whispered to herself, swinging away from the window.

She clasped her hands together before her excitedly. She desperately wanted her mother to approve of her marriage to Quick Fox. It would be wonderful if Dorothea stayed at Fort Meyers long enough to see and hold her first grandchild.

It would make everything perfect if her mother would decide to stay in this area forever. But Dayanara knew that particular wish could not come true. Her mother's longing for her beautiful home in Saint Louis would draw her there eventually. Even an old friendship wouldn't keep her mother from returning to her life as a pampered, rich woman, living in one of the largest mansions on the banks of the Mississippi.

"Oh, well, I shall enjoy her being here while I can," Dayanara whispered, leaving her mother's bedroom.

Knowing that she must take care of her uncle's belongings without her mother knowing it, she went toward John's bedroom. She was startled when her mother rushed back into the house, breathless.

"Darling, I forgot to ask you to do something for me while I am gone," Dorothea said, her voice breaking. "Dayanara, I have suffered too long over what to do with your father's belongings. It isn't right for me to keep them. I find . . . find . . . myself too often going through them to see if I can get the scent of him just one more time. And I even found myself . . . putting on his shirts in order to feel close to him again."

"Mother, *no*," Dayanara gasped. "I didn't know."

"When you are gone, I find myself thinking your father is sitting beside me, talking to me," Dorothea said, swallowing hard. "Dayanara, I know just how unhealthy that is. I must get his things out of here. Will you do it for me while I am at the dining hall? Place everything in the smaller trunk. I must keep the larger one for my dresses."

"Then what should I do with the trunk?" Dayanara asked, her voice breaking.

"I already questioned the colonel about that," Dorothea murmured. "He said to set it on the porch. He will see that it is taken care of. I'm not sure how. But that doesn't matter. I just need it done, Dayanara. Will you do it for me?"

"Yes. While you're gone, I shall do that for you," Dayanara said. She went to her mother and hugged her. "It is important to end your grieving and accept Father's death. Then you can begin the true healing, Mother."

"I know," Dorothea said, her voice sad.

Then Dorothea left Dayanara's arms. "I must hurry or I will lose my place beside Grace at the table," she said. "I have so much to say to her. Oh, so much!"

Dayanara smiled as her mother left again in a swish of skirts, and then Dayanara turned and glanced from one bedroom door to the other.

Behind one she would find her father's things; behind the other, her Uncle John's. Then a thought came to her that made her smile widen. "I now know how to get rid of Uncle John's clothes without burning or burying them," she whispered.

Yes, she would get her uncle's clothes and place them with her father's. No one would be the wiser.

But she would have to burn John's personal papers and anything else that would not look like her father's possession.

Her mother's decision to finally do away with her father's personal things could not have come at a more opportune time for Dayanara.

But it caused an ache in her heart to think of going through her father's things. Like her mother, she would smell her father's scent on his clothes, and as she held them out before her, she would see him in them.

She firmed her jaw. She knew she must pull herself together and get this all done before her mother returned.

If her mother caught her placing John's things with her father's, Dayanara would have a lot of explaining to do.

She didn't ever want to have to explain to her mother that the man Dayanara loved had put her uncle on an island, to be stranded until a paddle wheeler came past to save him. That information would certainly not help her mother form a favorable opinion of Quick Fox.

Then she began to realize just how hard it was going to be to explain to her mother about Quick Fox. Dorothea would never understand why Dayanara wanted to give up everything for him.

She smiled as she thought of her mother's reaction to the news that Dayanara was planning to give up a comfortable, luxurious home in Saint Louis to live in a tepee. She could just picture the look of horror on her mother's face.

But Dayanara would let nothing, not even her mother, dissuade her from what she believed was her destiny.

She proceeded with the task at hand, going first to her father's bedroom.

She trembled as she began sorting through his belongings.

She quickly understood how her mother could feel his presence, for Dayanara did, as well. As she touched, held, and sniffed the clothes that had been her father's, tears spilled from her eyes. Reverently, she folded them and placed them in the trunk, glad when everything — even his shoes and hairbrush and shaving equipment — was there.

"I will always remember you, Father," Dayanara whispered, then rushed to John's room. She knew she must move in haste before her mother returned and caught her.

She filled her arms with clothes from the dresser drawers and carried them to the trunk in her father's room.

After many trips, she had only one more drawer to go through. The drawer had socks and white handkerchiefs, and she hurried to empty it.

As she lifted the handkerchiefs, she gasped

and stared at what lay at the bottom of the drawer.

"The map," Dayanara whispered, her face aflame with anger at the certain knowledge that John had stolen it.

She sighed heavily as she took the map, folded it, and slid it into a pocket of her skirt, then hurried with these last belongings to the trunk. After locking it, she dragged the trunk out to the porch and left it there.

She then went to the fireplace and burned her uncle's other possessions.

Afterward, she returned to her bedroom, unfolded the map, and gazed at it. She supposed in a sense, she owed John a thank you.

If John had not stolen the map, she would have had no reason to become acquainted with Little Fox or his wonderful father.

"Yes, Uncle John, your theft caused me to meet the man of my dreams," Dayanara said, nodding. "Ah, what webs we weave when we deceive," she said, refolding the map and placing it in her top drawer.

She didn't need it now. She knew every inch of the way to the hidden valley.

"I owe you a big thanks, John, a big thanks!" She laughed, then went to the window.

The moon was high in the sky. A loon sang its eerie song somewhere along the river.

And in the distance she saw the reflection

of a fire in the sky.

She wondered if it was the large outdoor fire at the Cree village where even now a celebration was being held.

She longed to be there, but knew that soon she would be present at all celebrations. She looked forward to one in particular. Her wedding celebration!

A sudden thought struck her. If it was dark, how could John and his cohorts flag down the paddle wheeler and be seen?

She prayed that the paddle wheeler had reached the island before it got dark. If not, what would John do then?

It would be two more weeks before another boat came past that same spot in the river. Wouldn't that delay give John plenty of time to think up another way of taking revenge against Quick Fox and her?

That thought made a shiver ride her spine.

Chapter Twenty-five

Love is a spirit all compact of fire,
Not gross to sink,
But light, and will aspire.
　　　　　　— Shakespeare,
　　　　　　Venus and Adonis

Dressed in a serviceable skirt and blouse and her sturdy boots, Dayanara was once more at the site of the monster bones. This would be her last time there.

She had recorded her findings, describing the bones, their supposed age, and their condition. She had not attempted to unearth any of the buried bones. She had promised Quick Fox that she wouldn't do any digging. She meant to keep that promise.

Soon she would be speaking marriage vows to Quick Fox. She did not want to enter the marriage with lies on her conscience.

The sun was already high in the sky, the air dry, the wind whipping sprays of dirt here and there. Dayanara stopped and wiped her sweaty brow with the sleeve of her blouse. Her eyes moved around her, searching for anything noteworthy that might have eluded her.

She had chronicled her findings as best she could in her journal, and felt that her field notes would be invaluable to the naturalists at the Smithsonian Institute.

She had not wired them yet about what she had discovered. She was even beginning to wonder if that was the right thing to do. Now that she knew the Cree didn't want any more people snooping around, she worried about publicizing the existence of the prehistoric bones.

Most scientists would not listen to the Cree's pleas about leaving the bones intact. Too many would dig them up just for the glory of the achievement.

As it was, only a very few people at the fort and the trading post knew of the Cree's monster bones, and those few had no interest in old bones. Those at the fort were too concerned with keeping peace between whites and Indians, and those at the trading post were too busy trying to make money.

Dayanara was the only one who had ventured deep into Cree territory . . . except for her uncle, who had come for the hops plants.

And now he was gone. He knew better than to spread the word about the bones. He was cowardly enough not to take a chance that Quick Fox would come and kill him if he opened his mouth.

I hope he's afraid enough not to return, or tell anyone about what had transpired between himself and Quick Fox, Dayanara thought.

She hoped her uncle would never realize that Quick Fox's threats could not really be carried out. Quick Fox was not familiar with any land other than his own, whereas John was a man of the world. He could go anywhere in America to escape Quick Fox's vengeance against him.

So thirsty her tongue felt swollen, she reached inside one of her bags and pulled out a flask of water. She unscrewed the lid, took several big gulps of water, then replaced the flask inside the bag.

There was only one more place she wanted to examine. She began walking slowly toward it when a sudden gust of wind sent sprays of dust into her eyes, blinding her.

She took a few more clumsy steps as she tried to brush the dust from her eyes. When she could see again, she found herself standing where two flat rocks jutted up on either side of a narrow opening.

"What is this?" she whispered. "Where does it lead?"

She peered down a strange hole made in the rock. Her heart skipped a beat at the thought that she might have found a hidden place where more bones might be visible.

Leaving her bag beside the hole, she lowered herself down into it, then found herself suddenly hanging by her fingertips. The ground had dropped off suddenly beneath her.

Her fingers began slipping. She scrambled to hang on, scraping her fingertips raw.

She thought suddenly of snakes. What if this was a snake pit?

"Lord, please don't let there be any snakes down there," she prayed aloud.

Her body swayed as a sudden gust of wind came down the hole. Then she just couldn't hold on any longer. She closed her eyes and dropped.

The impact of her landing stung the soles of her feet. She stumbled forward, then landed awkwardly on her bare knees.

She cried out with pain as she felt the cut of sharp rocks against her knees; then, groaning, she pushed herself up to her feet.

She breathed deeply until the wild pounding of her heart slowed. Then she looked cautiously around as she moved slowly forward, the loose shale and gravel shifting under her feet.

Then she saw them. There were bones of all shapes and sizes glistening in the sun.

But there was something else, too. Dozens of snakes were coiled up amid the bones as though they were protecting the dead.

And she didn't know if these were human bones or animal.

She didn't dare take one step closer to see.

Thus far, the snakes didn't seem to be

aware of her presence. They seemed content to be where they were, and she knew she must leave before they discovered her.

One snake was enough to be afraid of; a snake pit like this was a living nightmare.

She began backing toward the opening. She had to find a way to get out of here. If she couldn't, she might be doomed to join the bones for eternity.

She retreated until she was standing beneath the hole in the rock through which she'd fallen. She gazed up at it, and her heart sank as she realized the impossibility of being able to reach up and pull herself back to safety.

Her eyes moved around her, then widened when she saw footholds in the rock leading up through the opening. Her heart pounded as she put her hand in one of the carved-out niches.

Her knees bleeding and aching from the fall, slowly she pulled herself up the rock. She almost cried from relief when she was finally back on solid land away from the bed of bones and the resting snakes.

She sighed heavily. She had had enough. She couldn't wait to be away from this place.

Her luck had almost run out a few moments ago. She didn't want to test fate any more today.

She lifted her bag, then stopped and stared at something she had not seen earlier.

"What is *that?*" she whispered, gazing at the tip of a leather-covered stick lying just beneath the ground.

She cushioned her damaged knees with her skirt as she bent down beside her newest find. She could see that the leather was brittle and cracked. The wood was peeling. The feathers were ruffled and shredded.

She wanted to touch the relic, to even pull it from the ground, if possible, to study it more extensively. But when she gently touched the stick, the feathers began to disintegrate in her fingers, and she pulled her hand back.

She still wanted to see more of the stick. Surely it wouldn't matter if she saw what it looked like. She had promised not to disturb the bones, but this wasn't a bone.

She swept aside the dirt covering it and slowly pulled out a stick that was long and curved on one end.

Now that she saw all of it, she realized it was beautifully decorated with fur and painted leather. Several strips of eagle feathers were attached to the crooked end. Those feathers looked as though they might fall apart at her mere touch, so she just studied them as she held the stick out before her.

Her heart was pounding with excitement at the thought that she might have uncovered an Indian artifact from long ago.

Then she shivered at the thought of possibly having disturbed a human grave. She hated the idea that she might have trespassed in such a way. She needed to know for sure.

She cautiously cleared more dirt away with her fingers, and when she saw no human bones, nor other signs that this was an Indian burial ground, she sighed with relief.

But sensing that she had wronged the Cree in some way by having uncovered something that was not meant to be seen or touched by a white person, something that might be sacred to Quick Fox's people, Dayanara decided to put the stick back where it belonged. It should never have been disturbed.

She had promised not to take anything from this place that belonged to the Cree. She would not even think about what value it would have to the Smithsonian Institute. She had to do what was right.

She had already overstepped her boundaries today. She wanted to get this stick back where it belonged, then leave this place and never venture near it again.

She realized abruptly that she had decided not to wire her final findings to Washington after all. If she aroused the Smithsonian's interest too much, the institute would send someone else to study the land. She could not risk it.

"Father, if you can hear me, I hope you

understand," she whispered.

Yes, finding this stick was what it had taken for her to know that she should never have come here. She had to do what she could to discourage others from following her.

She would send Washington a wire, but not with the information she had planned.

She would tell them that the venture was a disappointment after all . . . that there was nothing in the area worth studying.

After she sent the wire, she would sit down with her mother and explain how she had fallen in love with a powerful Cree Indian chief; how she would not be returning to Saint Louis with her.

She dreaded the conversation, for her mother had already lost her husband in this land. To lose her daughter, as well, might be too much for her.

But Dayanara had to live for herself, not her mother. She had her own desires, her own longings. She wanted to be with Quick Fox forever. She didn't care if she returned to Saint Louis ever.

Strangely enough, she now felt that her home was in this land, and she could hardly wait to live every day with the man she adored.

She smiled as she thought of Little Fox. She was anxious to see that he finally had a mother who cared about him.

As she began digging a deeper hole so that she could place the stick safely in it, she wasn't aware of someone watching her.

Quick Fox had left his horse tethered beside Dayanara's and had entered the hidden valley on foot.

He had just stepped around a bend in the rock when he had seen Dayanara studying the coup stick. He had purposely not gone any farther. He had decided not to interfere.

He had wanted to be right in thinking that she would do the correct thing.

He also knew that her discovery of the coup stick was a sign from above. He had prayed she would be guided by the spirits in her endeavor.

He had smiled when he had seen what she had uncovered, for it would give her the warning not to visit these hallowed grounds again.

It would persuade her to tell those who awaited news of her findings that they need not think about this land or the old bones again, that there was nothing worth studying, though in truth this place *was* precious . . . to the Cree!

Suddenly Dayanara felt a presence. She looked to her left.

She gasped when she found Quick Fox standing in the shadow of the bluff, his eyes on her.

With his face in shadow, she couldn't tell

whether he was angry.

Dayanara shifted herself so that her skirt blocked his view of the old stick.

She smiled awkwardly at Quick Fox as he came toward her, and she could see now that he definitely was not smiling.

Chapter Twenty-six

A woman would run through fire
and water for such a kind heart.
— Shakespeare

When Quick Fox held his hands out for
Dayanara and his expression softened into a
soft smile, she sighed with relief and took his
hands.

Their eyes locked and held. She wasn't
sure what to say. She was glad when he was
the first to speak.

"What you uncovered is called a coup
stick," he said thickly.

"I didn't intentionally uncover it,"
Dayanara said softly. She swallowed hard. "It
must have been exposed by the wind. When
I saw it, I . . . I . . . could not help wanting
to study it."

"It was then that you uncovered it?" Quick
Fox asked, his eyes holding hers.

He hated it when her gaze wavered and she
glanced down in shame.

It wasn't his intention to shame her. He
knew her well enough now to know that she
was an inquisitive person. He believed curi-

osity was a positive character trait.

But he did regret that her inquisitiveness had driven her to dig up the coup stick. Yet it was done. Nothing could change that.

It was now up to him to alleviate her guilt. He had watched her and seen that she was trying to get it back in the ground. He believed she had no intention of taking it or sharing her discovery with anyone else.

"Yes, it was then that I uncovered it," Dayanara murmured. She glanced quickly up at him again. "At first I did not plan to handle it. But it was as though something was there, urging me onward . . . perhaps my father? He would have loved finding something like this. He would not have been able to turn his back on it."

She heaved a heavy sigh. "And because I knew I was not going to take it away, I didn't see what wrong there was in taking it in my hands so that I could get a better look at it," she murmured. "It is so fascinating, Quick Fox. It is so ancient. Did I do any harm by looking closely at it?"

She was proud of Quick Fox's composure, of his show of understanding toward her. But he had not yet passed judgment. What would his final word be about what she had done? She was almost afraid to know. If she had done anything to harm her future with him, she would forever regret it.

"The true harm would have been if you

had claimed this ancient object as yours," Quick Fox said, his voice filled with warmth and understanding. "But since you were giving it back to the land, where it belongs, no true harm has been done. Let me finish covering it, and then I will explain what the importance of this coup stick is to a warrior."

Touched by his understanding, Dayanara slipped her hands from his and flung herself into his arms. "Thank you," she said, a sob of gratitude lodging in her throat. "Thank you for being so understanding . . . so loving. Quick Fox, I love you so much. Every new moment with you awakens more love in my heart for you. I'm sorry I did something today that might have threatened our relationship. Oh, so very, very sorry."

"My woman, your regrets are true," Quick Fox said, stroking her back with his hand. "And my forgiveness is just as true. Let us not dwell on it any longer. Let me cover the coup stick, and then we will leave this place. We shall return to our horses. I must return to my people. I left only long enough to come and ask if you would return with me to my village."

Dayanara eased from his arms, then gazed at him. "You want me to come with you?" she asked, her voice drawn. "You want to escort me from here, to be sure that I leave?"

"No, that is not the reason," Quick Fox

said. "I want you to go to my village with me and join the celebration. The time I have spent without you has not been complete for me."

His eyes devoured her loveliness as the sun touched her face with its light and the breeze fluttered her lovely hair about her shoulders.

"Will you return with me and join the celebration of hope and love?" he asked softly. "My people now understand that you are to be a part of my life. It is only right that they see us together at a time when the Cree are rejoicing over so many things. My people will have just one more thing to rejoice about — their chief's plans to finally share his life with a woman. They had begun to think I would never find that perfect woman. A man is only complete when he does. And a man who is not altogether complete cannot lead his people to his fullest capacity."

"And now? After we are married? Will you feel that completeness?" Dayanara asked.

"Only you can make me complete," Quick Fox said. He placed his arms around her waist and pulled her against his hard body. "My woman, soon we will share everything. Even children."

"To have a child in your image is something I long for," Dayanara said, her gaze sweeping over the handsomeness of his face. "I want a son first, Quick Fox. A son just like you, in every way."

Touched by her words, he brought his lips down on hers in a deep, trembling kiss.

He could feel her body straining against his and wished they were anywhere else.

He was longing to make love with her at this very moment. His body ached with the need.

But he had to practice control now more than at any time before, because he also had other needs to fulfill. His people's.

He could imagine them now dancing around the outdoor fire, singing, laughing, and reminiscing about the times they had shared before the tragedy of smallpox had fallen upon them.

Yes, he could feel the pull of his people, as well as the need to take some more private moments with his woman.

The lovemaking, though, would have to be delayed. But would not waiting enhance the pleasure?

Ah, yes, he had waited a lifetime for this woman; he could wait awhile longer for their bodies to be joined again as lovers.

He drew away from her. Gently he placed a palm on her face and stood that way for a moment, his eyes taking in her loveliness and sweetness.

But again reminding himself of what awaited him at his village, a time of joy and wonder, he stepped away from Dayanara and knelt beside the freshly disturbed ground where the coup stick awaited burial again.

Dayanara stood back as he gently scooped dirt onto the ancient Indian relic with his hands. It was with great reverence that he did this, as though he might be silently saying a prayer to the man to whom the coup stick had belonged.

When it was finally covered, to the last of its fragile feathers, Dayanara exhaled a nervous breath of relief.

She was glad when he stood again, took her by the hand, and led her away from the fresh mound of dirt.

After they reached their grazing horses, Dayanara smiled a quiet thank you as he lifted her into her saddle, then mounted his own steed.

"You will come with me, will you not, to take time to celebrate with my people?" Quick Fox asked.

"I would love to," Dayanara said. "But can we take some time to stop by the river so I can wash up a bit? I know I must look a sight."

"A sight?" Quick Fox said, lifting an eyebrow. "What does that mean?"

Dayanara laughed softly. "It means I know I must look terrible with all this dust on me and in my hair."

Quick Fox chuckled. "That was a strange way of saying it," he said. His eyes swept over her. "Even dust does not take away your beauty. But if you wish to bathe, then we shall stop."

"Thank you," Dayanara murmured, feeling suddenly bashful at his continued gaze.

"You are such a beautiful woman inside and out," Quick Fox said thickly. "No amount of dust in your hair or on your face can hide the woman you are. And you are my woman. The sound of those words on my lips is like a soft breeze on an early spring morning . . . wondrous to hear."

"I hope I never disappoint you and make you want to take those words back," Dayanara said, sighing. "You do know that our worlds are so different. They could collide. I will have so much to learn in order to live among your people and practice their customs instead of those I was taught in the white world."

"Our joined lives will work. My people will be your teacher," Quick Fox said. "And, ah, Little Fox. He will be eager to be the best teacher of all. My son is quite proud of having found you first. Were he some years older, I would have to compete with him for your affection. As it is, he admires you as a son admires a mother, for soon you *will* be his mother, Dayanara. When you marry me, you will not only gain a new people, but also an immediate family of husband and son."

"I will adore every minute of being all I

can be to you, Little Fox, and your people," Dayanara said.

She felt wonderful to know that soon she would be both a wife and mother. She would make Little Fox totally forget his other life.

"I see the shine of the river up ahead," Quick Fox said, nodding toward it. "*Kee-mah,* come. Let us get you more beautiful, and then hurry on to my people. Can you hear them? It is faint, but I can hear my people's songs coming to me on the breeze."

Dayanara looked in the direction of his village. "Yes, I hear it," she murmured. "And it's wonderful that they have cause to sing songs of happiness."

"This happiness will be lasting," Quick Fox said, his voice suddenly solemn. "Never again will I allow anything to separate my people into two groups. They will stay together and work out whatever faces them together."

"But don't you think that splitting your people saved many lives?" Dayanara asked, drawing rein beside the river as Quick Fox stopped his own steed.

"Yes, it did save lives, but it also took away much spirit and hope from my people," Quick Fox said tightly.

"Well, let's pray that nothing as terrible as smallpox comes your people's way again," Dayanara said, sliding from her saddle as he dismounted.

"Yes, let us pray and hope that nothing as

devastating as what my people recently lived through ever happens again," Quick Fox said.

He gave her a sideways glance as his thoughts went to the stories he had heard of white soldiers' attacks on peaceful Indian villages. If he ever faced that sort of threat, he would need his people fighting together as one heartbeat.

When he thought of such atrocities and looked at Dayanara, he could not imagine how any white person could be as bad as he had heard. How could one be so good and another so evil? Then all he had to think about was Dayanara's uncle and he had his answer!

"What are you thinking right now?" Dayanara asked, placing a hand on his cheek as he came and stood before her.

"You would not want to know, so I will not say it," Quick Fox said. When he saw a hurt look in her eyes, he smiled. "It has nothing to do with you. It is other people who entered my mind, filling my heart with bitterness."

He took her hand and walked with her to the riverbank. "Do what you must quickly, for I am anxious to be with my people again, and to have you at my side as the celebration continues," he said.

He drew his hand away.

As she knelt beside the river and began splashing water onto her face, and even into her hair, he sat down beside her on a thick bed of grass.

"Would you now like to know the meaning of the coup stick?" he asked, bringing her eyes quickly to him.

"If we have time, I would love to know," Dayanara said, her eyes searching his.

She wove her fingers through her hair as the sun poured its warmth onto the wetness.

She was now clean enough to make an appearance in his village.

The dust had even blown from her clothes as she rode along. And the river water made her smell fresh and clean.

"I will tell about the coup stick as we travel homeward," he said, reaching a hand to her.

She took it and rose with him.

After they were on their horses and traveling toward the Indian village, Dayanara listened as Quick Fox explained about the ancient stick. She was mesmerized not only by the sound of his voice, but also by the tale of warriors and coup sticks.

"It is considered more courageous, more meritorious, to touch a live enemy than to kill him. A truly brave warrior rides up to his enemy close enough to touch the man with his coup stick, but does not kill him," he explained.

"The action is called 'counting coup.' It was a coup stick that you uncovered today," he said. "The word 'coup' means hit or strike. A warrior keeps count of his coups by tying an eagle feather to the crooked end of the stick after each brave deed."

He slowly looked at her.

"Some warriors, when there were bloody wars between tribes, decorated their coup sticks with scalps along with the feathers," he said. "It was of great significance in warfare."

"Scalps?" Dayanara gulped out.

"That was when there were many bloody wars between tribes, not now," Quick Fox assured her.

"Thank goodness. I am so glad that you are sharing this with me, Quick Fox," she said. "It is all so interesting. Could more than one warrior count coup on the same person?"

"Yes, but the one who touched first won the most honor," Quick Fox said.

"Do you have a coup stick of your own?" Dayanara asked.

"There *is* a coup stick in my family," he replied. "But it is not one used by my hand. It belonged to my father, and his father before him. When my father died, it became mine. But I hope I never have reason to use it."

"I . . . do . . . also," Dayanara said, glad that his intentions toward her people were peaceful.

"Please, don't worry that I will tell anyone

what I have discovered here on the land that belongs to you and your people," Dayanara said. "I plan to wire Washington and tell my colleagues that the map was wrong, that it led nowhere important."

"You would do this for the Cree?" Quick Fox asked.

"Yes, I was wrong even to go to a place so sacred to your people," Dayanara murmured. "But I have always loved seeing old things. I love studying them."

"You will truly be able to give up these desires?" he asked guardedly.

"I have *you* now," Dayanara said, smiling at him. "And, truly, I won't ever tell anyone about what I've seen. That will, for the time being, keep people from coming to see if there really are monster bones buried near your people's village. Those who live at the fort and who frequent the trading post have heard about the bones. But as you see, no one has cared to go find them."

"They stay away because they believe the Cree will cast spells upon them."

"Yes, there are many people who believe in such things," Dayanara said, sighing. "But if one has a strong belief in God, one does not fear such things."

"You are strong in religion?" Quick Fox asked, realizing there was much he did not know about the woman he was going to marry.

But he knew the most important thing: Her heart was good. He did not expect any surprises that would make him regret falling in love with her.

"I have a strong faith in God," Dayanara said, nodding. "I am of Protestant faith. I pray often. Do you?"

"Prayer has led me from many doubtful moments in my life," he said, gazing suddenly heavenward. "Up there, among the clouds, there is someone who hears all things. It is good to know he is there."

Suddenly Dayanara was aware of being closer to the singing. She could even see the flames of a fire shooting orange sparks into the heavens.

"We're almost there," she said, uncertain how to feel. She was again apprehensive about whether she would be accepted by his people, yet anxious to begin new alliances that might last a lifetime.

After she was married to this wonderful man, she never wanted to give him cause to regret having chosen her over all the many other women who surely had hoped to have him.

"I am glad that you are with me at this time in my life," Quick Fox said. He nodded toward the village, which was now within eye range. "*Kee-mah*. Come with me. Let us rejoice together."

They both sank their heels into the flanks

of their steeds and thundered onward.

Soon they were sitting in the midst of Quick Fox's people. A platform had been erected especially for Quick Fox so that he could see everything — the dancing, the singing, and the games of the children.

Dayanara sat on the platform with him, on a thick cushion of pelts, along with his uncle who lay on a thick pallet of blankets. The old man was propped up so that he could see and experience everything with his people.

The wonderful aroma of food brought by the returning warriors filled the air. The meat hung cooking on spits over the cook fires that had been built a little distance from the larger central fire, around which the celebration was being held.

It was a smell that had been missing in the village for too long, but now the grease sizzled in the flames as it fell away from the cooking meat. There would soon be platters stacked high with roasted buffalo meat. Tonight when the Cree went to bed, their bellies would be warm and comfortable from the feast.

Dayanara was fascinated by all that was happening around her. She gazed past the grown-ups who were dancing and singing around the fire and found Little Fox among the children enjoying games.

"The children are holding an imaginary buffalo hunt," Quick Fox explained when he noticed Dayanara watching the young braves at play. "The one who is 'it' will bellow like a bull, while the other children try to catch him."

Dayanara laughed softly as she watched the game. Before long the children started in on another game.

"What the children do now is called a fire-stick game," Quick Fox said. "See how they are throwing burning sticks into the air? It is usually done at night, so that the effects are more prominent. The one who throws the burning stick farthest is the winner."

"There are many different games, aren't there?" Dayanara asked as she noticed children in another group juggling mud balls, while others ran races, and some pitched arrows at targets.

"The quietest game is played by the young girls of the village," Quick Fox said, nodding toward a small group of girls who sat in a circle close to the large outdoor fire. "They are playing cat's cradle, using a piece of string made from sagebrush bark."

"I played cat's cradle with friends when I was small," Dayanara said, smiling, surprised to find this common ground. "But I did not use string made from bark."

Dayanara took a startled breath when several warriors arrived in costume, their appearance bringing a halt to the other games and dances.

The people hurried to their spread blankets and sat down.

"What is going to happen now?" Dayanara asked, studying the way the warriors were dressed.

Each man wore a deerskin shirt and leggings painted bright yellow. Their faces were painted with yellow stripes, as well as other shapes and designs.

Each of the warriors also wore a dressed fox skin that had been slit in the middle. The head of each man was thrust through this hole, the skin spread out on his shoulders so the head of the animal lay on his breast and the tail hung down his back.

The whole skin was decorated with colored porcupine quills and bells, and polished buttons were placed in the eye holes of the animal.

A headdress of fox teeth, bored and strung, was stretched across the middle of the men's heads from ear to ear, a lock of their hair tied in front. The rest was combed straight down behind and adorned with four eagle feathers.

The lances they carried were wrapped with fox skins cut in strips, and tails of that animal were sewed on the handles every twelve inches or so.

Some also carried bows and quivers of arrows at their sides.

"The warriors will now perform the Fox

Dance," Quick Fox said, then grew quiet again when several drums and whistles began playing.

The warriors formed a line and started off at a swift pace, moving together in a snakelike motion. Then they jumped up and down, striking one foot immediately after the other on the ground while they sang with the music from the instruments.

When the Fox Dance was over, the celebration focused on eating.

Dayanara was handed a huge wooden platter of cooked buffalo meat, the aroma reminding her of the roast beef served at her family's dinner table each Sunday. The taste was as delicious.

She ate and laughed and drank a sweet drink from a wooden cup, while all around her people ate, smiled, and laughed. It was a good sight to behold, and Dayanara hated to leave.

But she did have one last chore to do today and she wanted to get it over with before it got dark.

She didn't want to have to ask Quick Fox to escort her to and from the fort, for he was enjoying himself with his people.

She had to go and tell her mother her plans . . . that she loved an Indian, and she was going to marry and stay with him.

She also had to wire Washington and tell a white lie to prevent people from pouring onto Quick Fox's land to see the prehistoric bones.

She wouldn't allow that to happen. Even when she imagined the honor her discovery could bring to her father's name, she knew she had to do what was best for her betrothed.

He was the most important person in her life now.

"I wish you did not have to go," Quick Fox said as he walked with her back to her horse. "But if you must, I feel that you need someone to ride with you. I can go. My people will not even miss me now. They are so happy, they do not need a chief's presence."

"But I want you to stay and enjoy the moment," Dayanara murmured. She stood on tiptoe and kissed him. "I won't be long. I promise. I will be here before the sun begins to set behind the distant mountains. We will be together tonight, Quick Fox, and every night from now on."

"There is to be a massive hunt tomorrow and I want you to accompany me and my warriors on the hunt," Quick Fox said, helping her up onto her saddle. "Will you go with me? I wish for you to see the marvels of the hunt."

"But I didn't know women were allowed on a hunt," Dayanara said hesitantly.

"They accompany the hunters, but stay far behind them with the travois on which they will transport the meat after butchering the catch of each day's hunt," Quick Fox said. "But I wish for you to accompany me on the hunt. I wish for you to be beside me on your steed. But this will be the only time. In the future you must stay with the women and do the woman's chore of butchering."

"Why do you want me to go with you on the hunt this time?" Dayanara asked, searching his eyes.

"Because I feel that it is important for you to know every aspect of my people's lives," he said. "And since you ride as well as a man, I feel that it would be good for you to ride with me. Will you? Will you accompany me on the hunt tomorrow?"

"Will the women resent me for doing it?"

"No, not since it is their chief who is requesting this of you."

"Then I will go," Dayanara said, smiling broadly. "In fact, I look forward to it."

"Hurry back to me, my woman," Quick Fox said, reaching up to place a hand on her cheek.

"I will," she said, taking his hand and kissing the palm.

He pulled his hand away and watched her ride off. His heart was filled with pride and love for this woman. He hated being away from her for even another moment.

But soon, they would never have to say goodbye again.

Smiling, he went back to his people and sat and ate some more, talked, and laughed, all the while watching for his woman's return.

Chapter Twenty-seven

How many loved your moments of glad
   grace,
And loved your beauty
With love false or true,
But one man loved the pilgrim soul in
   you,
And loved the sorrows of your changing
   face.

                — Yeats

When Dayanara arrived at the fort and went to her mother's cabin, she was surprised to find Dorothea entertaining a visitor. It was Grace, her mother's friend. They were sitting in the parlor, knitting and talking.

Dayanara hated to break up the happy pair, since it had been a long time since she had seen her mother so content, but she had to talk to her, and it must be a private conversation. What she had to say could send her mother into another whirlwind of despair.

That was the last way that Dayanara wanted her wonderful news to affect her mother, yet she had no choice but to tell her, and she didn't want to delay the telling any longer.

Quick Fox was waiting for her. He wanted her to share the rest of the evening's celebration with him and his people.

And she knew why that was so important. If she could become acquainted with them under the best of circumstances, now that they were finally all together again, surely those who resented her presence, her future with their chief, would have an easier time accepting her.

"Mother?"

Dayanara's mother turned her head with a start, then laid her knitting aside on a table, went to Dayanara, and gave her a gentle hug.

"Daughter, I'm glad you're home," she murmured. "And I hope this is the last time I have to fret over you."

She stepped away from Dayanara, yet still held her hands as she gazed into her eyes. "Tell me you're finished with that terrible bone-picking," she said, visibly shuddering.

"Mother, I wasn't picking bones," Dayanara said, her smile waning. "I . . ."

Realizing that Grace was listening to their conversation, Dayanara quickly changed the subject. She didn't want anyone else to know about the existence of the bones. She eased her hands from her mother's and went to stand before Grace.

"Mother has told me about you," she said, extending a hand for a handshake. "It's wonderful that you two have met again after all these years."

"Yes, it is wonderful," Grace said, accepting the handshake.

Dayanara felt the woman's hand quivering, and only then noticed that her whole body was trembling slightly.

Dayanara didn't think Grace was nervous about meeting her friend's daughter. The trembling seemed to be some sort of affliction that she had no control over.

"And Grace and I are not going to be saying goodbye again anytime soon," Dorothea said. She went and stood beside Dayanara, slipping an arm around her waist. "Daughter, I'm staying at the fort for as long as Grace does. Things in Saint Louis will be there whenever I do choose to return home, won't they?"

Dayanara's pulse raced at the thought of her mother being so close for her. If Dorothea had returned to Saint Louis, they might never have seen one another again, for Dayanara knew that once she was married to an Indian chief, her duty would be to stay with him, not travel to a city far from the Cree's homeland.

And she knew without even asking Quick Fox that he would never travel that far. His duties would keep him home.

"You are going to stay?" Dayanara said, her eyes wide. "Mother, truly? You are going to stay at the fort for a while longer?"

"Yes, and I wish you would stay with me, but I know it would be a boring place for a young, pretty thing like you," Dorothea said.

Then her mother's eyes brightened. "Unless you could meet some fine gentleman in uniform at the fort," she suggested hopefully. "Now that the women have joined the gentlemen, there are going to be occasional dances to keep the ladies from getting bored. Dayanara, you could attend the dances. You could be the belle of the ball."

When Dayanara saw where her mother's mind was taking her, her imagination already placing Dayanara in the arms of some cavalryman, she knew she shouldn't delay what she had come to say any longer. When her mother got caught up in a fantasy, it was hard for her to let go.

"Mother, we need to talk," Dayanara murmured. She glanced at Grace, then turned to face her mother. She took her hands. "Mother, I have something to tell you, and . . . and . . . it must be said in private."

She could tell that Grace had heard. She had already laid her knitting aside on a table and was pushing herself slowly up from the chair.

"I'll leave you two alone," Grace said, looking from Dayanara to Dorothea with a soft smile. "My husband should be out of his meeting and at our cabin by now. It seems all those cavalrymen do is have meetings." She laughed softly. "But I guess that's better than being out there shooting savages, don't you think?"

Dayanara turned pale and frowned at Grace's words.

"I don't believe there are going to be any Indian attacks anytime soon, especially from the Cree," Dayanara said. "You can go to bed at night and sleep without worrying about losing your scalp."

No sooner had the words slipped across her lips than Dayanara wished them unsaid. Grace's face had drained of color, and her trembling was now even more pronounced.

"I'm sorry, I didn't mean . . ." Dayanara began, but she knew that nothing would erase the thought of being scalped from the woman's mind.

"I will take my leave now," Grace said. As she walked slowly to the door, she seemed to watch each step she took with much care.

Dayanara thought Grace was beautiful for a woman of her age, which was the same as her mother's. She had not one streak of gray in her red hair, and her complexion was wrinkle and blemish free.

Dayanara could tell that in her prime, Grace had been ravishingly lovely.

"I shall see you soon at the dining table," Dorothea said as she went to the door and opened it for Grace.

Grace turned and gave Dorothea a gentle embrace, frowned at Dayanara, then left the cabin.

Dorothea closed the door.

She then turned and also frowned at Dayanara.

"What do you have to say for yourself?" Dorothea asked, sitting down and resuming her knitting. "What on earth came over you that would make you say such things?" she asked with an edge in her voice. "Don't you know that most women are frightened to death to know that savages are so close, that a war with them might break out at any moment?"

"I said I was sorry," Dayanara said. She sat down in a plush armchair opposite her mother.

"People are very mistaken when they call Indians savages," Dayanara said. "Mother, I have become involved with Indians of late, and all I can say is they are more civil than some white men I know."

She was thinking about her uncle and those men who had allied themselves with him.

"You . . . have . . . become involved with Indians?" Dorothea gasped out. "Dayanara, what on earth do you mean? You haven't told me anything about . . . about . . . Indians."

"Mother . . ." Dayanara began, going back

to that first day she had become acquainted with Little Fox, and how he had come to be with the Cree. She related everything that had happened that day, even going so far as to say that she had been at the Cree village.

"And, Mother," she finally blurted out. "I met an Indian chief. . . ."

As she explained her feelings for Quick Fox, she saw her mother's face grow paler and paler. Tears appeared in her eyes when Dayanara revealed her feelings for Quick Fox.

"The redskins have cast some sort of spell on you if . . . if . . . you are truly planning to marry one of them," her mother said, almost leaping from the chair she was so angry.

She grabbed Dayanara by the hand and talked directly into her face. "No daughter of mine is going to lower herself to marry . . . to marry . . ."

Dayanara saw that her mother was finding it hard to say that Dayanara was going to marry an Indian, and not only an Indian, a chief.

She cringed when her mother's fingers tightened.

"Mother, please?" Dayanara said, yanking her hand free.

"Dayanara, if your father were alive, he'd give you a spanking and send you to bed without supper," Dorothea said, her face crimson with anger. "But as I am the only parent left to reprimand you, I am ordering you to stay in this cabin for two weeks. Do you hear? By then the paddle wheeler should have returned for passengers. Dayanara, you are going to be one of them, and so am I. I am going to take you home where you can get your senses back."

"Mother, I'm not staying in this cabin for two weeks, nor am I returning to Saint Louis on any paddle wheeler with you," Dayanara said, her jaws tightening. "Mother, I believe you forget that I am twenty years old, and I most certainly have my own mind with which to make rational decisions. I have fallen in love for the first time in my life, Mother, and I will not give up this love. Not for you, not for anybody."

Suddenly her mother grabbed at her chest, began coughing, and staggered to a chair where she crumpled down.

"My heart," Dorothea gasped out as she looked up at Dayanara with tearful eyes. "Dayanara, do you see what you've done? I'm . . . I'm having a heart attack."

Dayanara sighed and fell to her knees on the floor before her mother. She gazed into her mother's eyes. "Mother, you've used that tactic before when you didn't get your way," she said, sighing. "Mother, this is Dayanara, not some stranger who might be alarmed and believe you are having an attack. I've seen the same act too often when you've tried it on Father. After he realized what you were doing, even he ignored you. So please, Mother, stop it. Do you hear? Stop it and listen to what I am saying. I . . . am . . . going to marry the man I love. And that man is an Indian. He is a proud, handsome, wonderful Cree chief."

"Lordie, oh, lordie . . ." Dorothea said, over and over again.

"Mother, please?" Dayanara said. "Can't you just this one time think of someone besides yourself? Mother, I want you to be happy for me. Can't you be? Will you meet Quick Fox? Will . . . you . . . please consider coming to the marriage ceremony?"

That really did it.

Her mother sank more deeply into the chair, and her body was racked with deep, hard sobs.

"Oh, Mother, I do understand how you are feeling," Dayanara said. "Yes, you had plans of my finding a rich gentleman and living in the lap of luxury in a mansion close to our family home in Saint Louis, so that we could visit often and sit and knit before a roaring fire on the coldest days of winter. But, Mother, that has never been my vision of happiness. Only yours."

"And so you will be sewing beads on moccasins in a drafty, cold tepee while your Indian husband is out hoping to find something to bring home for you to cook over the fire?" Dorothea said, her voice trembling. "Can you truly see that happening? You will catch your death of cold your first winter in a tepee. You will starve, for surely it's all but impossible for a husband to supply enough meat for his wife during the worst part of winter."

"There is a whole village of Cree who have lived their entire lives in tepees, keeping fed through the winter months," Dayanara murmured. "With such a man as Quick Fox as my husband, I will have nothing to worry about."

"You shall see, you shall see," Dorothea said, sighing heavily.

Then her mother did something that Dayanara had never expected after seeing her first terrible reaction to her daughter's plans. She actually scooted to the edge of the chair and embraced Dayanara.

"I love you, daughter," Dorothea said, her voice no longer trembling, but now steady and filled with warmth. "I want you to be happy. If marrying this chief is what you want, so be it. If it doesn't work out, so be it. You know I will always be waiting for you, should you choose to return home to me. I will be staying at the fort while Grace is here. That will keep me close by in case you need me."

"Mother, truly?" Dayanara said. She stared disbelievingly at her mother. "You will accept my choice of a husband? You can actually be happy for me?"

"Happy?" Dorothea said, cocking a very carefully plucked eyebrow. "No, not happy, but at least I am trying to understand."

Dorothea took Dayanara's hands again. "Are you certain you haven't been tricked in some way to feel this way about the Indian?" she asked, searching her daughter's eyes for hidden answers.

"No, I've not been tricked," Dayanara said, laughing softly. "I'm in love, Mother, deeply, passionately in love."

"Passionately?" her mother said, slowly lowering her hands. "You don't mean . . . ?"

"I mean passionately," was all that Dayanara would say, feeling that was enough to let her mother know she had been intimate with Quick Fox.

Her mother lowered her face in her hands, sobbed, then got control of her feelings again.

"When is the wedding?" she blurted out.

"As soon as it can be arranged," Dayanara said, still stunned that her mother had actually accepted her decision. Under other circumstances Dayanara would have been embarrassed to admit she had made love before exchanging marriage vows. But with Quick Fox, nothing seemed wrong, only sweet and wonderful, something to be cherished.

"I'll be there for you," Dorothea said softly. "I love you so much, Dayanara. I do want you to be happy. I'm sure that if things don't work out, you will have the sense to leave it all behind."

"That will never happen," Dayanara said. "My love for Quick Fox is too real . . . too deep."

Then realizing how quickly night was falling, Dayanara gave her mother an uneasy gaze, then reluctantly said something she knew would upset her mother.

"Mother, my life with Quick Fox will not begin after our wedding vows," she murmured. "I'm going to him now, Mother, tonight. I plan to stay. Please understand?"

A choking noise came from the depths of her mother's throat.

"Just remember this, Mother. Know that I am the happiest I've ever been in my entire life," Dayanara said. "That should make what I am doing more easy to accept."

Her mother's eyes were filled with tears as she slowly nodded. "Yes, I'll think of that when . . . when . . . I think of where you are, and with whom," she murmured.

"You will come for my wedding to Quick Fox?" Dayanara asked guardedly. Although her mother had already promised that she would, Dayanara felt the need to hear her say it again.

"Yes, I'll be there," Dorothea said, wiping

tears from her eyes. "I am your mother, am I not?"

"Yes, you're my mother," Dayanara said, then flung her arms around her. "Thank you, Mother. Thank you."

Then she left and hurried to her room. She began sorting through her clothes, deciding to take only those she felt she would need to be the wife of an Indian chief. She hoped to dress in buckskin soon, in order to blend in with the other women, so fancy, frilly dresses were most certainly not needed.

But she did pack her riding clothes.

She even decided to take her pretty underthings. Although she knew the Indian women didn't wear such things, she wanted to look pretty in all ways to her husband.

She smiled as she took a lacy, silk nightgown from her drawer and shoved it into her bag.

Chapter Twenty-eight

I arise from dreams of thee
In the first sleep of night,
When the winds are breathing love,
And the stars are shining bright.

— Shelley

As it turned out, Quick Fox decided not to allow Dayanara or Little Fox to join the actual buffalo hunt, but he made certain they were able to observe it.

"I'm kind of nervous, even if I'm not going to ride amid the buffalo," Dayanara said, giving Little Fox a weak grin.

"There is nothing to fear," Little Fox reassured her. "My father and his warriors are skilled at what they do. None ever get harmed by the buffalo."

"How soon will it be before the buffalo are near?" Dayanara asked, gazing intently into the distance.

"Soon, very soon," Little Fox said, cocking his head. "I hear them. Soon we will see them."

"I hear something like distant thunder," Dayanara said, aware of a sound she had not heard before.

"That is the thundering of their hooves," Little Fox said, nodding. He squared his shoulders as he sat on his pony beside Dayanara's horse. "I have watched before. On the first hunt, my father left me on this exact bluff so I could witness what I would be a part of when I become a warrior."

"Oh, Lord, look! It is such a grand sight," Dayanara said, gasping at the magnificent herd of buffalo that had just appeared along the horizon. There were so many, it looked as if a massive black blanket was being spread over the land.

"That will change quickly when Father and his warriors make their surprise attack on the herd," Little Fox said, straining his neck as he looked to the left, where down below they would soon see his father and the other warriors. He pointed in that direction. "Watch, Day. Soon you will witness firsthand the magnificence of the Cree hunt."

Dayanara followed Little Fox's gaze and soon saw the warriors on horseback, armed with bows and arrows, moving slowly and cautiously toward the unsuspecting herd.

She saw how Quick Fox and his men kept to the hollows and ravines, out of sight of the bulls as the herd moved ever closer.

When the herd got close enough, Dayanara saw Quick Fox give a signal with a raised hand. A moment later he and his warriors rushed out on horseback.

Yelling and dashing into the midst of the herd, they launched their arrows to the right and left.

The land seemed to shake under the tramp of many hooves. Cows raced onward in headlong panic. Bulls, furious with rage, uttered deep bellows, and occasionally turned to make a desperate rush upon the men who were pursuing them.

"Lord, keep Quick Fox and his men safe," Dayanara prayed as she glanced heavenward.

She watched the melee down below again as men and animals clashed. Nothing could surpass the spirit, grace, and dexterity with which Quick Fox and his warriors managed their horses, wheeling them among the frightened herd as they launched their arrows with unerring aim.

She gasped in terror when Quick Fox suddenly turned his horse and raced alongside a large, bellowing buffalo until his arrow was discharged.

Then springing away, Quick Fox's horse just barely escaped the charge of the wounded animal, and they were off in pursuit of another buffalo.

In the midst of the confusion, Dayanara saw how Quick Fox and the others selected their victims with perfect judgment.

"They are generally aiming at the fattest of the cows now, since the flesh of the bulls is nearly worthless at this season of the year,"

Little Fox explained, his eyes filled with excitement as he continued watching beside Dayanara.

In just a matter of a few minutes, each hunter had crippled three or four cows.

A single shot with an arrow was sufficient for the purpose, and the animal, once maimed, was left to be dispatched at the end of the hunt.

"My goodness!" Dayanara gasped. She had just seen Quick Fox shoot an arrow completely through the body of a cow, so that it struck the ground beyond.

"Quick Fox rarely wastes an arrow, but this hunt will cost other warriors several arrows, especially when they have to shoot at the bulls to get to the cows," Little Fox explained.

"It looks so dangerous," Dayanara said as she saw a bull chase a warrior's horse furiously, with several arrows sticking in its flank. She was glad that Quick Fox had insisted she stay far from the hunt.

"It is dangerous for those who do not know the proper skills," Little Fox said as he continued to watch the slaughter down below. "Hunting buffalo is a necessary task with its thrills, in order to furnish the tribe with meat to eat, skins for tepees, robes for winter wear, fat for cooking and for greasing the human body."

"I hope to help in some way after the hunt

is over," Dayanara said, looking over her shoulder, where down in another valley the women and children waited for the hunt to be finished.

"You will learn today how much of it is done," Little Fox said, nodding. "The women will be eager to have another helping hand. They will take the marrow for stews, sinews for cord and sewing material, and horns for ornamental purposes."

"I never realized that the buffalo hunt is seen as sacred. The ceremonies that were performed before the hunt were so interesting," Dayanara murmured. "I noticed that prayers were sent to the gods for many buffalo."

"But the warriors never pray for more than they need," Little Fox said. "There are but four or five months when the hair or fur of any animal is good to use, and the rest of the year only enough are killed for meat, clothes, and lodges. The men never kill just to be killing."

"I am so glad that Quick Fox led me here, so that I could see how this is all actually done," Dayanara said, her eyes following the man she loved and seeing the power of his bow and arrow as more and more animals were downed.

"My father feels that the more you experience the Cree way of life, the sooner you will adapt totally to their . . . to *our* . . . ways,"

Little Fox said, smiling at her.

"It's such an exciting day. And tomorrow will be my wedding to your father," Dayanara said, returning Little Fox's smile.

"It is good that the hunt came before the wedding so that our people will have plenty of food to serve at the wedding celebration," Little Fox said. "The hunt today is good, very good."

Dayanara smiled, for she knew that today marked the first true day of her life as one of the Cree.

She blessed the day her father had received the map. Without it, she would still be in Saint Louis, bored, restless, and unhappy.

As it was, she would never be bored or restless again. She most certainly wouldn't be unhappy. Quick Fox was offering her a life that would be anything but those things. She could never be happier, or more fulfilled.

Chapter Twenty-nine

Thou lost, not least in love.
— Shakespeare
Julius Caesar

The Cree were still away from their homes. The day had been long. The hunt was over.

There had been much butchering this day, much laughing and singing. The feast around the huge outdoor fire had been great.

It was late in the night now. Dayanara lay beside Quick Fox on a makeshift bed of blankets and pelts beneath the stars, with a warm blanket covering them both. She knew she should be tired enough to go instantly to sleep, but she couldn't. She couldn't forget that during the celebration of the successful hunt, she had not been able to shake an uneasy feeling. It was as though eyes out in the dark were watching her.

Yet when she had peered into the darkness beyond the fires, she had seen no one.

The same sense of uneasiness still haunted her.

She gazed past Quick Fox and saw that Little Fox was sleeping soundly a few feet away beside a close friend, blankets pulled up beneath both of the boys' chins.

She then looked at Quick Fox, who was sleeping just as soundly beside her. He had hunted vigorously and tirelessly today, yet tonight he still had had the energy to dance and sing until she couldn't see how he could move another step.

After his people had gone to their own blankets for the night, and Quick Fox had given Dayanara a kiss good night, she had found it sweet to watch him go to sleep. She just loved watching him sleep.

She lifted a hand to his face and gently smoothed locks of hair back from the scars he had kept hidden when they'd first met. She was glad he now accepted that the scars did nothing to take away from his nobleness. In fact, he now seemed to wear the scars as a badge of honor, for he *had* been victorious over the terrible disease.

Dayanara slid closer to Quick Fox. She leaned low and brushed a soft kiss across his scars, then stretched out again beside him. She didn't cuddle up to him as she wished she could. She didn't want to do anything that might awaken him. He needed his rest. Although the hunt had been successful and there would be no more hunting tomorrow, there was something else she wanted him to save his energy for.

Their marriage. Tomorrow they were going

to become husband and wife.

A thrill coursed through her at the thought of him being hers until the day she died.

"Mine," she whispered. "My sweet, noble husband."

As she said those words, her eyelids finally grew heavy with sleep. She sighed deeply, got more comfortable beneath the warmth of the blanket, then drifted off into dreams of tomorrow.

Suddenly Dayanara was startled awake by a hand clamped over her mouth. Before she could fight off her assailant, strong arms yanked her away from the blankets and dragged her from the camp.

No matter how much she tried to pull those arms from around her, or to sink her nails into the flesh of her assailant, he was relentless. He strode swiftly away from the sleeping Cree until he reached a tethered horse.

"Dayanara, you've messed up my life, and now I'm going to mess up yours," John growled as he threw her to the ground on her stomach, then sank down over her, straddling her and holding her immobile with the weight of his body as he tied her hands behind her and gagged her.

When Dayanara finally knew who it was that had abducted her, and she heard the cold hate in his voice, she realized that Quick Fox had been too lenient in her uncle's punishment.

Were the rest of John's men with him? If so, they would probably finish what they had started the other day. They would ambush the Cree, this time while they slept.

She tried with all her might to use her body to push John away from her, but he was too strong. She only now realized just how tiny and defenseless she was. She was at the mercy of a madman.

"I've got someplace special to take you, niece," John said, cackling a madman's laugh. "It's just you and me, Day. Just you and me."

His words brought her a small measure of relief. She now knew that she had only John to fear, no one else.

She didn't want to think what his plans were for her. She knew she might be living her last moments.

Her heart cried out for Quick Fox to awaken and find her gone. Or Little Fox.

"Let's go," John said, lifting her from the ground and tossing her over the back of his horse as though she had no more weight than a feather pillow.

He leaned into her face. "If you try and wiggle free of this horse, your death will come sooner than I have planned for you," he growled. "And right now I'm only including you in my vengeance. If you do anything to rile me, I'll go and shoot me a few Cree, too."

Knowing that he meant every word, Dayanara nodded, then hung there, the blood rushing to her head, as he mounted before her and rode off into the darkness.

"Your fiancé didn't truly think I'd do as he said, now did he?" John said, laughing again as he glanced over his shoulder at Dayanara. "My dear niece, I did board the riverboat along with the rest of the men, but when it approached the shore to miss a floating tree limb in the center of the river, I dove in and swam for the bank. I then went to the fort and while everyone slept, I stole a horse. My dear niece, I couldn't just allow you to have your dreams when I had lost a good portion of mine, now could I?"

Dayanara listened to his rantings and watched the terrain as he traveled onward. She knew it well enough in the moonlight to know that he was headed for the hidden valley of the prehistoric bones.

She glanced skyward. She could see the break of dawn along the horizon. The sky was growing pink at the edges as the sun made its way heavenward.

That gave her hope, for she knew that the Cree had planned to awaken at dawn and start homeward with their many travois loaded with freshly cut meat. There was much work to do back at the village, where the meat had to be prepared for the long winter ahead, and the pelts made into clothing and new lodge coverings.

If the Cree awakened soon enough, they would see that she was gone. Then John would pay for having gone against Quick Fox's orders.

"We're almost there, and then, Day, just you wait and see what I have in store for you," John said, chuckling. "You wanted to study those old bones? Well, darling, you're going to have plenty of time to do that. You see, you're going to join them. I've dug you a grave close enough to the bones that you will feel you are actually among them. Now isn't that ironic? One day when someone else comes to study the bones, they'll find yours, too."

Dayanara swallowed hard. She tried to wiggle herself off the horse, but nothing she did worked. She groaned as she felt her body ache from having been left in this ungodly position for so long.

"Well, my dear, you'd best begin praying to yourself for any forgiveness you might want to ask of the Lord, for you've just about reached the end of the line," John announced, stopping his horse.

He slid from the saddle, secured the reins to a tree, then lifted Dayanara from the horse's back.

Her arms still tied securely behind her, Dayanara was helpless. She looked up at her uncle with pleading eyes, yet knew she was not reaching him. There was such cold hate for her in his eyes that Dayanara felt a chill go through her.

"Do you know why I really came for you, Day?" John asked as he lowered her into the hole in the ground he had prepared. "To save you from living the life of an Injun squaw. The disgrace that that would bring into our family was too much for me to bear.

"So I'll just hide you away, and this is the perfect place to do it," John said, now standing over her as she trembled in the cold ground. "Since you love old bones so much, you might as well be buried with them forever."

Her heart pounding in her ears, the fear building, Dayanara tried to get to her feet, but John was there too quickly, holding her down with a foot.

"Now, now, Dayanara, you don't want to spoil my plan, do you?" John said darkly. He reached over, and with a shovel that he'd left near the hole, began shoveling dirt as he held her immobile with his foot.

Suddenly Dayanara was aware of a sound reverberating through the ground, a sound that from his vantage point John couldn't hear. He was too busy taunting her as he shoveled to hear the horses approaching.

Her eyes widened and she said a quiet prayer over and over again that Quick Fox would arrive in time, for she knew it had to be Quick Fox advancing on her and John.

Surely someone had awakened and found her gone. Someone who was a good tracker had surely found the tracks that led away from the campsite. They were following the tracks to the hidden valley.

Then John's eyes narrowed and he stood straight and peered into the distance.

Dayanara knew that he was now very aware of the approaching horses.

"Damn it all to hell," John said, leaping from the grave.

He ran to his horse and yanked his rifle from the gunboot. Just as he started to run to hide, he was surrounded by the Cree.

Little Fox leapt from his pony and hurried to the grave.

He jumped inside and brushed the dirt away from Dayanara, then leaned down and yanked the gag from her mouth.

"Day, when I awakened and found you gone, I was so afraid," Little Fox said, helping her to her feet. "I thought we'd be too late."

Dayanara coughed and wiped at the dirt that had gotten into her eyes. "You almost were," she said, a sob lodging in her throat. "But thank God, Little Fox, you awakened when you did, or . . . or . . ."

Quick Fox came to her. He lifted her into his arms and carried her away from the grave. "I chose the wrong way to punish that evil man," he said thickly. "I am sorry, Dayanara. So very sorry. If you had died, it would have been the man who loved you covering you with the dirt, not your uncle, for I gave him the freedom to perform such a cowardly act."

Tears filling her eyes, Dayanara reached a hand to his face. "Please never blame yourself for what my uncle has done to me," she murmured. "Just be grateful, darling, that you knew to come. I am so very grateful that I am in your arms and know that we still have tomorrows to share."

She realized that John was being held between two warriors who were questioning him.

"No, no one else came with me," John said, his voice quivering with fear. "I acted alone."

"I say we place *him* in the grave and cover *him* with earth," Red Feather shouted. "Quick Fox, this man deserves to die the same slow death that he had planned for your woman."

Suddenly John managed to yank himself free.

He began running toward the deep shadows of a bluff, then stopped and screamed out in pain.

He dropped to his knees as he clutched at his lower right leg.

"A rattler!" he cried. "A rattler got me!"

Dayanara saw the snake slithering away into the thick brush.

"Someone do something!" John screamed, his face aflame with a frantic fear. "Don't . . . just . . . let me die like this."

No one moved.

Quick Fox still held Dayanara in his arms.

Little Fox came and scooted close to his father.

And then John crumpled to the ground, his eyes wide, his breathing slowed down almost to nothing.

"Please . . . have . . . mercy . . ." he said, his voice barely audible.

Suddenly Quick Fox placed Dayanara on the ground. He rushed to John. He used his knife to cut his pants leg open; then he made a slit along the skin where the fangs had penetrated.

He started to lean down, to suck away the venom, but then stopped when John reached out and placed his fingers around Quick Fox's throat.

"Die, savage," John growled out.

Quick Fox choked and gagged, surprised that the dying man had such strength left in his hands, then lifted his knife and plunged it into John's chest just as Dayanara drew her pearl-handled pistol and aimed it at her uncle.

But the gun wasn't needed.

John's hands fell away from Quick Fox, his

eyes transfixed in a death stare.

Quick Fox surged to his feet.

Dayanara flung herself into his arms. "He was evil to the very last moment of his life," she sobbed out. "How could he . . . ?"

Quick Fox slid a hand across her mouth. "Say nothing more about him, for he is no longer your concern, or mine, or my people's," he said thickly. He looked past his shoulder at Little Fox. "Son, bring my horse closer. I want to take my woman home."

"Yes, home," Dayanara sobbed. "Please take me home."

"You know what today brings for us, do you not?" Quick Fox said, smiling into Dayanara's eyes.

"Yes, we become man and wife," Dayanara said softly as he kissed away her tears. "Our life begins today, Quick Fox. Truly begins today."

"*Huh,* today," he said.

She didn't look back as he placed her on his horse and rode away as John's body was lowered into the grave that he had dug for Dayanara.

Chapter Thirty

The summer hath his joys,
And winter his delights;
Though love and all his
    pleasures are but toys,
They shorten tedious nights.
— Thomas Campion

Fifteen years later

It had been a wonderful day of autumn. Little Fox had married an Assiniboines princess. The celebration was over. The Cree had retired to their cabins. Little Fox and Dancing Star had retired only moments ago to be alone in their newly built cabin.

Dayanara lay in her husband's arms as their four children slept above on a loft built especially for them.

All was well in the Cree village now that Quick Fox had decided to move it from its original site. Settlers had built many cabins near the old site, where two brand new forts had sprung up.

Dayanara's mother was doing well, too. She lived in her mansion in Saint Louis and kept busy among friends with her social functions and charities.

She had opened her heart and house to her friend Grace, whose husband had died from a heart attack only two years after Dayanara and Quick Fox had spoken their wedding vows.

Grace, whose legs had given out on her long ago, was confined to a wheelchair. But Dorothea made certain that her friend's mind was kept off her affliction by taking Grace everywhere with her.

Dayanara was touched deeply by her mother's devotion to her childhood friend. She was also touched by her dedication to her grandchildren, whom she saw at least once a year in the village. It was not an easy trip for a woman of her age, or Grace's frailty, for she accompanied Dorothea even there.

"Dayanara, you are in such deep thought," Quick Fox said as he turned to face her in the soft feather mattress that had come with a four-poster bed her mother had sent to them after they were settled in their new home.

Long ago, Quick Fox had accepted that his wife enjoyed many things that white women used in their homemaking. The thing that most impressed him, as well as the women of his village, was her sewing machine.

Now many women of the village owned

such a machine, thanks to Dayanara's mother's generosity.

"It's my mother," Dayanara said, turning to face Quick Fox. "I'm so happy for her."

Their naked bodies met beneath the blanket and strained together.

Dayanara's breath was already more rapid than moments ago at the touch of her husband's manhood against her leg.

She never tired of their lovemaking. In fact, each time it seemed more wonderful.

That truth was evident in the many children they had brought into this world. She was even pregnant again, but not far enough along to show yet.

"Your mother is a woman of good heart," Quick Fox said, slowly moving his hand over Dayanara's body, enjoying her quick intake of breath when he touched a sensitive place.

"Please do that again," Dayanara said, her voice thick with rising passion. "Please stroke me again there."

He smiled as he slid his fingers more deeply between her legs. As she opened them to him, he found her womanhood again and slowly stroked the swollen nub of flesh.

"I am amazed that it never feels any less wonderful than the last time you touched me there," Dayanara murmured. She sighed as the pleasure built. "Oh, Quick Fox, my head is swimming with rapture."

He thrust a finger inside her.

His mouth seized hers.

He gave her a long, deep, passionate kiss.

She reached between them and ran her hand up and down the full length of his manhood, eliciting a deep, guttural groan from deep within him.

He slid his mouth down and flicked his tongue over one of her nipples, then sank his mouth over it and sucked.

Dayanara's breath quickened with yearning.

She guided him inside her, and then wrapped her legs around his waist and rode with him as he began his deep, rhythmic thrusts inside her.

Again he kissed her, a kiss all-consuming, his arms enfolding her within his solid strength.

As their bodies moved together, Dayanara was keenly aware of the happiness deep within her.

She drew her mouth from his and reverently breathed his name against his lips.

"I love you so much," she whispered, moaning when his hands went between them and he cupped both her breasts.

The way he ran his thumb in circles around her nipples made Dayanara gasp with pleasure. She reached down and touched him when he withdrew and then entered her again with deep strokes.

Quick Fox was keenly aware of a spiraling ecstasy that burned within him as they gave each other endless pleasure.

He placed his arms around her and drew her even more tightly against him, his thrusts more rapid now, his groans of pleasure mingling with hers.

"We might awaken the children," Dayanara whispered, looking devilishly into his eyes as the fire from the fireplace in their bedroom cast a golden glow along their bodies.

"Then they will know the passion their mother and father feel for one another," Quick Fox said huskily, his eyes glazed and drugged with desire as he gazed down at her. "It is such a passion, my woman, that fuels my fire every time I am near you."

As one of his hands swept down her spine in a soft caress, the other held her tightly against him, intoxicating her with his kiss.

Suddenly their climax came together.

With a sob of joy she clung to him.

As their bodies grew quiet again, Quick Fox rained kisses on Dayanara's closed eyes, and then her brow.

"Husband, husband . . ." Dayanara whispered, everything within her singing and soaring.

She was as much in love now as she had been that first time she had seen Quick Fox and knew that it was their destiny to meet and marry.

Every day she awakened in his arms with a joy in life that she'd never known before him.

And their children. Ah, what a blessing they were to her and Quick Fox. Two boys and two girls.

The fifth? It did not matter whether it was a boy or girl, just as long as it was as healthy as the others that had been born of their love.

"Darling, I have something for you," Dayanara said, breaking the magical spell that their lovemaking had woven around them.

Quick Fox moved away from her.

He lay on his back as he watched her scramble from the bed and go to a trunk at its foot.

"What do you have that I do not know about?" Quick Fox asked as he leaned on an elbow and watched her lift the trunk lid and reach inside for something.

"It is something that I have made when you have been away from me on the hunt or in council," Dayanara said, taking a small buckskin bag from the trunk.

She carried it back to the bed and plopped down beside Quick Fox. "Open it," she said, her eyes wide with excitement. "I hope you like it."

He sat up, opened the bag, and reached inside.

"It is ingeniously done," Quick Fox said, studying the necklace that she had spent many hours making for him.

It was made of melted beads with a like-
ness of a fox hanging from a thin strip of
leather.

"I watched the women of our village and
studied hard and learned the art of melting
beads of different colors for the necklace,"
she murmured. "Do you see the fox? The
beautiful colors? The ground work is blue,
the figure white, and isn't the glazing so
smooth and pretty?"

"It is something I shall wear with great
pride," Quick Fox said. He handed it to her.
"Will you put it on me?"

Beaming, Dayanara crawled around behind
him, placed the necklace around his neck,
tied the thin leather strips, then scooted
around in front of him to see how he looked
wearing the necklace.

"It looks as though it truly belongs on
you," she said, smiling broadly. "And I'm so
glad you like it."

He reached out for her and lifted her onto
his lap, facing him.

He twined his arms around her and pulled
her closer. "My woman, my woman . . ." he
said huskily, his lips trembling as he gave her
a deep, long kiss.

Clinging to him, she gave him back his kiss
with a moan of ecstasy.

Her body pliant in his arms, he stretched
her out beneath him and again made love
with her.

Their worlds had come together those long years ago, their destinies intertwined the moment their eyes met and held. Their love had never faltered, instead growing stronger each day.

Theirs was a once-in-a-lifetime love . . . a love that would endure no matter what faced them.

"*Nei-mah-tao-yo,* you tremble," Quick Fox whispered against her lips.

"That is because I love you so much," she whispered back. "Kee. Come with me again to paradise, my Cree husband."

He smiled, then did as she bade him and their bodies quaked and quivered in another joined, wondrous, sexual release.

"*Huh,* yes, *huh.* . . ." she cried as she soared to the heights of bliss with her beloved.